BOOK 1:

THE BLUE PLANETS WORLD

SLEEPERS

BY

DARCY PATTISON

Mims House, Little Rock, AR

Mims House
1309 Broadway
Little Rock, AR 72202
www.mimshouse.com

Publisher's Cataloging-in-Publication data
Names: Pattison, Darcy, author.
Title: Sleepers / by Darcy Pattison.
Series: The Blue Planets World.
Description: Little Rock, AR: Mims House, 2017.
Identifiers: ISBN 978-1-62944-071-2 (Hardcover) | 978-1-62944-076-7 (pbk.) | 978-1-62944-077-4 (ebook) | LCCN 2017901372
Subjects: LCSH Extraterrestrial beings--Fiction. | Parent and child—Fiction. | Refugees--Fiction. | Science fiction. | BISAC JUVENILE FICTION / Science Fiction
Classification: LCC PZ7.P27816 Sl 2017 | DDC [Fic]--dc23

Printed in the United States of America

Other Novels by Darcy Pattison

Liberty
Longing for Normal
Vagabonds
The Girl, the Gypsy and the Gargoyle
The Wayfinder

SLEEPERS

THE GREAT WHITE

The Great White shark moved silently through the surf, propelled by short sweeps of its crescent tail. It had no conscious thought for what it was doing so close to shore. It just hunted. The water shone brilliantly under the Milky Way, and its myriads of stars reflected on the face of the gentle ocean swells.

A lone figure emerged from a dark beach house, trotted down the weathered boards across the dunes to the beach, scuffed through the soft sand and slowed to walk straight to the water's edge.

Wet sand under his feet now, Jake Rose threw a darting glare over his shoulders, and then turned to stare out to sea. He took a deep breath, letting the salty air fill his lungs, and suddenly the longing was overwhelming. I will go skinny dipping tonight.

Defiant, Jake removed his shirt, flip-flops, and swim trunks, tossing them beside a piece of driftwood. He splashed into the warm August surf until he was immersed chest-deep, and he scooped water to splash over his shoulders, his face, and his hair.

A hundred yards off shore, the shark heard the splash and stirred, moving toward the disturbance, an arrow spiraling towards a bull's-eye. The shark closed in, his dorsal fin cutting through the water less than a dozen feet to the teen's side.

At the sight, a shiver of fear ran down Jake's spine, but he was committed. Without stopping to think further, he bent his knees and dove, arms outstretched, splitting the glittering breaker.

Underwater, Jake's eyes adjusted to the dark. There it was, circling. The shark's row of teeth flickered, stark white in the gloom. Its circle collapsed inward until the shark darted past, just a few feet away from Jake's face.

Time to move, Jake realized.

Quickly, Jake inhaled, the gills under his arms undulating as they expanded and contracted with each breath. Water-breathing through his Risonian gills felt as natural and regular as breathing air through his human lungs. When he pressed his legs together, the villi wove together with what his father jokingly called a Velcro system that turned his legs into a long tail.

Jake swept his tail in a powerful thrust that sent him speeding away from the shark. But as he did, he felt a strange vibration in the water. Confused, he stopped and looked back at the Great White, who now held stationary just staring at Jake.

Perplexed, Jake waited for a repeat of the vibration. Nothing.

Had the vibration been an attempt at communication? he wondered. If he were home on Rison, there'd be no doubt. But here? On Earth? Clumsily, Jake flapped his hands, sending his own vibrations through the water.

With its short fins, the Great White beat out a series of vibrations in answer.

Jake attempted a rough translation: "Friend. We swim."

He repeated the exact vibrations back to the shark, and immediately the shark repeated the phrase: "Friend. We swim."

Crude, but effective, exulted Jake. They understood each other—after a fashion.

"Cousin," Jake called in a bubbly voice. "Before us is the open sea. Take me out to explore!"

The Great White didn't understand the words, of course. Nevertheless, he swam toward deeper water, pausing now and then, as if to be sure that Jake followed.

Jake reveled in the too-long-forbidden feel of warm seawater buoying him upward and the joy of a strong tail that sent him coursing behind the Great White. With wild abandon, Jake followed his guide. They were just two wild creatures off to explore the Gulf of Mexico.

THE FACE OF RISON

Three hours later, as the stars began to fade for the night, Jake left his cousin-in-the-ocean, un-Velcroed his legs, and wearily climbed up into the shallows. It took only a quick moment to reestablish his air-breathing; his lungs expanded with a gasp, and began a regular rhythm. He splashed through the breakers toward the driftwood log to reclaim his clothes.

"Feeling calmer?"

Startled, Jake turned to see his mother striding toward him from the boardwalk, a gray shape in the early-dawn. The beaches here on the Gulf of Mexico were lined with beach houses of all sorts—big, small, old, or new—mostly rental properties. The houses sat back from the shore far enough to avoid storm surges; that meant they were fronted by sand dunes, which were protected by environmental laws. Local ordinances required a wooden sidewalk over the dunes to lessen the impact of foot traffic. The gray, weathered boardwalks were scalding hot during the afternoon sun but cool in the early morning, so his mother was barefoot, her red flip-flops dangling from one hand.

Embarrassed, Jake turned his back and pulled on his swim trunks. On Rison, people often swam with no clothing, but he'd been off-planet now for three years, and he'd picked up the Earthling's reserve about naked bodies. Shivering in the early morning air, he put on his rash-guard t-shirt, too, and slicked his wet hair back out of his face. When he turned, he sidestepped a pale ghost crab that scuttled across his path. Mom settled onto the sand facing the eastern sky and stretched her legs out in front. She was small and athletic, with dark curly hair. She wore a black one-piece swimming suit under a red t-shirt. As usual, she carried her waterproof string backpack.

Jake flopped beside her and absently brushed at the white sugar sand that clung to his wet legs and toes. Leaning back, he gazed up at the sky. Dawn slowly lightened the horizon, and mother and son watched as Venus, the gleaming morning star, faded; Jake knew they were both thinking of their own star, Turco, half a galaxy away and invisible from Earth. In the distance, a couple of helicopters droned toward them, probably an early morning patrol—a common sight on the Gulf Coast.

Jake leaned forward, suddenly. "Mother, it's an amazing ocean. They say that Earthlings have only explored about 5% of it. Our scientists could—"

At her frown, he stopped. The conversation had been repeated too many times; he shouldn't start it again.

"Look," she said. "I know you're upset about the YouTube video, and I know that swimming is the best way for you to calm down. But it's not our ocean. You've got to think before you act."

"Of course, I'm upset." He barely managed to keep his voice calm. "You've put yourself out there as the 'Face of Rison.' You're painting a bull's-eye on your face!" Guiltily, he thought, I should have done the video with her.

Last week, when it was clear there would be a family vacation, Mom had asked if he wanted to be in the video. "It'll be more emotional and real for people if they see a family. We could tape it at the beach."

While still on the Moon Base and excited about moving to Earth, Jake had been horrified at what that notoriety could mean for him. Now that he was finally moving to Earth, and headed toward his grandparents' house, he wanted to just be like other kids, everyone equal. He wasn't a Face of Rison and never would be.

Mom had accepted his "No" without comment, taped the video alone, and uploaded it right before leaving the embassy for the beach.

And now, her excitement spilled over: "I just checked. It's had over a million new views. Overnight. It has a chance of turning the tide of opinion our way."

Jake spun away, trying not to think about his mother's face on the video, her impassioned plea for Earth to understand how bad the situation had become on Rison, her brilliant blue eyes as startling as her speech. She needed to startle Earth's politicians: Rison's scientists warned that the instability in their planet's core was increasing rapidly. Time was running out. There had been background video of volcanoes erupting with Risonians running—the Risonian Embassy video editors had done a great job in making it emotional. "Compelling," his mother had called it.

Viewing it for the first time four nights ago, Dad had said quietly, "You risk your life with this video."

Even more quietly, Mom had answered, "I'm here on Earth on September 3, 2040 because others have sacrificed so much. Life is a risk. I choose life."

Now, his mother's voice softened, as if to ease his frustrations. "Angry or not, you were forbidden to go for a swim like that. Promise me that you won't swim in Earth's oceans again."

A pang shot through Jake, and he gripped a handful of the white sand. The past three years living at the Obama Moon Base on Earth's waterless moon had been torture. He had longed for water, and now that they finally had this weeklong vacation near Gulf Shores, Alabama—he couldn't stay out of the water. He wouldn't.

He tossed the sand toward the ocean and avoided her request for a promise. Instead, he asked plaintively, "What will we do, Mom?"

She hugged him so tight that he thought of the human stories of mother grizzly bears, fierce and protective. The smell of Risonian seaweed that always hung over her was an odd, yet comforting perfume. "We'll fight for a place for our people. In the end, Earth won't let a whole race, a whole species, be destroyed."

Jake wanted to argue that Earth had done just that over the last few hundred years. The Dodo bird, the passenger pigeon, the white rhinoceros—humans had let these and so many more species go extinct. The short-term needs of the humans were more important than saving an entire species.

"We can trust the humans," Mom said. "We must trust them. But we must do this slowly. You can't just take off like a child and explore whenever you like." She stopped, her mouth in a tight line.

Jake knew the arguments she wanted to repeat, had repeated endlessly the last few days, and was glad she restrained herself. Like every other Risonian school child, he had learned English, the business language of Earth, and studied Earth geography, cultures, and history. The planets had first become aware of each other in 1999, but Earth had been content to let contact flag because they were 30,000 light years apart.

Rison couldn't ignore contact with Earth, though. It was motivated by the crisis over its unstable core; by 2010, Risonian secret agents had landed on Earth, and by 2015, Rison was teaching English in their schools. Since then, the interest in Earth language and culture expanded so that many Risonians learned multiple Earth languages. Because Earth was the only planet similar enough to their own within reach of their starships, the blue planet was their only plan for evacuation, their only plan for survival. Jake knew what was at stake and why he shouldn't explore the oceans. But he also knew that Risonians needed real experiences on Earth, not just book knowledge; Risonian scientists needed to explore Earth's vast oceans to uncover its secrets and find ways to live and thrive.

"What are you two doing out so early?" Dad's baritone voice boomed from the boardwalk behind them.

Jake scrambled up, relieved that Dad had arrived before Mom forced him to make a promise he couldn't keep. He held out a hand to pull Mom up, too.

She linked her arm with Jake's and waved, calling merrily, "Come and join us for a walk on the beach. Maybe we'll find a shell or two."

"Great idea," Dad said. "I set out steaks for breakfast. A walk will work up our appetites." He was olive-skinned, fit and trim, with just a hint of grey at the temples. His dark eyes twinkled, and he pulled his military-issue sunglasses from the top of his head, slipped them on, and headed toward his family.

When he reached them, Mom let go of Jake and lifted her chin to Dad, who scooped her into a tender hug.

Jake turned away, embarrassed. They'd been like this all week, as if he'd been thrust into their honeymoon. His discomfort was partly because he was forced to see his mother in a new light. Back home on the planet Rison, Jake had lived with his mom and stepfather, Swann Quad-de. They were distant cousins who married for political reasons, consolidating power into one united front; the result, as expected, was that Swann was now Prime Minister of Tizzalura, the largest country in the northern continent. Jake had known for a long time that Swann wasn't his biological father; Jake was a test-tube baby, the result of a laboratory experiment in combining alien and human DNA. Only three years ago he'd learned the identity of his real father.

He remembered the conversation perfectly. Mom had explained, "We're evacuating you to the Earth's moon." She stared over his head and spoke in a too-casual voice. "By the way, you'll be with your biological father, Lt. Commander Blake Rose."

Startled, Jake asked, "You know my biological father?"

"Yes," she shrugged, but it was too nonchalant. "He was on the first Earth-Rison contact mission as the U.S. Navy's comparative anatomy physician. He did the test-tube experiment that created you."

Jake tried more questions in the weeks leading up to his departure, but his Mom cut him off. Instead, she bustled about helping him pack for the Moon, stopping often to pull him into a hug and whisper, "I'll miss you."

He answered stoically, "I'm a Quad-de. We'll survive." The Quad-des were politicians, always involved in the government of Tizzalura. He only hoped to earn the right to be called a Quad-de. It was bad enough to leave Rison, but it was worse to have to replace Swann Quad-de with a mere human.

Jake had expected to hate Commander Rose, but Dad had been a total surprise in many ways; in the last three years, they'd learned to like each other—except when they behaved too similarly, like when they both got stubborn in an argument.

When Jake had first met his biological father, he'd called him by his first name, Blake. Jake didn't remember when he made the transition to calling him Dad, but it just seemed natural now.

Behind him, Jake heard Dad's gruff voice, "Dayexi—so beautiful."

His mom laughed—as she hadn't in a long, long time.

Jake cringed and blocked out their private moment by stretching out on the soft sand and flopping one arm over his eyes. He yawned, ready for a nap after his long swim.

A moment later, though, his mom kicked sand onto his legs and said, "No naps. We'll walk, and then we'll eat steak and eggs, and then you can—"

A phone rang, a jangling noise against the rhythmic surf. Mom stopped, her nose wrinkled deep with worry. Risonians were so close anatomically to Earthlings that it would take a casual observer a while to notice the nuances between the species. Earthlings from Asia have a slightly different eye created by the epicanthic fold. In a similar way, Risonians looked different but it was hard to pin down exactly what that difference was. Of course Risonians had underarm gills and the Velcro-like legs, but you didn't see that at a glance. Risonians had a slight wrinkle on the bridge of the nose, a sharper chin, and slightly bigger eyes. When Mom was worried, her nose wrinkle deepened.

Now, she pulled her satellite phone from her backpack and turned away to answer it.

Mom had been allowed this week long vacation, with the provision that she was on-call and couldn't go anywhere without the phone, the latest in communication technology. Surprisingly, it'd been silent for four days, giving them four days of peace, of being together as a family. Jake suspected his parents had been in regular contact since he'd moved to Earth's moon, but Dad had been private about his feelings for Dayexi—till this week. Jake didn't understand how his mother could value a human over a Risonian, especially a Quad-de. But they were his biological parents, and even if Jake was a test-tube baby, he supposed Mom and Dad could still like each other. These four days were like a glassy sea with no wind. Strange, yet peaceful. A calm space—a time set apart.

Now Jake was filled with a sense of foreboding. Sitting up, he startled a ghost crab that scurried sideways and disappeared safely into a hole in the wet sand.

Dad pulled off his sunglasses and stood with his head bowed as he listened to Mom's side of the satellite phone conversation.

"Yes, sir," she said. "Right away, sir."

And Jake knew: the family vacation was over.

Dad raised an eyebrow at Mom.

A flash of fear passed over Mom's face, and she nodded at the approaching helicopters. "Anti-Sharks. They're coming for me."

Dad sprang into action, his years as a Navy officer taking over. He kissed her—fiercely—and then thrust her away.

"Into the water," he ordered. "I doubt they've seen us yet; they're still out of range. We'll distract them. You know what to do."

Without a wasted movement, Mom stuffed her flip-flops into her backpack, along with her t-shirt. She sealed the waterproof closure, slipped the backpack's strings over her shoulders, trotted into the water and dove, disappearing under the waves.

A sudden loneliness washed over Jake. He didn't know when he'd see his mom again, and he wished she'd looked back to wave good-bye.

Dad gripped Jake's shoulder and turned him around. They trotted across the sand to the boardwalk and crossed the dune to their two-story beach house. "Hurry. No slip-ups."

Already, Jake felt the tension building in the pit of his stomach. "I know what to do," he growled.

Passing the grill that sat on a concrete pad near the bottom of the stairs, Dad clicked the electric lighter, and the flame sprang up. By the time they got things cleared up inside, Dad could be out here grilling their breakfast steaks.

Because of possible storm surges this close to the ocean, the ground floor under the house was mostly parking spaces under the house and a storage room. Jake climbed the stairs to the main level. Inside the dim beach house, Jake spun around, searching for anything that would reveal that a woman had been here for the last four days. The rental was decorated in beach chic, with seashells and paintings of boats and fishermen. Mom had brought almost nothing with her, and she was meticulous, keeping everything that belonged to her in her string backpack or in a tiny bag that Dad would soon take care of. Jake shoved a glossy women's magazine amidst the other magazines in a basket. Otherwise, it looked like she'd never been here.

"I'll change." Jake sprinted to his room and pulled on long flannel pajama pants to hide his own Velcro-legs.

Suitably dressed, Jake trampled down the stairs to the grill and ripped open the white butcher paper to reveal three small steaks. Three. That was easy to explain, though; human teen boys were infamous for their huge appetites.

Dad raced downstairs and tossed the seasoning and cooking tools near the grill. He still held Mom's small bag and looked around frantically. Finally, he ran to the trashcans near the road. He pulled out a trash bag, undid the twist ties, and stuffed Mom's bag at the bottom of a pile of shrimp shells from their shrimp feast the day before. Nodding, he replaced the twist tie, slammed the trash can lid back into place, and trotted back to the grill.

On the beach, the helicopter dropped lower, and the sound of its blades whomp-whomped louder and louder until the helicopter hovered directly above the spot where Jake dove into the ocean earlier. Five men slid down ropes to the sand, machine guns tucked under their arms and wearing helmets and Kevlar vests. Dropping to the ground, the men spread out and trotted toward the beach house.

Dad calmly sprinkled lemon pepper and salt on the steaks and then turned to face the oncoming soldiers.

The leader called, "Where is she?"

Jake's stomach clenched in fear, but Dad was calm.

"What's going on?" Dad replied in his best military voice. "I am Navy Commander Rose, and this is my son, Jake Rose. Is this a military operation? Am I needed back at the Obama Moon Base? You could've called, you know."

The soldier hesitated, and then motioned for the other to stop. Quietly, he said something into a headset.

Jake admired Dad's cool demeanor, appreciated that his direct approach had managed to stymy them. Any delay gave Mom more time to swim farther out into the ocean depths—and she had to escape! Jake wasn't sure about military technology, but he worried that if she were in shallow water, they might be able to use heat-sensors to find her. To hide his agitation, he bent to check the gas flame of the grill and adjusted the dials to shoot the flames higher. He then straightened up to glare at the soldiers.

"I'm sorry to bother you, sir," the soldier said. "But we've had a suspicious report." He tilted his head slightly, listening to the headset. Then he squared his shoulders. "Commander, sir. My orders are to search this beach house."

"For what?" Commander Rose sounded outraged. "My son and I are on vacation from the Moon Base, and we were just about to have steak and eggs for breakfast. What sort of reports? What are you looking for?"

Defiantly, the soldier said, "Sharks."

Jake remembered the sleek skin of his swimming companion that morning. Why had Earth nicknamed Risonians as Sharks? They weren't anything alike. He couldn't help it; he laughed. "Sharks live in the ocean, not in a beach house."

"Risonians, sir." The soldier's voice turned hard. He didn't like being laughed at.

Dad's voice was equally hard, and his eyes flashed. "And just who are you, anyway? Special ops? Or just a vigilante group, anti-Sharks taking illegal guerrilla actions?"

"Captain Cyrus Hill," he said, "from the ELLIS Forces. Sorry, sir. Orders." Like all the soldiers with their gear on, Hill looked bulky, awkward and hot. Under his helmet, his ruddy face glistened with sweat even this early in the morning. His nose spread prominently across his face, broad with large nostrils. To Jake, he looked about the same age as the younger officers on the Moon Base, maybe mid to late twenties.

Hill lifted his machine gun slightly and motioned to the others to move forward.

Jake's tension built as two circled the house, shaking the dune grasses to make sure no one was hiding nearby. One flipped off the top of the trashcan, and Jake watched with his peripheral vision, not daring to look directly, lest he give away his anxiety. The man's nose wrinkled at the rotten seafood smell, and he replaced the lid.

"You're not well trained," Jake wanted to sneer. Using a bad smell to hide something should've been an obvious ploy. A savvy soldier would have been more suspicious, instead of put off.

Two men in camouflage, but without discernable insignia, pushed past Dad and Jake and charged up the stairs. Jake took a half step to stop them, but Dad gave a tiny headshake. Jake stopped, but felt his worry expand with each step they took upward.

A third soldier deliberately bumped into Jake and shoved him up against the stair's railings. "And just who are you, anyway? Shark-lovers?"

Almost trembling with pent-up rage and fear, Jake reared back and shoved his fist at—Dad's hand caught his arm before he could connect with the man's stubbly chin.

Dad said firmly, "No."

Dad spun and kneed the man's crotch and shoved his shoulders. The man landed heavily in the sand, stunned for a moment. Quickly he recovered and surged up toward Dad, ready to fight.

"Grant," warned Captain Hill. "Back off."

Grant hesitated.

"That's an order," Hill said harshly.

Grant sullenly picked up his gun and went to kick at dune grasses.

Jake grabbed the steak tongs and clicked them together to keep himself from exploding. He fumed: he could've taken on the man. Why does Dad treat me like a kid?

Dad spun to the Captain and glared, fists clenched. "You're way off here. We're on vacation from the Moon Base. We're just cooking steak and eggs for breakfast."

Hill shrugged. "Orders."

"Whose orders?" Dad demanded.

The soldier said easily, "If you must know, General Puentes. He doesn't care if people know. He's a patriot and everyone knows that, too. We're ELLIS forces."

He emphasized the "ELLIS" in a way that made Jake shiver. ELLIS was an international organization created in 2000 as a result of an answer to the infamous Aricebo message. On November 15, 1974, from Aricebo, Puerto Rico, Earth had broadcasted a binary message toward the edge of the Milky Way Galaxy. They expected the message to take 30,000 years to reach someone and 30,000 years for a message to return. Instead, on April 1, 1999, a mere 25 years later, an answer came—and it wasn't an April Fool's joke. It was a repeat of Earth's binary message along with extra information that specified a location near the center of the Milky Way.

Rison had been sending probes widely and intercepted the message. Rison orbited the Turco, a tiny star in the midst of a previously unknown globular star cluster about 25,000 light-years from Earth. Astronomers knew there were many such globular star clusters in the Milky Way. Because Earth was part of the Milky Way, though, it was rather like a human who wanted to see his own back; it was impossible to see without special tools. Astronomers named Turco's globular star cluster the Liller-2, or LL-2 for short. The name had been incorporated into the organization's name: ELLIS stood for Earth-LL Interstellar Security. ELLIS Forces were given the task of controlling all contact with the aliens. Within ELLIS, Jake knew that some factions hated the Risonians, but he hadn't witnessed it before.

The two soldiers in camouflage clattered down the stairs. Jake gripped the tongs so hard that the edges bit into his palm.

The lead soldier shook his head at the Captain.

Captain Hill grimaced. "You checked the bathrooms? Any sign of longer hair, like a woman's hair, in the sink or tub?"

Jake's knees went weak. Had Mom wiped down all the surfaces before she came out to the beach?

The soldier sighed heavily. "We checked. Nothing."

Jake straightened his spine and stood even taller, a touch of pride in their perfect execution of the escape plan. He and Mom were Quad-des. These Earthlings wouldn't find her.

Captain Hill turned to Dad, "Sorry to bother you, sir. If you do happen to ever see a She-Shark, tell her we're on her tail. We'll find her."

Relief loosening his tongue, Jake taunted, "Are you sure that's wise? Sharks have sharp teeth. They bite."

Captain Hill's face darkened. "Freaks! Exactly why we have to find her. And bite back." He raised his gun threateningly.

Jake sucked in a breath at the viciousness of the response. On the Moon Base, because his father was an officer, Jake seldom heard gossip, especially not about the Risonians who were working with the Navy. Everyone spouted the official government position that peaceful relations were imperative. Jake had watched videos of protests arguing against letting the Risonians come to Earth, but nothing could have prepared him for this extreme Anti-Sharks sentiment. He wanted desperately to consider the humans as equals, but they made it hard. He thought of his mom, so passionate for the cause of the Risonians, who desperately needed a haven on Earth. Proving to Earth that they came in peace seemed hopeless.

The Captain continued, "After that video posted this week—well." He shrugged. "We'll find her."

Dad said coolly, "What video?"

Captain Hill laughed harshly. "Haven't seen it yet? Look up the 'Face of Rison.'" He said it with almost a sneer.

He turned away and waved his free hand in a circular motion; the soldiers turned and jogged toward the helicopter. Over his shoulder, Grant made a last jab: "Don't worry, Shark-lover! We'll be watching you, too."

He raced across the sand toward the waiting helicopter.

Jake sagged against the stair rail and stared after the retreating soldiers. The helicopter took off in a whirr, and thankfully, it followed the beach again, not going out over the Gulf. Maybe they didn't have heat-sensors on board, or maybe they didn't really know that Mom had been there. Either way, she was safe. For now.

Abruptly, Dad sat on the bench of the picnic table and let his face sink into his palms.

Jake put a hand on his shoulder. "Dad?"

Dad's lean form seemed to shrink a couple more inches, and when he finally raised his head, his face was wet with tears. "We just wanted to have a few days as a family. We thought the Labor Day weekend would be safe." He shook his head. "Foolish."

"It's okay, Dad." Jake said. Only it wasn't. Mom wasn't here to break the eggs into a bowl and whip them till frothy with only a fork. Determined to be strong, he stomped upstairs to the kitchen, bringing back the skillet, butter, eggs, small bowl, and a fork. He set the skillet on the fire and dropped in a pat of butter. He broke four eggs into the bowl and used the fork to beat and beat and beat them, even though he was sure that he could never match Mom's technique.

When he saw Jake thumping away at the eggs, Dad smiled grimly and whispered. "She's safe."

Jake poured the eggs into the sizzling skillet. Barely able to speak, he croaked back, "For now."

"For now," repeated Dad solemnly. He stood and moved to the grill. "We'll eat, pack up and leave."

Jake knew the contingency plan. Mom would swim a couple miles to a Florida state park where they'd rented a cabin for the week under a different name and paid for it in cash, so that there was no way to trace them. She had a stash of clothes hidden there and a rented car that would only be traced to an elderly lady who didn't exist. Mom would be at the airport in a couple hours and back at the Rison Embassy in New York

City by nightfall. Risonian Ambassador Dayexi Quad-de would be back at work in the morning.

Around the same time his mother would arrive in New York, Jake would be in Seattle—no, not Seattle proper, but on Bainbridge Island, which sits in the middle of Puget Sound. That was Dad's family home where his parents, Sir and Easter Rose, still lived. Jake's Earthling grandparents, the strangers he'd never met. Dad's recent promotion to Commander came with a top-secret assignment, which meant Jake couldn't live with Dad any longer. Instead, Jake would live with his grandparents and go to an Earthling high school. They had shipped ahead most of his clothes and things, and a room was waiting for him. After the ELLIS Forces, he realized that he'd have to be very careful at his new home and school. No one could know who he was. Wasn't that what he wanted, to be on an equal footing with his fellow students? But now, it was imperative that he hide his heritage. No slip ups.

Looking up, Jake saw that the day had barely begun; the sun was still a ball hanging on the horizon, sending drifts of red across the early morning clouds.

So this was Earth. His new home.

TRIPLE-SHOT VENTIS

Coffee fascinated Jake. Dad never drank coffee, and during Jake's time on the Obama Moon Base, Dad had never allowed him to try it. But Dad had been busy, distracted by the myriad of details he had to take care of to leave Jake in his parent's care. And then, he left. Jake was alone on Bainbridge Island. He drank coffee and drank coffee and drank—and barely slept.

On Saturday morning—it was 10 a.m., a cool, late summer morning, just three days after school had started on a Wednesday—Jake walked into Blackbird Bakery, his third coffee shop of the day.

A girl turned from the cash register. Dark, straight hair framed her face, and her bangs swung slightly, just brushing equally dark eyebrows. Amidst that frame of glossy hair, her face glowed with life. Seeing him, her eyes went wide for an instant, and fleeting emotions rippled across her face, and were gone. Businesslike, she asked, "What can I get started for you?"

Distracted by the case of pastries, he mumbled, "Triple-shot venti."

"Good choice," she said, and her face changed from surprise to approval.

Jake looked up from the pastries to watch her closer and wondered if her face was always so open and her emotions so easy to read.

The girl turned to the espresso machine, moving with a cat-like grace, with no wasted movements, and humming as she worked. Soon steam hissed into a metal pitcher of milk, and her hum turned into a trill, soft and sweet. The sound stopped when she slipped her phone from her back pocket, read a text, and thumbed a quick reply. When she turned back to the espresso machine, the humming started again. Jake realized that her music wasn't quite a melody; it was just a musical background for her motions. It caught at Jake, and he couldn't turn away. She shoved the phone back into her pocket and sent him a curious glance.

This was Jake's fourth triple-shot venti since 8 a.m., when he'd set out to try every place in town that served coffee.

After the bleak Moon Base, Bainbridge Island was a lush paradise. Connected to the mainland by one bridge to the north and a busy ferry system to the east, it was a protected place, Dad had said. A safe place.

For Jake, the past week had been a blur of meeting his grandparents, Sir and Easter, enrolling in the local high school, eating strange Earth foods, and slipping exhausted into bed at the end of each day, only to squirm, wide-eyed, unable to sleep because his body rhythms hadn't adjusted yet to Earth's Pacific time zone. Night after night, he slipped out of bed to sit by his window and stare at the stars and wonder about his home star, Turco, or to stand on the porch and listen to the call of waves lapping at the shore, or to fire up his laptop and watch Mom's YouTube video. Wildly popular, the number of views rose and rose, even as the comments ran hot and cold. Worry over his Mom and Rison's fate tugged at Jake, but all he could do was drink more coffee.

Dad left, away on his secret assignment for the Navy. Alone, Jake strolled around the island, cataloging the lush variations in colors from yellow-green to pure green to blue-green. School had started three days ago, but the nameless crowds had left him feeling even more isolated. Coffee kept the loneliness at bay.

"You want an Earth muffin to go with that?" The girl poured the three shots of coffee into a white porcelain mug and filled it with hot milk.

Suddenly, Jake's heart thumped loudly in his ears. Did she suspect something? He stammered. "Wh-what's an Earth muffin?"

The girl handed him a menu and pointed to a listing.

The Earth Muffins had carrots, zucchini, pumpkin seeds, flax and other stuff that Jake was pretty sure didn't usually go into a muffin, which was just a piece of bread. He wasn't sure why vegetables made it an "Earth" muffin, but it looked like it had nothing to do with Rison. He was safe. "Okay," he squeaked. "I'll try it."

"We've got special coffee mugs on sale, too, if you're interested." She pointed to a line of mugs on the top of the counter.

They were works of art, each hand-painted with a skyline of Seattle.

"Who did these? They're interesting." He was starting to regain his composure; his voice was almost normal. Maybe he'd buy a mug for his mom sometime.

"It's a business that I'd like to build up," she said. "I only work here so I can sell the coffee mugs that I paint."

From behind the counter, an older man gave a short laugh. "You work here for the money and to meet cute guys."

"Got that straight," she retorted. She picked up the triple-shot venti and offered it to Jake.

"Thanks." Jake was rewarded with a smile that suddenly made his knees weak. But no other barista had made Jake's senses tingle like this one, and he watched the coffee-girl's hands move as if in slow motion.

When she saw that he was too distracted to take the mug, she set his drink on the counter and wrapped his muffin in a brown wax paper. Turning to the register, she pulled out her phone and set it beside the cash register.

"You new in town?" she asked.

Jake could barely nod, he was so intent on watching her pink-painted fingernails tap the cash register. He managed to ask, "Who are you?"

"Good question." She looked him straight in the eye, and a flood of words poured out. "I'm a human female who lives on Bainbridge Island. I'm an athlete, a painter, a barista, a lover of carrot cake, a student of biology—so are you, you're in my class. I'm a laugh-a-minute when I get going, but I seldom get going."

Jake just stared. She was in his biology class? The first three days had been such a blur that he didn't recognize her at all.

She was obviously on a roll because she kept talking. "Or maybe you want to know what I'm not. I'm not a cheerleader or an A+ student. I'm not a believer in the tooth fairy. You'll never find me eating eggplants or Brussels sprouts or asparagus."

Jake stammered, "No asparagus." She was fascinating and confusing all at the same time. Her accent, so different from what he'd heard during their week in Alabama, was great. He wanted her to keep on talking, so he could keep on listening.

"Here's an unusual skill I have," she continued, "I am a star-gazer, and I can name any constellation you point out."

Suddenly, Jake started laughing. "You're amazing, is what you are."

She grinned back at him.

Her smile, wide and welcoming, called to him like a siren; it pierced him, and yet, it was also a pure pleasure just to see her. He wanted to know everything about this girl, not just that she liked carrot cake but not asparagus. "Let me rephrase that question," Jake said. "What's your name?"

"I'm Emmeline Tullis. Call me Em." She glanced at her phone, frowned, tapped something—pink flashing up and down—then looked up again.

Em. He liked that name. "Jake," he squealed, his voice still refusing to fully cooperate. "Jake Rose." Even after three years with Dad, it sounded strange sometimes to use Dad's surname, Rose, instead of his adoptive father's surname, Quad-de. He'd been Jake Quad-de for eleven years, and Jake Rose for only three years.

"You new in town?" she repeated.

"Living with my grandparents."

She raised an eyebrow.

So he continued, "Sir and Easter Rose."

"The dentist in Seattle?" She frowned slightly, "My sister, Marisa, works for him."

Jake wondered if she was frowning about her sister or his grandfather. But he only said, "Good. Maybe we'll run into each a lot."

Jake handed her a twenty. Earth money still confused him, but his parents insisted that he use cash instead of a credit or debit card—as they had on the Moon Base—that would leave a digital trail.

When Em took his money, their hands brushed; Jake jerked his eyes up, surprised by—what? Something. Her touch—it reached inside him somehow. Her eyes widened slightly, too, he was sure of it. She set his change on the counter, and Jake wondered if that was to avoid touching him.

He backed away and sat in a booth where he had a good view of the counter and Em—the human female that was in his biology class. How had he missed her? He sipped his coffee and nibbled his muffin, not even tasting it, just watching her with other customers. Listening to her melodic hums that accompanied her work. She glanced at him once, twice—but casually, sweeping the shop to see if any customers needed anything. When there was a lull, she went around collecting empty coffee cups and offering refills. And always, she fiddled with her phone. Addicted to it, he thought. It was an Earth habit that he hadn't picked up yet. His parents would likely forbid it as another digital trail.

The string of bells on the door jangled, and Jake glanced over. Startled, he realized the man who had just walked in looked eerily like that soldier, the captain from Gulf Shores. Trembling with surprise, Jake quickly twisted away from the door so his back was toward the man. Peering around, he watched the man take off his cap to reveal a military crop and a broad nose. It was Captain Hill.

What was the captain doing here on Bainbridge Island? Was he tracking Jake?

The door jingled again, and an older man with thick glasses walked in to stand beside the captain. Jake was startled to recognize his biology and civics teacher, Mr. Blevins. He had a thick graying mustache that looked like a fuzzy Earth caterpillar.

Jake shrank further into the depths of his booth.

"Morning, Coach," Em said from behind the counter. "The usual?"

But Mr. Blevins taught biology and civics. Why was Em calling him Coach? So far in biology, they'd only been given seat assignments, lectures on Blevin's grading system, received textbooks, and talked about lab safety. In civics, it was the same, except instead of lab safety, they had a long lecture about their major project of the first semester, a research paper. And in both classes, they'd talked about the freshman class trip to Mt. Rainier. Apparently, it was a big tradition because everyone had been excited about it. Outside the classroom, though, Jake knew nothing about this particular teacher.

"The usual," Mr. Blevins said. "Have you met Captain Hill? He's ELLIS Special Forces." Blevins paused to let Em fully appreciate his friend's prestigious job.

Em said, "Of course, I know him. He took my sister Marisa to the senior prom."

Captain Hill squinted. "Em? You're all grown up! I didn't recognize you."

Mr. Blevins took off his eyeglasses, polished them, and put them back on to peer at Em with puzzlement. "You're Marisa's sister? You don't look anything alike."

"We're both adopted, you know," she said.

Mr. Blevins nodded, and then slapped his friend on the back. "Cy's just been posted in the area for a special assignment. He likes Americanos." He laughed. "A good patriotic drink. And throw in a couple of those Earth muffins, too."

Wow! This man is proud of his friend, Jake thought.

"Got it." Em turned to the espresso machine but turned back to wave at the line of coffee cups. "We've got special prices on the coffee mugs, too, if you're interested."

Mr. Blevins smiled and said, "You paint those, right? I'll get mugs for Christmas presents, I promise."

"I'll hold you to that." Em hummed and fixed the coffees, while her boss set two muffins on individual small plates.

Mr. Blevins reached for his plate, but the Captain said, "I'll get them. You just find us a table."

"I can carry my own," Mr. Blevins said, and picked up one of the plates and a cup.

Captain Hill picked up his coffee and muffin but turned back. "What's Marisa up to these days?"

"She works for a dentist in Seattle." She shrugged. "Officially, she still lives here on the Island."

"Officially."

Em rolled her eyes and stared up at the ceiling. "Yeah, well, she spends the night in Seattle a lot. Two years ago, she found her biological mother."

"Good for her," Captain Hill said. "She always wanted to do that."

"Well, anyway, she stays with them a lot." She shrugged like it didn't matter. But Jake thought that it really did matter. A lot.

"Married?" asked Captain Hill.

Em shook her head, no.

Captain Hill said, "Maybe I'll call her. Thanks."

Jake was overwhelmed. ELLIS Forces had some "special assignment" for this captain here in the Seattle area? Were they here for him? Did ELLIS know who Jake was? No. They likely only knew he was Commander Rose's son.

While at the beach house, Mom and Dad had drilled into Jake the need to keep his identity secret. "No one must know you're the son of the Risonian ambassador," Dad said. "No one must know that you're half-human and half-Risonian. Very few know that's even possible. My commanding officer from the first contact mission with Rison didn't include it in his official report."

Mom's voice had been the most passionate in the discussion. "I am working day and night to win a refuge for Rison here on Earth. And back home, Swann is working to calm down the Risonians who just want to attack Earth. We don't want a war; we just need a place to evacuate our people before Rison's core implodes."

"How long before that happens? What's the current prediction?" Dad asked.

"Two or three years. Maybe less. Time is short," Mom warned. Dad laid an arm protectively over her shoulder, and they turned as one to glare at Jake. "You must be invisible."

But now, the captain who led the search for Mom at the beach was here on Bainbridge Island. Surely it wasn't an accident.

The two men settled in to the table next to Jake, but thankfully, with their backs to him. Jake held immobile, trying to be invisible so he could shamelessly eavesdrop.

"How was Gulf Shores?" Mr. Blevins asked.

"Fine," said Captain Hill.

"Did your assignment go well?"

"No. We missed our target."

He meant Mom! That video had put a bull's eye on her face, and this man was taking aim. Jake's stomach cramped.

Then: "You know that I'm here on special assignment?"

"Yes."

"I need to go through your old photos," Hill said apologetically.

"For what?"

Silence.

The old man cleared his throat. "Look, I know you're working on something about Rison, and you think bringing that up will upset me, will bring back old memories. It's okay. Just ask. What do you need?"

"Okay," said the Captain. "I'm looking for photos of the Ambassador's son. The Quad-des have kept him out of the news, and the most recent picture we have is four years old. You know we have software that will age up a person's image, and I just wondered if you had anything better than the fuzzy photos online."

Jake's mind swirled. They were looking for pictures of him. But why would Mr. Blevins have pictures of Jake? Old pictures. This was crazy.

Mr. Blevins answered, "After Julianne died, I almost threw away all the old pictures from Rison. But for some reason, I kept them. You're welcome to pick them up and look."

"I'm not sure when I can get by," the captain said. "I have to take the late ferry back to Seattle."

"If I'm not there, just look in the storage room at the back of the garage," Mr. Blevins said.

"Thanks. I hope we get lucky. ELLIS convinced the National Enquirer and other newspapers like that to put out the word to its paparazzi, offering $10,000 for a photo of the kid. Maybe we'll get it."

"He was a nice kid—"

And then—Crash!

Spinning around, Jake took in the scene. Em's phone was in one hand, and an empty tray in the other. She'd apparently come around to gather empty cups, and had been concentrating on her phone to the point that the whole tray of dirty cups had spilled onto the captain's lap.

She really shouldn't text and work at the same time, Jake thought. Then he wanted to swat his head for how obvious that thought had been.

Dark coffee ran down the captain's jeans, and one thick white mug lay at Em's feet with the handle broken off.

"Oh!" Em cried. "I'm so sorry." She jammed the phone into her back pocket and—

The captain shoveled the coffee cups and napkins from his pants, shooting out of his seat and knocking Em backward into a table, which overturned with another crash. Em wind milled her arms, causing the tray she was still holding to go flying and crash onto the floor, too. Somehow, she kept her balance and didn't fall herself.

Anger surged in Jake. This bully thought he could push women around. Captain Hill poised like a cobra about to strike, his arms held tightly away from his sides like a tightly wound coil. His wide nostrils flared, and he took a step toward Em, clearly barely controlling himself.

Em cringed, shrinking into herself, and raised an arm in self-protection.

Captain Hill said, "You silly—"

"No! Leave her alone." Jake leapt up and shoved the captain's back. "She didn't mean to do it."

The captain whirled, fists ready to strike. Mr. Blevins grabbed his arm, stopping the swing.

The captain froze anyway and hissed, "You!"

Too late, Jake remembered his mother's preaching. "Grow up. Think before you act."

Em was saying, "It's okay, Jake."

But it wasn't okay. What had he done?

The other cashier, the older man who must be the storeowner, rushed over calling, "Everyone calm down, now. Just a clumsy waitress. No need to fight."

Jake sank heavily into the seating of his booth, legs sticking out into the aisle. But the captain was in his face. "What are you doing here on Bainbridge Island?"

"My grandparents live here. The Roses."

Blevins tugged at the younger man's arm. "The Roses have lived on Bainbridge for twenty years or more. Sir Rose is a dentist. Leave the boy alone."

"Where's your father? Where's the Commander?" the captain demanded.

"On assignment."

"Where?"

Jake shrugged. By now, he was regaining some of his composure and certainly wasn't going to answer this jerk's questions. "No idea. Dad doesn't exactly tell me all about his Navy assignments."

Anger blazed across the captain's face. He jabbed a finger at Jake's chest, almost yelling now. "He's negotiating with that Shark ambassador, isn't he? Where are they?"

This time, Mr. Blevins jerked his friend's arm, forcing him to turn. "Leave it."

The two men stared at each other for a moment before the captain squared his jaw and nodded. Through clenched teeth, he told Jake, "Don't worry. We're looking for the ambassador's son, and we know he's in the Seattle area. When we find him, we'll find her."

The captain pulled up, ramrod straight, as if at attention. He ran a hand through his curly hair and backed up a step, obviously trying to calm himself. "Okay, Okay." He reached into his pocket, pulled out a five-dollar bill, and threw it on the table.

To the shop owner, he said, "No problems here. We're leaving." He glared at Em but said nothing more. He stalked out.

Mr. Blevins shrugged a quick apology at Em and the owner, and then followed the captain.

Jake leaned his head back against the booth's cushions, stunned. The ELLIS captain who had tried to capture his mom was here on Bainbridge. And ELLIS knew the ambassador's son was in the area and were trying to get a current photo of Jake. But what did it mean? Why would his biology and civics teacher have old photographs of Jake? That had to mean he'd been on Rison at some point. And that was impossible.

If Jake thought he needed caution before, now it was drilled home. He must be invisible. Frustrated with the new culture or not, he couldn't turn to anyone else for help.

JAKE'S SIREN

Em touched Jake's shoulder, and he startled, jerking around in his seat. For a moment, the coffee shop windows blurred and grayed, like a cloud had gone across the sun.

"Sorry." Em held up her hand in surrender. "I didn't mean to make you jump. I just wanted to say thanks for sticking up for me."

She held out another cup of coffee. "Free." She waved a thumb toward the owner. "Everyone got scared and started leaving, so he's giving out a round of free coffee. Sorry, it's not a triple-shot."

Jake took the coffee and sipped; it was so hot it almost burned his tongue.

Even now, with his new worries weighing on his mind, Em's casual grace, her easy way of moving—she took his breath away. "Um. When do you get off work?"

She pulled out her phone.

Of course, he thought, she's glued to that phone.

"Thirty minutes," she said.

Jake needed information. Everything about high school was confusing, so different from his schooling on the Moon Base where he just sat at a computer for five hours a day; in the mornings he'd done a Risonian correspondence course, and in the afternoons, an Earth correspondence course. No interaction with other teenagers.

"Do you have time to visit?" he asked hesitantly, not sure how to ask. "I'm new on the island and have so many questions." He gave her a small smile.

Em smiled. "Sure. If you can wait."

Jake nodded in relief. Maybe he wasn't making a fool of himself.

While he waited, Jake listened to Em's random humming and tried to think what to do. Mom had forbidden him to call her unless it was a matter of life and death. Phone calls were too easily traced, so he had to do it through encrypted websites, which meant he'd have to wait till he got home to his computer. It made Jake's head hurt just to think about the possible public outrage and repercussions if anyone found out about his parents. Besides, Mom was so busy with her Ambassador duties that he didn't want to bother her.

And Dad was out of touch on his top-secret assignment. Jake knew he could get a message to him in an emergency, but this wasn't an emergency.

Sir and Easter, Jake's Earthling grandparents, were kind, polite, and were plainly trying to help him get settled into school and life on an island. Sir was a slightly taller version of Dad, athletic and tanned. Easter ran a neat, efficient home, making Jake think of a librarian who kept all her bookshelves alphabetized and dusted. Even on Rison, they'd had the equivalent of a librarian, and as far as he could tell, the character qualities of Risonian and Earth librarians were equally regimented. But he didn't know his grandparents well yet, didn't trust them. When they asked about life on Rison, he barely answered because it was so different, they wouldn't understand. Life on the Obama Moon Base was easier to answer because that was an Earthling base. Anything to do with intergalactic politics, Jake strictly avoided for now.

He had no one to turn to. It didn't seem wise, though, to ignore all of this with Captain Hill's presence on the island or what he had overheard—the ELLIS Force was looking for Jake.

When Em finally took off her apron and came to his table, Jake was ready to get away from his own thoughts. He remembered the manners that Dad had been trying to teach him and pulled open the coffee shop door for Em. He motioned for her to go ahead of him. She flashed him a smile—his heart thumped harder—and went outside.

"I only live a mile away," Em said. "On nice days, I just walk." She put on a Chicago Cubs baseball cap and pulled her long hair out the back.

"I'll walk you home," Jake said. "Is that okay?"

When she nodded, he tingled in anticipation. He'd never had a long conversation with an Earth girl before. Well, not with a Risonian girl, either. He'd left Rison about the time he was figuring out that girls were something different. And exciting. The Obama Moon Base had no other kids his age; it had been a special concession to let him live there with Dad. For a moment, he worried that he'd latched onto the first girl he ran across. But no. He'd been around enough to recognize that Em was special.

One thing about the Moon Base, there was plenty of time to read. Jake had read everything he could about Earth, especially its oceans, even folklore. Risonians could breathe easily on land or in the sea. They reasoned that Earth was 70% water, but Earthlings all lived on land. Surely, Earth could share their oceans and save a race of people. On paper, it sounded reasonable, but of course, the politics were immensely more complicated than that.

One old story came back to him now: mermaids sitting on rocks, combing their long hair, and singing to entice unwary sailors to their death. A siren's song.

For the last three days, the new Earthling high school had overwhelmed Jake. He'd seen other girls, heard other girls. Since Em was in his classes, he was sure he had seen her, but only as a part of the mass of students. Seeing her individually here at the coffee shop, Em was different: she was his siren, he thought in a daze. She called to him like no other girl had ever done. He would've waited eight hours for her to get off work. He would've walked her home, even if it were all the way across the island. He found himself strangely just wanting to be near her, to get to know her better.

He stopped himself: was he going overboard here? From the movies he'd watched with his dad on the Moon Base, this was how the boy-girl thing worked on Earth. Somehow, though, he wondered if movies made a good model for how he should behave. He shook his head: movies were all the guidance he had.

Jake remembered that the first thing movie guys did was talk to the girls. Conversation. He could do this. Make an effort at conversation. "That was Mr. Blevins, the biology and civics teacher, right? But you called him Coach?"

Em nodded. "Coach Blevins. Everyone calls him that. He's been here about five years. Teaches biology and civics. And coaches the swim team."

Jake shrugged to himself. If everyone else did it, he'd call him Coach Blevins, too.

They turned off the main street onto a side street that lacked sidewalks. Instead, beside the road was a swath of waist-high plants with fluffy yellow flowers that rippled in the light wind, a yellow lake in the midst of green foliage.

"You swim?" Jake asked.

"Sure. I do backstroke and IM."

"IM?"

"Individual medley," she said. "That means I swim one or two laps with each of the strokes: free style, backstroke, breast stroke, and butterfly."

Jake was struck by a sudden vision of Em in a racing swimsuit and speeding through the water. It spooked him how much he wanted to see her swim. To distract himself, he asked, "Are you fast?" But he already knew that she would be; she didn't have a cat-like grace, as he first thought, but the grace of a powerful swimmer.

She checked something on her phone, and then held it up and pointed to what looked like a list. "3rd in the district in back stroke, and I'm fighting for first in IM." It wasn't bragging, just a statement of fact.

Jake nodded, afraid to ask more lest he seem like a total idiot. He knew that his father had been on the Bainbridge Island swim team, but he didn't know much more than that. He wasn't even quite sure what a "district" meant. These were things he could ask Easter and Sir about; in fact, it would actually give them a topic for conversation for a change.

Em smiled, a sudden flash of white teeth. "Before Coach Blevins, the Bainbridge swim team was a joke. But since he came five years ago, we've built a strong team. We took the state meet last year. He drives us hard, but we win. I think everyone on Bainbridge likes him."

"Where'd he come from? Was he always a swim coach and teacher?"

Em frowned, "No idea. I think he's Canadian. He knows his science, though."

Jake decided that he'd have to do some research on Coach Blevins. There was something fishy about Blevins owning photos taken on Rison, especially photos that might show Jake as a child.

Em stopped and turned to look him up and down. "Say, are you a swimmer? We sure need more guys. What stroke are you best at?"

"Oh, I don't swim," Jake said, without conviction. "I do a little freestyle, but I'm not very fast." If he understood their terms right, his leg-tail would be akin to doing dolphin kicks instead of the flutter kicks required by freestyle.

"That's okay," Em said. "Swim team speeds you up. You work on your form and your times and before you know it—"

"No." Jake had to stop her. He desperately wanted to be on the swim team, to be in the water all the time. Or rather, to have the freedom to come and go, in or out of the water, as he liked. He wanted to go home to Rison. But Rison was dying, and he had his orders from his parents; no one could know who—or what—he was.

Only a few blocks from Puget Sound the houses were large with civilized lawns. Rison houses on land were often made with ebony volcanic rock polished to a gleam; Earth houses, by contrast, were constructed from a variety of materials, from stone and brick, to logs or wood siding. Such a different world, thought Jake.

"Okay, okay. I get it," Em said. Her face was bright red, and she started walking fast again, this time at a fast pace as if to get away from his refusal to consider swim team. "I just love swim team, and I get overly excited about it. I want everyone else to be as excited as I am. I'll back off." She took off her baseball cap and waved it at her face.

"No, no." Jake almost trotted to keep up. "I mean—oh, I've just been teased a lot because I can't swim. Because really, I just can't."

"Oh."

There was a world of uncertainty in that "Oh." Jake wanted to please her, to say that he'd give swim team a try. No. He had to convince her. "I'm too scared of the water."

"That's all?" She gave a nervous laugh. "We can help with that." She stopped waving her cap at her face, but fumbled with and dropped it.

Quickly, Jake picked up the blue cap, but he made no move to return it. He tried again. "I'm scared of the water because I don't have the right lungs for it." That part was true at least. His lungs weren't good Earthling lungs; they were good Risonian lungs that could breathe air on land, while his underarm gills breathed in the sea.

"That's just technique. Coach Blevins can help you with your breathing—"

"No."

They stopped at a street corner where one road went downhill toward the water while the other stayed on higher ground. Em looked over his head, obviously embarrassed now.

She held out her hand for her cap. Jake stepped closer, and reaching to the back of her head, pulled her shiny pony tail through the back of the cap, and settled it on her head. For a moment, Jake stared into her eyes, a warm sienna, and felt like he was falling.

Em sucked in a breath and jerked her head away, breaking eye contact. "Oh. Well, if you ever want to come and watch, we practice early mornings." She waved downhill. "Well, thanks for walking with me a while. I live down that way, and I'm sure it's too far for you. You have better things to do." With a tap of her thumb, she wakened her phone and concentrated on the screen.

She was giving him the brush-off.

Jake bit back the words he wanted to say: You're beautiful. I would walk—or swim—anywhere with you.

Em turned, and with a half-wave, she strode away.

He let her go.

He stood watching until she turned the corner. Em was his first friend on Bainbridge Island. At least, he hoped they'd be friends. It was going to be hard, he realized, to resist the swim team. He wanted to belong, to be on equal footing with everyone else. But he wasn't equal. He was a Risonian and a Quadde.

Discouraged, he turned to trudge further on to his grandparent's house on Yeomalt Point. It wasn't home, not yet, maybe not ever.

His thoughts turned back to Captain Cy Hill and his friend Coach Blevins. They were investigating him. Jake didn't know the ways of Earth yet, nor did he know how to look into someone's background. He'd have to be patient, but he'd eventually figure out what was going on. He could maybe search the Internet or maybe find out more about Coach at school. It might take him a while, but Risonians were patient fishermen; in the end, he'd hook the two men and reel 'em in.

Lungs vs. Gills

Jake walked into Bainbridge High School on Monday morning—the first full week of class—with one goal: to be invisible. That's what his parents expected, and that's what he would deliver.

He didn't want or need to be noticed. He just wanted to be one of the crowd. He sidled close to one group of students, close enough to be on the fringes, but not so close that someone would single him out. Once inside the brick building, he drifted from group to group. Always close enough that someone might think he belonged, but never so close that he invaded the group's space.

The day went well until Coach Blevins's biology class.

"Our first unit is anatomy and physiology," Coach said. He flipped on the holo-projector and pulled up a set of 3-D slides of major organs.

"Sometimes it's easier to understand anatomy when we compare it to something else." A second set of 3-D slides opened on the right side of the screen.

Instantly, Jake recognized Risonian anatomy. Lungs vs. Gills. The so-called Velcro legs. The wrinkled nose that was the result of internal flaps that closed off the Risonian nose so water didn't fill their air-breathing lungs.

"Humans vs. Sharks." Coach spat out the words. "They may resemble us physically, but think of all the science fiction aliens that look like insects or slugs or monsters. These anatomical differences may not be huge, but their mentality is completely foreign. Alien." Coach pointed at the gills, and his hand trembled, in what Jake thought must be anger.

Jake cringed. What had happened to make Coach Blevins hate the Risonians? he wondered. Coach must have been on Rison at some point to have pictures of Jake. But when? And what had happened to him while there?

Coach was lecturing about blood. "Risonians have hemoglobin to carry oxygen, but also myoglobin, which is—well, some people are of the opinion that it's more efficient. But the Risonians have to have twice the blood, so it's a trade-off. They're also dependent on a different molecule that's been named magma-sapiens." Coach barked a short laugh. "Late night TV comedians call it the hot-man molecule."

A titter ran through the class, and made Jake shiver in frustration.

One side of Coach's mouth curved up in a lopsided grin.

Jake sat straighter and glared. Coach was deliberately making fun of Risonians. It was a dangerous game for Jake to say anything, but he should just let it pass without drawing attention to himself. Still, his stomach clenched.

Coach continued, "The function of the magma-sapiens, though, is to keep Risonians warm when they slink away to the cold depths of the ocean."

From the back of the room, someone heckled. "Hey, does that make girl-Sharks hot mamas?"

Coach Blevins smirked but kept talking. "Humans need wet suits to survive the cold of Puget Sound except on the warmest summer days. Wet suits, glove, boots, and a headpiece—humans will freeze if anything is exposed."

"I was wondering why all the girls were so frigid," came the call.

The class groaned.

Coach Blevins cleared his throat and became serious. "Think about this difference in how humans and Sharks regulate their temperatures. What would it mean if Sharks colonized our oceans?"

Coach ran a finger down his seating chart, his hand still trembling with anger. He called, "David Gordon."

He looked up expectantly, waiting for David to say something.

"Um. They could live in the Arctic Ocean away from human population centers." Seated in almost the center of the room, David slumped in his desk, his long legs filling the aisles. He also had a long face and long nose, like a bottlenose dolphin.

"Yes, what else?"

No answer.

"Emmeline Tullis," Coach Blevins called.

All morning, Jake had tried hard not to look at Em. Last week, he hadn't been confident enough to even lift his head to look past one row. Now, he glanced sideways across the room to where she sat by the wall. Her pink hoodie made her dark cheeks look rosy.

"They can go where we can't go," Em said. "They could hide, ambush us, or just disappear and do anything they wanted."

Wait! Was Em anti-Risonian? Maybe she was just saying what Coach wanted to hear. Still, Jake frowned.

"Exactly right!" Coach exclaimed. "Would you invite someone dangerous to live in your house? Of course not!"

Pulse racing, Jake couldn't hold back the words: "Are the Risonians dangerous?"

Now, Coach sounded vicious. "I know people who've worked with the Sharks: those aliens pretend to be friends, and then they lie and turn on you. Threw my friend to the wolves. You can't trust them."

Jake blinked in surprise. Where did the venom come from? He had to find out more about this man.

Blevins walked down the aisle to stand in front of Jake. "Jake, right? You're new here. What are you, for or against the Sharks?"

Looking right and then left, Jake found every eye turned toward him. The classroom, with its white plastic skeleton in the corner and the black-topped laboratory desks, seemed suddenly dangerous. He wondered if these students would turn on him if they knew about his parents, if they knew who he was.

"Well?" Blevins demanded.

"Neither," Jake said. "I'm pro-life. Creatures have the right to try to live, and that's all the Risonians are trying to do: survive."

Coach snorted. "Survive? Yeah, if they move here, it will be survival of the fittest. And there's no guarantee that humans will win." He spun to point at the rest of the class.

"There's a good biology question. What do you think? Are humans physically superior compared to Risonians, or vice versa?"

Jake wanted to laugh. Of course, the Risonians had the advantage in almost any comparison of anatomy. He gripped the edge of his chair to keep his hand from shooting up to continue the argument.

Just then, the bell rang. Jake let out a breath he didn't know he'd been holding. Escape. For now.

He grabbed his backpack and joined the throng rushing through the door and into the hallway. Glancing back, he saw Coach Blevins was still glaring at him.

Yes, Jake thought. It was definitely time to find out more about Coach Blevins and Captain Hill.

BREAK-IN

After supper, Jake told Easter, "I think I'll run a couple miles."

"Enjoy the weather while you can," Easter said. "We'll be into the fall rains soon enough."

Jake pulled on tight running pants to hide the villi on his legs, a short sleeve t-shirt, and a baseball cap. In the top of his bedroom closet, he'd discovered his Dad's collection of baseball caps, and now he grabbed an old NYPD (New York Police Department) cap that had seen better days. When Dad got around to visiting again—whenever that might be—Jake would ask him about the collection. In the meantime, Jake had decided to try a different hat each day.

Evergreen trees towered on either side of the road, making the deserted road feel like a huge tunnel. Breaking into an easy trot, Jake tried to understand the last twenty-four hours. Coach Blevins was Canadian but had somehow landed here on Bainbridge Island. Jake had glanced at Coach's bookshelf and had been surprised at the mathematical, volcanology, and biology journals stacked there, some of the most technical scientific journals published, if Swann was right. And Swann had kept track of most of Earth's scientific journals.

If Blevins understood half of what was in those journals, he was a genius; what was he doing just teaching high school? Jake suspected that at some point Blevins had done volcano research: volcanologists were the only Earth personnel who had access to Rison, and thus, would have old photos taken on Rison. The volcanology journals supported that theory, but it made it even stranger that Blevins was now teaching high school biology.

He turned left at the next block and steadily wound through neighborhoods until he stood in front of Coach Blevin's house. It was still light—sunset in early September was about 7:30 p.m.—but it was now or never. If he understood right, Coach would be busy with swim team for another hour or so. Jake had watched enough detective shows that he knew what he had to do: break in and search Blevins's house. Of course, those shows were just fiction, he knew that. But he'd also read about real Earth detectives, and concluded that—when you suspected someone of questionable activity—it's just what you did on Earth. As Sherlock Holmes would say, "The game is afoot."

Looking all around, Jake saw no one. He pulled on a pair of gloves to guard against fingerprints. Taking a deep breath, he pulled the brim of his cap low on his forehead, and crossed the road, heart beating crazily. He'd never broken into a house before, in fact, never been around Earth housing before.

Blevins's house was a one-story ranch, small, and obviously had seen better days. The garage door sagged, and the roof had patches of moss. The garage's side door stuck, needing a shove to open, but it hadn't been locked. Jake shrugged to himself: detective work was easy.

Inside, the garage was empty, which probably meant that Blevins still parked his car there on a regular basis. In his short time on Earth, Jake had already learned that many garages were storage rooms, not protection for cars.

Coach Blevins had told the captain to look in the storage room at the back, so Jake crept across the open space, spotted the door, and opened it. He found a light switch, and when he realized that there were no windows in the room, he flicked the light on and closed the door.

The storage room was narrow, piled with boxes near the door, and at the other end, thick canvas covered several large shapes. Blevins was clearly a neat man: every box was labeled with large black printing. Julianne's clothes. High school annuals. Rison photos.

Jake's hand trembled as he pulled the photo box from under the others and set it on the floor. Kneeling, he peeled off the yellowed tape and opened the cardboard flaps. He felt like he was peeling off a couple years of Blevins's life, and Jake didn't know if he'd like what he'd find. Inside was a jumble of photos, newspaper clippings, and a couple photo albums. Jake whistled. These were old. No one kept stuff like this anymore; everything was digital.

He pulled out an album and flipped through it: badly faded color photographs and even a few black-and-whites. Really old. Probably Coach Blevins's parents or maybe grandparents. Next, he discarded a yellowed newspaper dated December 25, 1999. Why Coach Blevins kept that newspaper, Jake couldn't figure out. To one side, a stack of 8"x10" black-and-white photos caught his attention. On top was a sight Jake recognized, the Cadee Moon Base. His breath caught. Seen from a spaceship, the Moon Base was a square block of buildings, and behind it loomed Rison. Jake wished it were a color picture, wished it showed the blue oceans. Rison and Earth were so much alike: about 70% of Earth is covered in water and 80% of Rison. Jake touched the photo of his home planet and let the homesickness wash over him. Usually he blocked it, turned it off. But now he longed to see his pet kriga—a monkey-like animal he had named Bell. He had photos of Bell and himself sleeping in what Earthlings would call a hammock, and photos of them sharing a frozen dessert much like ice cream. Even three years later, some nights he still wanted Bell to cuddle while he went to sleep. Before tears could well up, he set aside the photo.

Glancing at the next photo, he froze. It showed his stepfather Swann Quad-de and another man who were shaking hands. Judging from Swann's image, it was taken maybe six or eight years ago. The face of the other man looked familiar, but Jake couldn't place it. Something, though, stilled his hand, and he couldn't put it down, as if instinct told him that this photo was important. The man was clean-shaven, but the hairstyles then had been longer and shaggier. Who was it?

A noise sounded from outside in the garage, probably the garage door rising. Jake leapt up, and flipped off the light. Blinded in the sudden dark, Jake picked up the box of photos and felt for the stack of boxes. He heaved the box onto the top of the stack. He couldn't tape it shut, but he could make it less conspicuous. The last photo he had looked at, the black-and-white of Swann Quad-de and somehow-familiar man, Jake shoved into the waistband of his pants; he wanted to look at it in more detail. Finally, he squeezed behind the boxes and hid. The growl of a car pulling into the garage made him cower and cover his head. Jake gulped and forced himself to relax. Behind the short wall of boxes, he slumped, his back against a wall. The stolen photo poked his ribcage, but he wasn't giving that up.

The growl of the car suddenly stopped, and Jake tried to stop breathing.

A car door slammed.

A tiny crack of light shone at the bottom of the door to the storage room.

The door opened and a shaft of light poured in. And then the overhead light came on.

Jake gulped air, and then squeezed his lips together to ensure silence. Fear throbbed, making his heat beat wildly. He peered through a small opening between the boxes.

Whistling, Captain Hill walked into the storage room, strode to the right, and stopped at a wall map that Jake hadn't noticed. It was a topographical map, one that showed the mountains and valleys of a landscape in great detail. At the center someone had drawn a red circle and written numbers in a black marker: 45° 51'14.16"N; 121° 45'35.71"W.

Jake realized they were GPS coordinates, an Earth method of finding exact locations on Earth using satellite data.

Captain Hill tapped the map and muttered, "Soon."

With his fingernail, he peeled tape from the map, pulled it off the wall, and folded it. Captain Hill knelt and flipped open a large case in the corner of the room that Jake hadn't noticed when he came in. Hill slipped the map into the side of the case, and then pulled out a white metal thing that unfolded to show four legs, and set it on the floor. From the case, he removed a propeller and blew on it to make it spin.

A drone! The case had four propellers that could screw onto the four legs. What was going on?

The Captain stood on a small stool to reach the cabinet's top shelf and carefully stepped down holding a package. When he turned, Jake got a good view of it: the black plastic was plastered with universal symbols warning, "Poison" and "Brown Matter."

Jake watched in horror as Captain Hill fitted the package into the payload area of the drone. A single drop of Brown Matter—it was unthinkably dangerous.

Red Matter, Brown Matter—Rison physicists had debated the structure of matter in the universe for decades. Red Matter wasn't just theoretical, but it was hard to produce in a lab because it was hard to contain it. Besides, physicists predicted that a critical mass of Red Matter could cause a singularity, or a black hole, so few experimenters wanted to risk dealing with it. Brown Matter was a cruder form of Red Matter with slightly different properties; instead of collapsing into a black hole, it merely absorbed energy. A hundred years ago, Risonian scientist Oliver Saboo had proposed that Brown Matter could absorb the energy from a volcano about to erupt. When they finally tried it 50 years ago, he was partially right. Brown Matter absorbed energy, pulling up even more energy from the planet's core, which could make a dormant volcano explode. In the short term, a volcano's activity could be worse. But over the long run, the Brown Matter did sink deep and calm down volcanic activity, volcano by volcano across Rison, and it seemed to have no side effects. However, over the next five decades, the Brown Matter sank even farther into the core than predicted, kept absorbing energy, and cooled the planet.

At some point, scientists realized that the energy absorbed by the Brown Matter and the increasing pressure from the depths of Rison's core was slowly purifying and transforming the material into Red Matter. Eventually, the Red Matter particles would be attracted to each other until they formed a critical mass and created a singularity. In other words, the planet would implode into a black hole.

Over the years, the delivery of Brown Matter had been miniaturized. The box that Captain Hill held was about half the size of a cereal box, but it could hold anything from a few nanograms to a full gram of Brown Matter. The rest of the box was a containment field called a Penning Trap. Penning Traps were electromagnetic fields created by an octupole magnet. It was like creating a bottle with no walls and was considered the safest way to contain and deliver Brown Matter.

Captain Hill sat cross-legged on the floor and drew a worn paper notebook from the cabinet. Flipping through it, he whispered to himself. "We'll have our revenge, yet. That volcano will blow."

Horror struck Jake. Captain Hill was actually thinking about using the Brown Matter on an Earth volcano! It was madness! The short-term effect could pull even dormant volcanoes to life.

Hill's phone rang: the ringtone was a classic alien sound effect.

"Yes?" he answered.

Then: "Sure, I'll stick it in the oven now. I'm just looking for those photos, and then I'll catch the last ferry back to Seattle."

And: "Okay, see you soon."

He stuck the phone into his back pocket, packed up the Brown Matter and the drone, and carried the case to his car. The car door slammed, and then the house door opened.

It was Jake's chance to get away!

He tiptoed to the storage room's door, opened it a crack, and peered out. Captain Hill was just walking into the house from the garage, a dark silhouette in the lighted doorway.

Jake waited, counting to 20. But he dared not wait longer; Captain Hill would soon reappear. He opened the door and darted into the garage. The large door for the cars to enter and exit was closed, so he went to the side door through which he'd originally entered. The door was stuck again. Jake tugged, the door making a scraping sound on the concrete floor.

"Halt!" It was a military-style order, given with the assurance that it would be obeyed. A quick glance told Jake that Captain Hill had come out of the house and was pointing at Jake.

Ignoring the order, Jake yanked the door, finally dragging it open, and dashed out. Panicked, he pounded down the street, no plan except to get away.

Behind him, Jake heard the stomp of Captain Hill's boots giving chase.

Jake ran lightly, glad now for his running outfit and running shoes. Car lights glared, forcing Jake to slow for a second before darting across the road. Captain Hill was catching up, obviously a strong runner. Jake saw a path ahead and darted into the Grand Forest, a 240-acre park of second-growth forest with miles of trails. He hoped it would be easier to find places to hide there.

Dashing through the towering woods, he thought he might be right. Captain Hill seemed slower, less sure, in the darkness. Suddenly, Jake's foot caught a root, and he fell heavily, thumping his head. He sat up, shook his head, and almost passed out. Stumbling up, he ran again, but slower, Captain Hill thundering up behind him.

Finding a deeper strength from somewhere inside, Jake lengthened his stride. Dark shadows flickered past, and he was afraid he'd trip up again. But he had to go faster. He pushed himself harder, moving faster up a steep incline, then down and up again through another steep area.

Captain Hill was breathing loud, maybe not in as good shape as Jake had first thought.

But Jake's head throbbed. He needed to stop and breathe, too. There, beside the trail was a stand of ferns, chest high. Jake shoved through the wall of fronds and sat abruptly, forcing himself to a stillness that let him blend into the Grand Forest. He had just disappeared. He hoped.

Captain Hill thundered past, huffing and puffing, pushing up yet another incline. The dark shadows had deepened, and it was getting hard to see anything.

Waiting, Jake breathed heavily. He was scared of being caught, but oddly, it was his mother he feared the most. If he were caught, her smoldering frustrations with the pace of negotiations would spill over and burn him. Humans might call them Risonian Sharks, but they had no idea how angry his mother could get. Oh, she wouldn't touch him; Rison parents rarely spanked or hit their children. Instead, her disappointment would be a sword that stabbed his heart.

Captain Hill would be back soon, and Jake had to escape. He wondered if Captain Hill had gotten a good look at him or could identify him. The woods were dark now, and Jake could take a chance getting close to Captain Hill if he had to. But it was still better to just outrun him. Jake darted up and back the way they had come.

Immediately, he heard Captain Hill circling back to find him. Though he had rested briefly, Jake was still panting, and he had to pause, bend over and gulp air. He couldn't run much longer; he had to stop and fight.

Jake crouched under a fern, and just as Captain Hill dashed past, Jake swarmed upward and shoved the man to the ground. Captain Hill rolled head over heels, landing flat on his back. Instantly, Jake was on top, flailing with fists at Captain Hill's face.

The captain screamed, "Halt!"

For the briefest instant, Jake hesitated, instinct making him want to obey. Captain Hill heaved upward with his legs throwing Jake up and over his head to land sprawling on the forest floor.

They both staggered to a standing position and squared off in the dark woods, with only scraps of starlight coming through the forest canopy. Jake's ears rang, fear drowning everything else. It might look exciting in a movie, but this chase stuff was way overrated. Captain Hill was military, trained in armed combat. Jake, as a politician's son, had received hand-to-hand combat training, but he was unsure of himself, untested against a human. And now, Swann's voice replayed in his head. "If there's a way to avoid a fight, that's the best."

Looking at the steep terrain, Jake thought he saw a chance. He rushed headlong toward Captain Hill, his momentum giving him strength, and shoved the startled man.

Captain Hill waved his arms wildly for a moment, and then fell down the incline behind him, rolling a couple times. He groaned—he was alive!—but didn't move.

Swann's voice came again in Jake's head: "And once you have your opponent immobilized, leave."

Jake turned and ran. Behind him there was only silence.

□ ☆ ☆

Jake opened the back door, shoes in hand, intending to sneak upstairs to his room. But a voice stopped him.

"Where've you been?" Sir asked.

Jake shrugged. How could he explain the night's adventure to his grandfather?

Sir shook his head, bald scalp gleaming in the shafts of light from the street lamps outside. In a reasonable voice, he said, "I used to wait up for your father just like this. He always tried to sneak in, too. Doesn't work, you know. You have to talk to me sooner or later."

Jake set his shoes beside the staircase. When he'd reached the road, he'd been aggravated to find that Dad's old NYPD hat was missing; but it was too dark and too dangerous to go back into the woods to find it. He went to the refrigerator. "May I please have some milk?" Cow's milk was one Earth drink he'd learned to appreciate.

"Of course," Sir said. "Then come and sit with me." He went out to sit in one of the rocking chairs on the front porch.

No good options. Jake took his milk and sat in the other rocking chair. For a few minutes, they just watched the stars, both overhead and how they reflected in the waters of the Sound. Across the water from Yeomalt Point, Seattle's skyline twinkled, and on the horizon a glow was growing where the moon would rise soon. Jake shifted his chair to the right so he could see the stars better, and he wondered how things were faring for his stepfather. Guilt washed over him again. He should've been there on Rison with Swann, not here on Earth. But Swann and his mother had been adamant about him leaving Rison.

"When I come to Earth," Swann had said, "you'll show me around. You'll be the one to help me get settled."

They both knew it was unlikely for Swann to ever come to Earth. Even if they'd started evacuating Rison a year ago, there was no way they could get everyone off-planet. No way Earth could accommodate all the Risonians.

Sir cleared his throat. "Do you want to tell me where you've been?"

Jake rubbed his temples and sighed. He desperately wanted to tell him, wanted advice and help. But not from Sir. Where was Dad? Anger ruffled through him and settled into a dull headache. Anger that he was here on Earth with his father, while Swann was back on Rison in danger. "No, I'd rather not talk about it."

"Thought you might say that," Sir said. "Well, I'm here. I'm ready to listen any time. I can help, but only if you let me."

"Thank you, Sir."

"If you plan to be out late again, call me. I don't want Easter worried."

"Yes, Sir."

His grandfather rose. "Well, goodnight."

Jake waited a few minutes, letting his grandfather go upstairs first. With a last glance at the Milky Way galaxy, he went upstairs to the bathroom. He found some headache medicine in the medicine cabinet—close enough to Risonian pain medicines that they usually worked for him. He swallowed the pill and brushed his teeth. Back in his room, Jake pulled off his t-shirt, then paused to smooth out the photo of Swann Quad-de and the strangely familiar man. Who was it? It was an important clue, he was sure. Jake yawned, tired from the night's race through the woods. Tomorrow, he promised himself, he would find out everything there was to know about Captain Hill and Coach Blevins.

SLEEPER CELLS

School was buzzing with the news: Coach Blevins's house had been broken into, and the captain from the ELLIS Forces had a slight concussion. It was a scandal for the island. ELLIS forces were at the Blevins's house, going through everything for clues. The only thing they'd found so far was a battered NYPD baseball cap that could've come from anywhere.

Anything else was just speculation because ELLIS Forces were refusing comment. The Kitsap Sun's online Police Blotter had no more details to add, either.

Even Coach Blevins said nothing, though it was clearly hard for him.

Coach just kept repeating to everyone, "If you have information on the incident, please report it to the ELLIS Forces Hotline number."

Jake rubbed his eyes, which felt like sand from so little sleep; he had tossed all night, worried that Captain Hill might be hurt badly. It was a relief to know it was a "slight" concussion. Jake ran a hand over the back of his head, as if he was the one with a concussion. Slowly, he forced his hand to reach down and pick up a pencil; he had to keep his hands busy, even if his mind was still reeling.

Blevins stopped in mid-sentence and said, "Jake. Stop tapping the pencil."

Jake nodded curtly and dropped the pencil.

Still, he couldn't help but wonder why, after all the excitement, why was Coach Blevins even trying to teach a class today? Blevins was a traveling teacher. He taught biology in a science lab on the first floor and civics in a second story history classroom with maps on the wall instead of skeletons in the corner. The rest of the day, he was in the athletic offices in the gym.

Coach pulled down a wall map, but it rattled in his hand, and the cord slipped out of his grip, letting the map pop back up with a bang. Grimly shaking his head, he pulled it firmly until it settled into position. The map showed Seattle and its surrounding areas, including Puget Sound and Bainbridge Island.

"Nidoto Nai Yoni," Coach Blevins intoned. "Does anyone know what that means?"

Civics was always silent: 5th period was right after lunch, and food made humans sleepy.

This time, though, Bennie Chalmers spoke up. "That's Japanese. Translated, it means, 'Let it not happen again.'"

From somewhere at the back came a voice, "Of course, you know that."

Bennie was the freshman class's history nerd. The football coach described him as a fireplug, and he played on the offensive line. He shaved his head for football season, but he let it grow long and shaggy during the off-season. He wore an XXL football helmet, so everyone joked that he had a big head to cram facts into, and it was crammed with history trivia. He liked letting that trivia leak out.

Coach Blevins nodded his approval. "Who knows when and why it was spoken?"

"March 30, 1942," Em said promptly.

Jake swiveled to stare at her. She seldom volunteered information about anything. Swim team required massive intake of food, which then made her sleepy after lunch. She usually pulled her hoodie over her head and slumped in her seat to snooze.

Coach said, "Go on." He clearly was interested to see what Em would say, too.

"U.S. Army soldiers forced 257 men, women, and children from Bainbridge Island to board the ferry for Seattle."

Bennie couldn't be outdone by a casual historian. "They were taken to an internment camp, mostly to Manzanar, California. Although some later went to Minidoka, Idaho."

Em and Bennie glared at each other. She was trespassing on his turf, and he wasn't going to let her be the class expert.

"Yes," Coach Blevins agreed. Wearing soft khakis, a school t-shirt, and a pair of sandals with socks, he always looked like a grandfather who'd seen better days. "In today's terminology, the government worried that there might be sleeper cells of people spying for Japan. People who lived here in the U.S., but who still held loyalty to their country of origin."

Em threw back the hood of her sweatshirt and sat up straighter. "But that's just it. These were American citizens who just happened to have Japanese ancestors. How dare the government question their loyalty and send them to prison."

"It's not that easy," Bennie said. "Pearl Harbor had just been bombed by the Japanese. Everyone was terrified that the war was coming to the mainland."

"It is that easy!" Em cried. "Soldiers came and picked up American citizens, and the soldiers had their rifles fixed with bayonets. Bayonets! Little kids were terrified. Soldiers with knives on their guns were shouting at them."

For a moment, the room was quiet. Jake felt the outrage and thought he followed what they were talking about. The people of Japanese descent were seen as aliens, foreigners who were so strange that no one could predict what they'd do or where their loyalties might lie. Still—they were American citizens. Didn't that count for something?

Bennie spoke now, low and passionate. "Don't talk to me about bayonets. My grandfather was in the Philippines when it fell to the Japanese army. He evacuated to the island of Corregidor, where a small force held out for a month. On 1/16th rations." Bennie almost spit out the words. "Starving. Killing anything they could—snakes or rats—and eating it raw, just to stay alive. When they finally surrendered and went to the prison camp, the Japanese soldiers were brutal. If an American soldier made any kind of trouble, they'd make him stand in a field in front of everyone. And they'd use him for bayonet practice. Stabbing him. Over and over. Till he was dead." Bitterness tinged his words, and Bennie kept shaking his head. "Don't talk to me about bayonets."

"That's horrible." Em's eyes were wide, and she waved a hand as if she could make the mental images erase. "But don't you see? They were soldiers. The people taken from Bainbridge were civilians. Citizens. American citizens."

Everyone leaned forward, tense, looking from Bennie to Em, waiting for the next blow to fall. Jake admired Em's passion for the people who were considered aliens. Rison would need people like her when they moved to Earth, people who would speak out and defend their right to even exist. He'd wanted to be open with her and tell her that he was half-Risonian. But besides his parents placing a taboo on that information, Jake also worried about what Em would think. Would his heritage send her running away from a friendship with him? Maybe she was more open than he'd assumed.

Suddenly, he realized that he was probably the only kid in the class who was grinning like a looney at Em, making a fool of himself. Quickly, he looked down at his sandals. But his shoes were brown, a warm sienna color, just like Em's eyes. With a groan, he turned to stare at Coach.

The silence grew. Coach Blevins crossed his arms and just looked from Em to Bennie and back to Em.

Once, Em took a deep breath as if to speak, but then shook her head.

Bennie nodded, as if he'd made a point.

Into the tension, David Gordon spoke slow, measured words: "Are sleeper cells real?"

Jake twisted to stare back at David where his long legs were sprawled across two aisles. He'd noticed David in a couple of his classes; the mass of students was slowly resolving into individuals. David pitched for the baseball team and was captain of the sculling team. Apparently, he was also a peacemaker because his question had defused the tension. Visibly, the class relaxed, some slouching down again and closing their eyes.

"Are they real?" repeated Coach Blevins.

"Well, sure," Jillian Lusk said. She was always taking photos with her cellphone and posting them all over. Jake had already developed a sort of sixth sense about her, and when she came into sight, he left if he could, or at least ducked behind someone. She didn't know it, but a photo of him was worth a lot.

Coach said, "Elaborate for us."

Jillian just nodded at Bennie to take the discussion where he wanted.

"During the Cold War," Bennie said, "sleeper cells made sense. You could send people to live in the U.S., and no one really knew who they were. They were in place, though, should Russia ever need them."

Jake only vaguely knew about the Cold War; it was another Earth history thing to bone up on.

Em said lazily, compared to her earlier passion, "Does the U.S. have sleeper cells overseas?" She yawned widely.

"Do we?" Coach Blevins echoed.

"We must," David said. "If they have them, we have them."

Jake wondered if there were sleeper cells of Risonians on Earth. Were there Earthling sleeper cells on Rison? Did it go both ways? But a sleeper cell on Rison would be in danger of getting blown up with the planet. Would they risk that? There was enough talk on Rison about invading Earth that Earth probably had spies in place. The species appeared so similar, but it still was hard to blend in. Jake only managed it because he was half-human. But wouldn't a group of humans stand out on Rison, just as Risonians stood out on Earth? Just like the Japanese-Americans stood out against the mostly white population during World War II?

Coach Blevins grinned now, enjoying his role as a provocateur. "Does the possibility of sleeper cells justify putting U.S. citizens into jail?"

"Naturalized citizens?" Em asked. "Or born-here citizens?"

Bennie said, "Does it matter which? Are naturalized citizens second-class citizens?"

The complexities of the discussion—indeed of the whole political and cultural situation in 1942—made Jake's head swim. But what he did understand was this: "different" meant enemy. If that was how Earth treated people they perceived as "aliens," even from the same species, it would be hundreds of years or more before Risonians could ever be accepted—if it ever happened. But then, again, struggling to be fair, he wondered what Risonians would feel if they'd been asked to allow Earthlings to live on their planet. Nothing was black and white.

"For Monday," Coach Blevins said, "write a two-page opinion essay on whether or not it was right for the government to put Japanese-American citizens in jail. Be sure to defend your opinion with facts. And don't wait till Sunday night to start."

Earth school—so much homework! On Rison he'd had schooling, too, of course. But it was more hands-on, mostly one-on-one tutoring, mixed in with some large-group lectures on Earth culture. Sure, that's because he was the son of a politician. He didn't care; the tutors had been great. Here, he was stuck in class with so many others—up to 25 at a time—that he felt lost. The teachers didn't know or seem to care if he understood the material. It was up to him. Before this, teachers had taken responsibility to make sure he understood things. Now it seemed like kids were one big super-student to the teacher with no individuality at all.

At least it was easy to hide his ignorance, because no one ever called on him.

Maybe Easter would know how to do research and write an essay that would satisfy an Earth civics teacher.

The bell rang for the end of class, and as they streamed out of doors, Coach Blevins called, "Remember: if you hear anything—anything at all—about who may have broken into my house, call the ELLIS Security Hotline."

And Jake wondered: when the Japanese-Americans were jailed, was it in the name of "homeland security"? Did homeland security mean that someone had to give up his or her rights as a U.S. citizen? When ELLIS Forces finally found Jake, what would they do in the name of interstellar security?

MADE YOU LAUGH

After school, Jake caught Em in the hallway. Or, at least, he tried to.

Em stood in front of her locker and shuffled things around. This was the second week of school, but already stray pieces of paper floated out.

Jake wondered how she could ever find anything in there.

She had a backpack slung over one shoulder, and a gym bag dangled from a longer strap below that. With her left arm, she hugged two textbooks with papers falling out against her pink fleece jacket while she juggled keys and her phone in the other hand.

"Need help?" Jake took her textbooks and reached for her gym bag, but she shook her head.

"Thanks, I can do it."

"Yes, but I can help." Gently, he tugged on the bag.

The strap broke and slithered off Em's shoulder. Jake was left with the bag dangling from the broken strap that he held. Apparently, the zipper was broken, too, because clothes and shoes spilled out.

"Oh!" she wailed.

Quickly, Jake picked up a piece of clothing and held it up. It was white with elastic and two big circles. No, they were perfect half-globes. As if someone had taken planets, cut them in half, and scooped out the insides. Around them, kids laughed and pointed.

"Hey, does it fit?" someone called, and everyone laughed harder.

Em jerked the globe-thing from Jake's hand, her face bright red.

"What?" Jake said.

Em rolled her eyes and stuffed everything back into her gym bag. On top, she dumped her textbooks, so the heavy weight would hold everything inside. She hugged the bag to her chest with one hand while she slammed her locker shut with the other. Paper hung half-in, half-out at the locker's bottom, but she ignored it and stalked away.

Jake fell into step with her.

She walked briskly, looking straight ahead and refusing to look at him.

"Did I do something wrong?" he asked.

"Um. Nothing but hold up my bra for everyone to see." She rolled her eyes and tossed her dark hair in a motion that Jake understood was annoyance.

"Oh." What's a bra? Jake wondered. Why is it bad to hold it up? Easter is going to have to explain this one. "Sorry?"

She stopped and turned to him. "Look. Why're you following me?"

"That day in the coffee shop? I took one look and fell in love." He gave her a lopsided smile to let her know it was a joke. But inside, his heart was pumping crazily.

"You must think opposites attract." Her phone buzzed, and she pulled it from her pocket, tapped something, and then looked up.

Jake waited patiently until he was sure he had her attention. "Are we opposites?"

"Duh. You don't like to swim, remember? The only way to my heart is through the pool."

Jake was ready for that. He'd spent a couple hours looking up swimming pool jokes on the Internet. "Why do girls have trouble swimming?"

She shrugged.

"Because they don't have boy-ancy."

Em groaned. "That's bad."

Jake was quick with another joke. "Where do Zombies like to swim?"

Em raised an eyebrow and shook her head.

"The Dead Sea."

She did laugh at that, a low, musical laugh. It thrilled him, like her constant humming and singing did; it set his heart to pounding even harder.

"Where'd you find those jokes?" she asked. "They are awful."

"Internet," he said. "Want to hear some more?"

"Sure," Em sighed. She turned to walk toward the doors again, and he fell in with her, and this time, they kept talking all the way until Em's turnoff toward home. He told bad swimming jokes, and she chattered about the swim team, of course, but it didn't matter what she talked about. He had made her laugh. If he did it once, he could do it again.

PHONING HOME

That evening, after finishing his homework and watching the movie, "E.T. Extra Terrestrial," with Sir, Jake tried to call Swann Quad-de on Rison. The movie and watching Em fiddle with her phone all day made him want to hear his stepfather's voice. Wanted to hear him say, "We're Quad-des. We'll make it."

He didn't do it often. Besides being expensive—Mom would pay it but would squawk at him later—it was tricky because it required the use of a U.S. Army ansible that had a strong enough signal to reach Rison.

Following the procedures for the Risonian diplomatic corp that Mom had given him, Jake logged into the computer accounts for ansible access, but he kept getting a 404 Error, which mean the webpage didn't exist.

Jake had been dreading this moment for a long time. Earth had cut off access to Rison, even for the diplomatic corp. The Embassy had their own ansible, so they could reach Rison outside of Earth's channels. But few outside the Embassy's immediate office would have access. Some businesses traded with Rison—technology companies and specialty companies such as online classes for English. Quickly, he checked the site he'd used most often, RisonEnglish.edu, and wasn't surprised when he got a 404 Error for it, too.

Finally, Jake used the encrypted security phone access channels and called Mom. She confirmed it: Rison was cut off from commercial channels of communicating with Earth.

"Why?" Jake asked.

Mom sighed. "Negotiations are tricky right now. And there's a huge solar flare from Earth's sun that's blocking messages, too. I think it's a combination of both of those. It'll be back up soon. I hope."

Jake grunted. That sounded reasonable; he just hoped Mom wasn't keeping anything back.

"Do you want to send a message to Swann?" Mom asked. "I can pass it along."

"No," he said. How could he tell Mom that he wanted advice about a girl?

"Sorry," Mom said. "I know he'd love to hear your voice."

Jake hung up reluctantly and thought about the loneliness that tinged Mom's voice. It was little comfort. Jake desperately wanted a father-son chat about so many things, not the least of which was Em. Milk, rocking chairs and E.T. with Sir didn't work. Dad was off on some lousy assignment, out of contact, and Jake had no idea when he'd return. Swann would've listened. At least, Jake told himself that. Swann was always busy with his political duties—being away for three years made it easy to forget, but he'd always tried to make time for Jake. Didn't he?

Frustrated, desperate to fill his own ache of loneliness, Jake slipped on headphones and cranked up the volume, listening to his favorite Risonian opera about the mythical founder of the Killia, the capital of Jake's home country of Tizzalura. Dad had told him the story of how Rome was established by twins, Romulus and Remus, who had been raised by wolves. Killia had been one of the first Risonians to leave the ocean, and he had fought wild beasts to establish a city on the high volcanic plateau. The songs were full of animals roaring, clanging battles, and a love that stretched from the highest volcanic mountains to the deepest oceans. Full of life, Risonian life. It was his music. He was a Risonian, and he would listen to opera all night long if he wanted, he thought defiantly.

BETRAYED

Sir and Easter Rose lived a mile and a half from the high school, right on the beach of Yeomalt Point. The first night when Easter had led Jake upstairs to his bedroom, she said, "This will be wonderful, almost like having Blake come home again for a while. You'll sleep in his old room."

The room at the top of the house suited Jake. The windows opened wide and let in the sea breeze that both tortured him since he was forbidden to swim and comforted him with its smells. Like on the Moon Base, he put his strongbox of Risonian mementos at the back of his closet. The closets were huge, though, almost as big as his entire room on the Moon Base. It would take a while to feel at home in such space.

On Rison, the Quad-de estate perched on the edge of a small cliff overlooking the ChiChi Sea, which roughly translated to Pleasant Sea. Behind them, the city of Killia sprawled across a plateau. His stepfather's house had been half on land and half in the sea. The kitchen and bedrooms were mostly on land, along with one small living area. But the main living room and the ballroom were underwater. Moving between water-breathing and air-breathing was normal for Risonians.

Rison. How much longer would it survive? A day, a month, a year? Scientists predicted only two years, but no one really knew. The volcanic eruptions were more frequent; the earthquakes, stronger. The planet's core had become more and more unstable, the result of fifty years of trying to control volcanoes with Brown Matter. As if anyone could control nature! What fools they'd been.

He'd still be there if his mother hadn't accepted the position of Ambassador to Earth. It was her assignment that prompted her to insist that Jake live with his Earthling father.

At the spaceport on the Cadee Moon Base, she hugged him hard and joked ironically, "My little shark, going to the dry, dry moon of Earth." She shook her head, curls bobbing gently. "At least your father can help make a place for you on Earth. You have a chance that few other Risonians will have."

Jake hadn't understood then. But as tensions between Rison and Earth progressed over the last three years, he started to understand just how desperate Rison was. Their planet was going to implode, and a couple billion people would die unless they could evacuate to somewhere. The Cadee Moon Base was already overflowing. Construction progressed as fast as possible, but there was no way it could ever accept more than twenty or thirty thousand. They desperately needed a planet.

Dad had once explained to Jake the difficulties of finding another habitable planet. Earth's Kepler Space Observatory was meant to find habitable planets similar to Earth. Kepler trained photometers, very sensitive light meters, onto a tiny section of stars and monitored them, looking for small variations of light that might indicate a planet had passed in front of the star. It wasn't a short-term project because a planetary orbit around a star took months (counting in Earth time). Once a dimming of light was found, scientists had to wait for it to repeat before they could speculate it meant a planet. Scientists then calculated if the planet was in a habitable zone; humans were delicate creatures with limited temperature tolerances. If the planet was too close to its sun, it would be too hot; too far away, and it would be too cold.

Even once it was determined a planet was in the habitable zone, it still had to be a rocky, water planet. And beyond that, humans would have to be able to reach the planet with current hyperdrive technology.

The universe was so vast that finding a habitable planet close enough to be helpful was just as hard for Risonians. By sheer luck, one of the Risonian exploration drones had intercepted the Aricebo message that Earth broadcast in 1974. Risonian scientists interpreted it, sought its source and answered the message in 1999. It was sheer luck that Earth was similar to Rison. Sheer luck that Rison already had hyperdrives under development that could reach Earth in a reasonable time span. And sheer bad luck that in all that time, no other planets presented themselves as alternatives. In the end—it was Earth or nothing.

Earth. Risonians had only asked for colonies in the oceans. Humans lived on land. Surely, they could share their planet and give refuge to another species that lived mostly in the water.

Well, he wasn't going to solve the problems of the universe by daydreaming. Jake shrugged off his worries, pulled his bedroom windows shut for the day, and went to look for Easter.

He found her with her head bent over her laptop. She had her workspace set up right under his room so that she overlooked Puget Sound, too. For an old lady of almost sixty, she was still active. Her dark hair had highlights—she had appointments once a month to color it—and she wore clothes only slightly outdated. She certainly didn't look old, but she didn't look young, either.

"What kind of computer work do you do?" Jake asked politely.

"Websites for churches," Easter said. "I'm webmaster for a dozen different churches."

"Is that hard?"

"No," she said. "But there's a constant stream of emails from the church staffs who want this or that updated, or have this or that problem with their site. Lots of little tasks to do each day." She laughed. "It's fun."

"I need to look up some information."

"Sure. What do you need to know?"

"Coach Blevins, the high school swim coach. I need to know his background."

Easter's mouth tightened in disapproval. "Why?"

Jake considered telling her everything, but there was too much to explain. "I just need to know something about him. He's paying too much attention to me at school, and I'm worried that he may suspect something."

Easter said, "But—" She stopped herself. "Okay. But if you need help, Sir and I are here. Or contact your dad. Promise me that."

Jake's throat felt thick with emotion. They all wanted to help, but really, there was little anyone could do for him. He was the alien here, and he had to find his own way.

Without a word, she set him up on one of her desktop computers, showed him a few advanced search tools, and let him work.

Boring at first, Jake quickly drilled down on information about the coach, surprised that Coach Blevins didn't exist until five years ago; no records existed for the man before then.

When he realized that, Jake started looking for volcanologists who had visited Rison and had a wife named Julianne, and he easily found Julianne H. Yarborough, wife of volcanologist Glen Yarborough, Ph.D.

Jake sat back in surprise, staring at the black-and-white photo of Swann and the younger human. No wonder he looked vaguely familiar. It was Coach Blevins—before he used the name Blevins. And Jake had met him on Rison.

 ☆ ☆

It was 2033, Earth calendar; Jake was seven years old.

Swann Quad-de burst out of the front door of their house, stern-faced bodyguards trotting to keep up.

Jake had been seated cross-legged on the paving stones waiting, but now scrambled to his feet. By then, Swann had already blustered past and through the gates to the estate, leaving Jake to trot after him.

Swann towered over the guards, at least a head taller. Deeply tanned, short blond hair—he was a striking man in his prime. Just now, his face was splotched with red, which made Jake cringe inwardly. Whoever made his father mad had better look out.

Jake's bodyguard trotted a step behind him. Killia's streets were crowded, people coming and going on government business, the biggest industry of the city, so the small party wound in and out of the throng. The air was hot from the nearby volcanoes and dusty from ash; only the dark shadows of the stone buildings provided any scrap of comfort from the heat.

Jake finally caught up and asked, "What's wrong?"

"Earthlings," Swann said shortly.

Jake groaned. Was it ever anything else?

Swann glanced at him, intense blue eyes glaring until he pulled himself back to the present and slowed his pace so that Jake could walk instead of trot. In a kinder tone, he asked, "Ready for this fight?"

Jake just nodded, not trusting his voice. He'd be fighting Adan, the biggest of the seven-year-olds, who was about a third again as heavy as Jake. He'd need speed to escape.

His hand went to his belt, to the emerald green, carbon-fiber knife that Master Bru Paniego had given him. Master Bru was his current combat tutor, a Boadan fight master from the southern Bo-See Coalition. Jake couldn't imagine what bribes and payment Swann had given the man to entice him to come north to Killia as Jake's tutor.

Next week, his Boadan tutor would be replaced with an aquatic combat tutor—Jake's tutors alternated aquatic with dry land fighting specialists—because Swann wanted Jake trained in every kind of hand-to-hand combat known on Rison. Of all the tutors so far, Jake had liked the short, squat Boadan best. Master Bru expected Jake to neither ask for nor give quarter. And he taught Jake more about simple gut reaction fighting than anyone. Jake's fighting on the fight floor may not have improved—today was a big test of what he'd learned from Bru—but Jake thought that if he ever got in a street fight in a Bo-See country, he might have a chance of escaping alive. A slim chance, but a chance.

"Remember: do as much damage as possible, as fast as possible," Swann said.

Jake sighed at the unnecessary instructions, "Yes, sir."

But Swann got that far away look again and repeated softly to himself, "As fast as possible."

Jake shuddered and pitied the Earthling who'd made Swann angry.

"Your weapons, sir."

Three massive soldiers blocked the entrance to the fight floor. Dressed in scarlet military uniforms, even their faces were scarlet from the heat of the day.

Reluctantly, Jake handed over his Boadan knife and watched Swann give up four concealed knives, two strapped to his legs under his own red uniform, one strapped to his forearm and one in a holster at the pit of his back. Every politician was armed these days because tempers ran as hot as lava.

The air was heavy with a sulfur smell from the volcano visible just northwest of the city. Jake was sweating, a light sheen across his chest as he took off his shirt and shoes, getting ready to step onto the fight floor. It was a bare dirt ring that Swann could cross in ten quick steps, but Jake's shorter legs would need twenty steps. Surrounded by a thick, black metal wall as tall as Jake, it gave no place to run and kept everything at close combat.

Jake had no time to fret because his opponent entered from the opposite side. Even at seven, almost eight, Adan Utset's chest hinted at muscles that Jake would never have. Staring at Adan, Jake wanted to rub his fingers over his own ribs, his chest muscles, and his arm muscles to make sure they were even there.

"You're scrawny now," his mother always said. "But when you're a teenager, you'll put on muscles."

Swann leaned over and murmured, "Be sure you survive to fight another day."

Jake groaned to himself. Swann expected him to lose. The best he was hoping for was survival.

Jake threw out his chest and breathed deeply. He opened the metal door and stepped onto the hard-packed floor.

Instantly, Adan charged, arms outspread to grasp the smaller boy.

But Master Bru had prepared Jake well for surprises; the Bo-See were known for street fighting. At the last moment, Jake sidestepped, pivoted on his foot, clasped both hands together and crashed his fists onto Adan's neck. If Jake had been larger, it would've felled Adan or even knocked his breath away. Instead, Adan stumbled, caught himself and awkwardly turned.

But Jake had already danced away, across the ring. Close combat would kill him. His only choice was to force the bigger boy to chase him and hope that he tired.

Wary, Adan closed on Jake. Off to his right, Jake saw his tutor leaning over the wall, grinning from ear to ear. Master Bru hadn't seen the boys on the fight floor before and had been anxious to observe. It was obvious that part of the appeal of tutoring Jake was to spy on the Tizzalurians; Swann had accepted that and hadn't worried about hiding anything. What was the point when their planet's days were numbered?

Adan stepped closer, but this wasn't a square fight floor where he might corner Jake. Instead, Jake slid right along the curved wall, escaping—except Adan lunged, and caught Jake's ankle, toppling them both. As he rolled, Jake scrabbled at the ground, digging in his fingernails, and managed to grab a scrap of dirt. Adan lumbered to his feet and started forward again. Jake waited for the bigger boy to get closer, and then flung the dirt at Adan's eyes.

From somewhere, he heard Master Bru crowing. It was a street tactic, not something often seen in a Tizzalurian fight.

Adan wavered, fists rubbing at his eyes.

And Jake remembered Swann's edicts: Attack the attacker.

Jake gathered his feet under himself and leapt, tackling Adan, the larger boy almost defenseless because he was still trying to get dirt out of his eyes. They rolled together on the ground, and again, Swann's edicts echoed in Jake's mind: Do as much damage as necessary, as fast as possible.

Jake shoved Adan, keeping him on the ground until he could straddle Adan's chest. He pummeled Adan's face, half of his blows falling uselessly on Adan's forearms which were thrown up as protection. But a few blows got through the defense. They weren't as hard as Jake wanted—he hadn't the muscles to really hurt someone.

But Adan howled, "Enough!"

Instantly, Jake stopped hitting and just sat on Adan's chest heaving, trying to breathe the thick sulfurous air. Still straddling the bigger boy, Jake rose to his feet, and then stepped to the left, and held out a hand to Adan.

Reluctantly, Adan took the hand. Jake braced himself and pulled, barely managing to help Adan rise.

The larger boy's chest, back and face were streaked with red dirt.

Jake turned first to Master Bru, whose long white beard nodding in approval. And then to Swann, who wore a grim smile.

Exiting the fight floor, though, Swann just slapped his back and said, "As fast as possible!"

There wouldn't be more words of praise, only a dissection of what Jake could have or should have done differently. But the slap was enough. Swann was pleased. A warmth spread through Jake, a glow that would carry him through many a tutoring session from the next fight master.

It was the next morning that Jake met Dr. Yarborough, the man who had so angered Swann.

Jake had come back from his morning swim. Coming up out of the water, he had paused to quickly readjust to air-breathing, and then bounded up the steps into the Swann's day-office. Their estate was built with thick granite; it kept out heat but made for poor sound quality, as the rooms echoed badly.

"No!" Swann's angry words bounced off the stone walls and floors. He was hunched over, his tall form bent to speak to someone much shorter—a human.

Jake had seen many humans because they came through his household regularly to talk to his stepfather, who was the prime minister of Tizzalura. Politicians and scientists—mostly Earth volcanologists—came regularly to Killia to consult. But Jake hadn't quite gotten used to humans: there was something odd about their smooth noses, or the proportions of their limbs.

Swann Quad-de jabbed a finger at a computer display. "You should have given our scientists credit in your reports."

The scientist waved a hand, as if to dismiss the argument. "They were published in Risonian scientific journals, not Earth journals. Another language. Another planet. It wasn't relevant."

Quad-de's voice lowered, and Jake stopped cold. He'd heard that note of anger in his stepfather's voice before, and it never ended well. Quad-de said, "You quoted others' work and didn't give them credit. That is unacceptable."

"And you'll do what?" The scientist tried to deflect the Risonian minister's anger. "You'll ruin me?"

Quad-de said simply, "Yes."

Jake shivered, remembering Swann's angry voice, "As much damage as possible, as fast as possible!"

He must've jerked or made some movement because at that moment Quad-de turned his head to glare at Jake. Heart pounding in fear, Jake stepped backwards. His stepfather's face was screwed up like he's just eaten a sour *kwitch,* and his neck muscles bulged like they did after a session with a punching bag. "Go. To your mother. Get your breakfast."

Jake fled, his footsteps slapping on the stone floors and echoing behind him.

☆ ☆ ☆

That Yarborough! The one who was disgraced within the volcanology scientific circles. People still warned, "Don't make a Yarborough mistake." And everyone knew they were talking about interstellar plagiarism. You must cite your interstellar sources, whether Rison or Earth was the source. Swann's retribution had indeed been swift and damaging.

Apparently after that disgrace, Yarborough had changed everything. His face was different, like maybe he'd had a nose job or something; he wore a mustache, short hair and thick glasses. Even knowing that Blevins had to be Yarborough, Jake was amazed at how well the simple changes worked as a disguise. And then, to make a new life, Yarborough had become Coach Blevins, a high school biology and civics teacher and a swim team coach.

But there was no doubt: Coach Blevins was Yarborough.

Now, Jake could start to trace some of the anti-Shark movement in the ELLIS Forces. General Puentes, who had sent in the beach helicopter, was friends with Yarborough/Blevins. No, it was worse: they were brothers-in-law, having married sisters. Both wives were dead now, but the connection clearly remained strong between the two men. They still jointly owned a hunting and fishing cabin on the upper peninsula of Michigan.

Why had Blevins chosen to teach on Bainbridge Island? Did he know about Jake's Mom and Dad?

This was even worse than Jake had imagined.

PANIC ATTACK

Early Friday morning, Jake locked his bike to the bicycle stand outside the Aquatics Center. The sun was barely over the horizon, and the parking lot held only scattered cars.

Pulling open the door, a damp chlorine smell hit Jake's senses. On the Obama Moon Base, he'd often used the Navy's pool, which was a one-man affair that gave him enough privacy to keep his identify hidden. The chlorine smell of Earthling pools was the same, whether on the Moon Base or on Bainbridge Island.

The large room resonated with a noisy roar of churning water.

It was foolish to be there, Jake knew, but he just wanted to watch Em swim, to see how she moved in the water. When Em explained about early morning practices, she'd said that Coach Blevins usually had another meeting on Friday morning, so parents ran the practice, a sort of Casual Friday in the pool. That sounded like a good time to sneak in and watch Em.

The pool was large, but still not Olympic-size, Em had complained.

Looking around, Jake's heart sank. There, pacing beside the pool was Coach Blevins.

A swimmer touched the far end of the pool, and Blevins reached down to tap the swimmer before he could turn and start back down the pool's length. Blevins demonstrated a stroke with his arms while yelling something over the roar.

A longing welled up in Jake so intense that he thought his chest might explode. I want to be part of this!

He wanted to swim with others who loved swimming, to be part of a team, to work hard—together—to swim faster than anyone else in the state. The hustle and bustle of the practice fascinated him: as much as he knew he should, he couldn't leave now.

The huge room was brilliantly lit, but Jake spied a relatively dark corner. Quickly, he hid in plain sight by leaning against the wall and becoming as still as a shadow.

Slowly the constant movement took on form. The girls practiced butterfly strokes in the right-hand lanes while the boys backstroked in the left. Each swimmer—he had finally located Em in a lime green swim cap and could follow her—did six laps, then sat out for a couple laps to rest or to talk with Coach.

When it was Em's turn to rest, she stretched out in a patch of sun just starting to spill into the room. Jake knew he should stay hidden, but he wanted her to know he was here. He strode over and tapped her swim cap.

When she turned, her eyes widened, and she smiled and patted the floor beside her.

Jake squatted on his haunches and shook his head. "Too wet."

She shrugged her understanding. Nodding to the noisy pool, she asked, "What do you think?"

Jake stared at Em. She propped herself up by leaning back on her elbows, which made the muscles on her shoulders and arms more prominent. Jake had already thought she was beautiful, but in a swimsuit, she was stunning. He could barely concentrate on answering her question, but managed to say, "Interesting." He nodded toward the girls swimming butterfly and asked, "What's a polar bear's favorite stroke?"

She rolled her eyes and shrugged.

"Blubber-fly."

Em rewarded him with a wry smile.

Oddly, from the men's locker room, strolled a man in khaki pants.

Jake shuddered. It was Captain Hill. He probably wanted to talk to Coach Blevins about the break-in before he caught the Seattle ferry to go to the ELLIS offices, something that Jake knew he did most days. Now Jake regretted leaving his out-of-the-way shadows.

Quickly, Jake said, "I'll let you get back to practice."

Em nodded but looked disappointed. She shoved up to sit cross-legged and watched him retreat. While Captain Hill was turned away, Jake quickly returned to his shadow to hide again.

Coach Blevins blew a whistle, and slowly swimmers dragged themselves up and out of the pool to gather at the side opposite from Jake. Em stood and walked around the pool to join the group. Everyone except one girl was out, sitting by the pool and ready to listen, when Coach started yelling.

"That's good for this morning," Coach said. "After school, we'll do sprints. Build up your stamina."

The girl still in the pool had stopped swimming and was holding onto the side of the pool near Jake, breathing deeply. No, she was gasping.

Coach Blevins moved closer to the seated group and stumbled slightly on a towel. He kicked it away, face suddenly red, and stood stiffly. "Our first meet is just a week away." The acoustics in the poolroom forced Coach to shout.

The girl rasped louder now, and a couple swimmers turned to her. But no one seemed to realize that she was really having problems. In slow motion, her hand drooped off the pool's side, and she sank underwater. Her hands splashed, frantic to grasp the pool's side again. For a moment, Jake thought she'd be okay, but when her face broke the surface a moment later, she was gasping, and before she could draw a good breath, she went down again. She was in trouble.

A few more heads turned her way, but still no one moved to help her.

Reluctant, but determined to help, Jake darted from his dark shadow and dove into the water, fully clothed.

A few quick strokes, and he reached her side. She swatted at him before managing to pull him under. It was no problem breathing for him, but she struggled wildly. With one arm, he wrapped her arms at her side where she couldn't slap at him. The pool wasn't very deep, so he shoved off the bottom and used his momentum to thrust upward enough to shove her out onto the pool's side.

Em was there, tugging at the girl, and then Captain Hill was there, pushing Em aside. Captain Hill felt for a pulse and checked the girl's breathing. She gasped, deep, racking breaths, and her eyes were wide with terror.

Captain Hill sat in front of her and pulled her face toward his. "It's okay," he said. "It's just a panic attack. Slow down your breathing. Look at me."

His voice was calm but insistent. The girl ripped off her swim cap, and dark hair tumbled around her face. Her wide eyes focused on the Captain.

Coach Blevins ordered someone, "Call 9-1-1. Get an ambulance here."

Captain Hill breathed deep and blew out slowly, giving the girl a pattern to follow.

Still, she wheezed, "I. Can't. Stop."

"Yes, you can. Breathe with me. Deep breathe, that's it. Blow out, and count to three. 1, 2, 3. That's it."

Hill's voice almost hypnotized Jake into inaction. Swimmers knelt nearby—not too close, but nearby—and they breathed in unison.

Coach jerked Jake's arm and pulled him out of the water. "Where'd you come from?" He stared at Jake, and his expression turned puzzled, his forehead wrinkling. "I know you from the coffee shop, and—what class?"

Water poured from Jake's jeans, and his tennis shoes squelched. The Moon Base pools were chlorinated, but this one had chlorine so strong it reeked. Either they had recently put in chemicals, or else they used more than the Moon Base pool. Already, his skin chaffed from the irritants, and he wanted to rip off his t-shirt.

Em stepped to his side. "Coach, this is Jake Rose from civics."

Jake nodded and shrugged to make the Coach turn loose of his arm. "I thought I'd watch a practice or two." He waved a hand at the back wall. "I could see that she was in trouble."

The Coach's eyes narrowed. "You're in my civics class—and Biology class, too. Right?"

Coach glanced at the girl, whose breathing had finally slowed, and then his eyes settled back on Jake, studying him as if trying to evaluate the breadth of his shoulders, the reach of his arms to decide if he could turn Jake into a competent swimmer or not.

Jake felt like a racehorse being evaluated by a big-dollar gambler who wanted to know where to put his money. He pulled off his shoes and upended them, water dribbling out.

In the distance, a siren wailed.

Jake said, "She's okay now. I'll just run home and change so I can get back before school starts."

"Bring back some swim trunks." Coach Blevins grabbed a white towel from a bench and handed it to Jake, with trembling hands. "Afternoon practice starts at 4 pm."

A student almost drowned—no wonder Coach's hands trembled. Jake's stomach was still fluttery, too. "Thanks." Jake took the towel and turned to go. "But it's not for me."

Coach caught his arm and spun him back. He was slightly bow-legged or he would've been taller than Jake. Still, they stared eye-to-eye.

"Why not?" Coach said.

Jake realized that he was in trouble. His parents had been firm: Don't get noticed. Stay in the background. Be invisible. Now, Coach Blevins, the most anti-Shark person on Bainbridge Island—the scientist who'd been disgraced by Swann Quad-de—was staring him in the face. Again. Where Coach was concerned, it seemed like Jake couldn't stay invisible. Sooner or later, Coach would connect him with the Quad-de family, and then what? Jake struggled to control his face, to keep it neutral; he struggled to move normally, instead of dashing away. With a forced casualness, he said, "Just not interested."

"Coach, come talk to the mother." Captain Hill held out a cell phone.

Coach had one last word for Jake, though. "Well, if you get interested, show up any time."

As Coach walked away, Jake wanted to collapse under the weight of his charade.

Fortunately, everyone was watching the paramedics carry in a stretcher.

Everyone except Em. She grabbed another swimmer and pointed to Jake's wet jeans. "You got a spare pair of sweats for him?"

Jake nodded, grateful that someone was looking out for him, and especially grateful that it was Em.

The boy shrugged, pulled sweats from a gym bag, handed them to Jake and went back to staring at the EMTs.

Quickly, Jake went to the boy's locker room and found an empty changing stall. Afraid that someone would look under the door and see his Velcro-legs, he climbed onto a bench, awkwardly stripped off the wet jeans and stood squeezing out water until the jeans were just damp. He dried off with the white towel and started to pull on the sweats.

Jake heard someone come into the changing room, so he froze.

"Anyone in here?" called a voice that Jake recognized as Captain Hill.

He looked down to see if he'd dropped anything on the floor. His tennis shoes lay on the bench, and its shoestrings dangled. Quickly, he bent and jerked them up.

Silence.

"I looked under the doors; no one is here," said Coach Blevins.

Jake's core had gone cold; he hugged himself to keep from making any sound.

"You have an appointment next week. You'll get a second opinion."

Silence.

"Okay?"

"It's Parkinson's. You know it is."

Silence, again. Jake wondered what they were doing. If they were hugging or just staring at each other or trying not to stare at each other. He didn't know what Parkinson's was, but it sounded like the Coach might be sick or something.

Captain Hill cleared his throat and said briskly, "Look."

"It's the Quad-de boy?" Coach said. "The picture you took from my house last week?"

Jake trembled, afraid to move. Water from his jeans and shoes dripped onto the floor. To him, each drop was a drumbeat calling to the two men, saying, "Look in here."

"See what our techs did?" Captain Hill said.

"That's him, aged up?" Coach sounded confused. "What he'd look like today?"

Jake wanted desperately to see the aged-up photo. Then he could figure out a disguise, something simple like Coach Blevins had done to disguise himself.

Captain Hill said, "It's the way one program would picture him today. I'll have printouts from two more before the end of the day. The problem is that we know how to age up a human, not a Risonian. Our people have adjusted the programs, but we're not sure that any will work well. We still need the paparazzi to get a photo of him."

Jake reached up and grasped the top of the stall. If he silently pulled himself up, he could peer over the stall. It was unlikely they'd look up. But with a silent headshake, he let his hands fall. Too foolish, he decided.

Coach said. "Looks a lot like Swann Quad-de."

Holding his breath, Jake wondered. Are they seeing what they expect to see, a Risonian? Of course! They didn't know he was half-human, so when they aged up his photo, they'd used algorithms developed for Risonians. Captain Hill hadn't recognized him from the photo—and he'd just gotten a good look at Jake—so probably his half-human side had complicated things enough to make their program ineffective.

Other voices entered the locker room, talking about the ambulance and the EMTs and homework.

"You'll be okay?" the Captain said. And Jake wondered about the half-worried and half-lonely note in his voice. Obviously, he was worried about his older friend. How bad was the—what was it?—Perkins or Parkins?

Their voices disappeared.

Peering out, Jake saw swimmers coming in to change for school. He fled, dashing out of the Aquatics Center to climb onto his bicycle and pedal home in the chilly air, his damp shirt making him shiver in the cool autumn air. Each push on the pedals screamed at him, "Danger!"

He'd gone to watch Em. That part had been as amazing as he'd expected, her speed and grace put her far above anyone else. And he longed to be part of a swim team. He should've known, though, to stay away from the pool and away from Blevins.

It's Em, he sighed. She's my siren.

Maybe, like the mermaids of Earth legends, she would do nothing but lure him into danger.

THE HARBOR SEALS

When Jake walked in from school on Friday afternoon, Dad was sitting at the kitchen table with Easter eating a chocolate cupcake, a smear of chocolate on his upper lip. He wore jeans and a t-shirt and looked weird without his Navy uniform. Dad and Easter stopped talking when he entered.

Dad rose to give Jake a hug. "I've got a couple days off," he said.

Jake grinned. After the incident at swim team that morning, he'd decided to talk to Sir and tell him everything. He didn't know how much Sir and Easter already knew about his mom, and he'd been dreading the explanations. Of course, they knew she was the Risonian Ambassador. But did they understand what she was negotiating for? The decision to ask Sir's advice had been rock solid, a necessity, a cold hard place inside him. Now, those tensions softened and bent like dune grasses blown in the wind; relief flooded through him. Dad was here. He could talk to Dad.

"But only a couple days," Dad grimaced, then shrugged. "I'll have to leave in 48 hours."

Jake's grin faded, and he filled in the unspoken words. The Navy had only given Dad a 48-hour pass, and there's nothing Dad could do about it. Desperately, Jake wanted to ask where Dad was stationed and about his assignment. At least on the Moon Base, they'd been together in the tiny quarters every night. Dad had taught him to play checkers, and he had taught Dad to appreciate the finer points of Risonian opera. They both loved watching NBA basketball games, only bemoaning that Seattle didn't have a pro basketball team. Jake even played around with fantasy basketball for a while, getting help and advice from Dad. He'd gotten used to having Dad around. It'd filled the empty hole left by Swann. And now, he felt hollow again. Sir and Easter were nice enough, but they'd never be able to take the place of his stepfather or father.

Easter put a glass of milk and a cupcake in front of Jake.

"Thanks," he mumbled, and then pulled the cupcake paper off to one side. His mouth full of chocolate, Jake tried to think;

he was doing lots more thinking these days. If he told Dad too much, his parents might put even more restrictions on what he did. Already there were too many rules. The rock-hard decision froze inside him again, but this time, it was a decision to stand-alone. Mom and Dad were too busy, and Sir and Easter just wouldn't understand.

"Let's go fishing tomorrow," Dad suggested. "I've been telling you that I'd take you fishing for three years now."

Jake swallowed hard. Last year, nothing would've kept him from a fishing trip with Dad. Once a year, on New Year's Day, they ate salmon and crab—Dad spending lots of credits to have the seafood shipped up to the Moon Base—and dreamed of the day they'd eat it fresh. If they were alone together, though, Jake knew he'd spill everything. He felt pulled into two jagged pieces. He didn't want Dad to worry; yet, he longed to be asked the right questions so he could tell him all.

No.

It was time for him to start making his own decisions. He could take care of Coach Blevins without Mom or Dad stepping in. "I need to go to the library tomorrow," he said. "Research paper in civics is due on Monday."

Dad frowned slightly. "Oh." Then his face cleared. "Ah, a girl?"

"No!" But Jake had protested too quickly, too loudly.

"We'll go fishing early. Set your alarm for 5:30, and we'll be out and back before the library opens." He stood and slapped Jake's back. "What do you say? Pizza for supper? Our usual?"

Jake nodded absently and said, "Sure."

"Say, are you going to play on the high school basketball team?"

Jake shrugged. "Probably. If they let me wear tights." But he was remembering the first time he'd met Dad and the first time they played sports together.

☆ ☆ ☆

The Obama Moon Base sprawled across the Peary Crater, close to the moon's north pole, featuring a spaceport with bays for a hundred or more spacecraft and a small naval station. After the Risonian spaceship docked, the Risonian Captain himself escorted Jake to a small room, where his biological father waited.

Jake recognized the man from his mother's photos. The Risonian Captain briefly introduced them, shook Jake's hand in farewell, and left the room. Both stoic, Jake and Captain Rose merely nodded at each other, and Jake had followed the tall man whose easy stride looked just too much like his own. They wound through corridors until Jake was thoroughly lost, until Captain Rose stopped before a small white door, bowed slightly and said, "Be it ever so humble. . ."

Jake looked at him blankly.

"Oh," the Captain looked away and shrugged. "It's just an Earth saying. Be it ever so humble, there's no place like home. This is my apartment."

Walking in, the Captain's windowless rooms were small by Risonian or Earth standards. But Jake would have a room of his own for privacy, something he knew was a luxury on the Moon. It was barely more than a closet, but still, it was his. He'd hoped for windows so he could watch Earth—the other blue marble—but none of the crew quarters had windows. The Peary Crater was situated high enough above the surface that it was always in the sunlight, with no dark times that would create extremely frigid temperatures. Instead, it was a balmy minus 50 Celsius year-round. The disadvantage was that constant sunlight created havoc on human's biorhythms; in order to create sleep cycles of day and night, crew quarters had no windows and operated on artificial lighting timed to Greenwich Mean Time on Earth.

Jake had to settle for an occasional visit to the observation gallery to look at Earth.

Though the enlisted men ate all meals in the cafeteria, Captain Rose's cabin had a tiny galley kitchen, a wall of shiny metal. Captain Rose opened two cabinets to reveal boxes of food and told Jake, "Eat what you want. Make yourself at home."

Jake nodded at the third cabinet with a questioning eye.

Captain Rose looked embarrassed, but opened it and said, "My collection."

On the narrow shelves sat rows of *umjaadi* globes. It was a Rison tradition of small globes full of water and aquatic species that could live in an enclosed space like that. They were named after the *umjaadi* starfish, the most common animal in such an enclosure. Often an *umjaadi* starfish could live in a globe for two or three years; after they died, it was still a fascinating bit of Rison. So—Commander Rose was a sentimental man.

These globes sparkled in the artificial light. Jake wanted to look closer, but his father shut the cabinet with a sharp click and asked, "Hungry?"

Captain Rose fixed sandwiches—dry smoked meat between two pieces of bread—and they sat at a small table and stared at each other and chewed.

Finally, Jake set down the remains of the sandwich. "I'm done. Thank you, sir."

"About that. You're right to call me, 'sir.' It's a sign of respect, and you should use that term for everyone you meet. But you'll need to call me something else. You can use the Earth term, 'Dad.' Or, you can just call me by my first name, Blake."

Jake brushed his hand over his pants leg, taking comfort in the feel of the green blade strapped to his thigh, and a smaller one on his back. As Swann had promised, the Earthling's security hadn't detected it because the carbon blades didn't set off the metal detectors. He was glad that this man was so direct and just laid out this tricky bit of Earth etiquette so clearly. "Thank you, sir, for explaining that. I'd prefer Blake."

Blake nodded, leaned back, arms stretched across the back of his chair. "Want to play basketball? I'm off duty the rest of the day."

Jake shrugged. He knew the term "basketball," of course, and had actually watched videos of the sport a couple times. But it made no sense. Why did Earthlings play so many games with balls of every shape, size and color? "Why would I want to?" he asked.

Blake nodded decisively. "Of course. Good question. Come. We'll shoot hoops, and I'll try to answer that question."

Blake handed him a set of clothing and motioned for Jake to go to his room and change. Donning the sweat pants, t-shirt and strange shoes that Blake handed him, Jake felt like he was playing dress up. He took a few extra minutes to open his strongbox and make sure that his mementos from Rison were safe: he'd only brought a few things. Knives, of course. A couple things from his long-gone best friend, Stefan Dolk, who had died last year. Several memory devices full of photos and videos of other friends. Sentimental things. He put the strongbox on the bottom shelf of his closet. He might not look at it often, but it was comforting to have something from Rison here on the Earth's Moon. So—was he a sentimental person like his biological father? Jake closed the door firmly and went out.

Blake was waiting for him wearing shorts. Jake realized that his own pants were part of the price he'd have to pay for coming to Earth. To hide his identity, he could never wear shorts lest let people see his Velcro-legs.

A few minutes later, they strode through another confusing maze of corridors. Walking to the gym beside Blake, Jake felt even stranger. He was on Earth's Obama Moon Base, walking through sterile white pressurized corridors to a common room that was used to play some game with a ball. Play. It was wrong on so many levels.

Blake handed him a brown ball and showed him how to bounce it up and down. After a few bounces, Jake watched his father—was this stranger really his father?—heave the ball toward a metal circle. When the ball went through the circle—hoop, Blake called it—Blake called, "Three points!"

Retrieving the ball, Blake threw it to Jake, saying, "You try it."

Jake caught the ball, but just stood and asked defiantly, "Why would I want to?" He was a Quad-de. What was he doing here?

Blake held out his hands, and Jake threw the ball back to him. Blake shot again. The ball rolled around and around the metal circle before falling through and bouncing away to ricochet off the wall. Blake chased it down and turned back to Jake, who hadn't moved.

"OK," Blake sighed. "You want answers. But it's not easy." He bounced the ball up and down rhythmically, the noise echoing in the chamber. "Dayexi tells me you're pretty good at hand-to-hand combat."

Jake shrugged, torn between bragging and not speaking. The Quad-des were always good at fighting. What did Blake expect?

Blake nodded. "OK. I know you've taken the top honor for your age group for the last three years. Yes?"

"Yes." At home, his knife rack had held the specially made trophy knives for the last three years. Reluctantly, he'd left them, of course, no room for vanity in his hasty evacuation. He remembered Swann coming into his room to say goodbye and running a hand across the collection, tears in his eyes, and a bit of pride in his crooked smile.

"On Earth, our teenagers don't do hand-to-hand combat," Blake said.

"But you have wrestling."

"Yes, but it's a sport, like basketball. It's not combat like you have on Rison." Still, Blake thumped the ball up and down, the motion automatic. "Do you know what testosterone is?"

Jake shook his head.

"You're what? Eleven years old? You're about to hit your teenage years, which means your life will be ruled by testosterone for the next decade. Testosterone is the human male hormone, and you'll likely get your share of it. It's what makes males more aggressive than females. Teenage boys need some way to be aggressive, and in centuries past, they might have gone to war or fought or done a number of things to channel the aggression in ways that helped society. But then, Earth became more civilized. We decided that hand-to-hand combat was too harsh, too cruel, too—well, uncivilized."

Jake's anger flared. Hand-to-hand combat was the most civilized, fair, and just method of physical exercise. The Tizzalurian traditions went back for centuries. Furthermore—but Blake was still speaking.

"But that didn't stop young men from needing an outlet for their aggression. They still needed some way to, well, hit someone, to shove, to fight. Teenage males need socially acceptable ways to be aggressive."

Jake nodded slowly, letting his anger ebb away in an effort to understand. When he stepped onto the fight floor, there was a certain wild pleasure in knowing that he could let himself go and just fight. And that feeling had grown stronger this last year. If Earth teens were denied hand-to-hand combat, they needed something to replace it.

Blake continued, "Rison has codified the hand-to-hand combat, created rules about it, and structures that award praise to the most aggressive and most skilled. On Earth, we created sports that serve the same function. Our young men play football, soccer, basketball, volleyball, golf, and so on as a substitute for battle. Instead of sending them to war, we put them on a basketball court. We tolerate—no, we expect—a certain amount of violence: shoving, tripping, hitting. Within limits, of course. If they went off to battle, we'd expect a certain number of injuries; and we get that on the sports fields. Broken legs, bloody noses, concussions—no one demands that we stop the sports simply because there are a few injuries. We accept those injuries as battle wounds; they are the price our society pays for being civilized and allowing young men to be aggressive only on the sports fields.

"When you step foot on Earth, you must understand that hand-to-hand combat will not be tolerated. That means you need another outlet for your anger, your aggression, your need to be physical."

Jake stared at Blake with a growing respect. This was a clearer and straighter explanation of Earth sports than he'd ever heard. It actually gave him a clear decision, to either join Earth's sports or to totally control his own aggression. "This is clearly understood on Earth?"

Blake gave a short laugh. "Oh, no. It's poorly understood on Earth. It's just my conclusion." He stopped bouncing the ball—dribbling, he called it—and threw the ball to Jake.

"On Earth," Blake said, "we roughly separate the sports by body types. If you're big and heavy, you play football; if you're tall and skinny, you play basketball. For those who are tall and skinny, but not very coordinated, they do sculling, which is a sport where they row long, skinny boats. For short and fast players, there's soccer. For stocky kids, there are things like bowling or golf or tennis or baseball."

Jake hefted the brown basketball, and let his hands pass it back and forth, feeling its weight. "So many sports!"

"Something for everyone. You're going to be tall, like me, so basketball is a logical sport to try. Doesn't matter where you come from, or who your parents are. On Earth, males need some way to be aggressive in a socially acceptable way."

Jake mimicked Blake and leapt upward; at the top of his leap, he awkwardly shoved the ball toward the hoop. It went through! Complete luck! And yet, elation shot through him. Blake's insights were perhaps unusual for an Earthling, but exactly what Jake needed. To succeed in passing himself off as an Earthling, he needed wise advisors. Maybe if he thought of Blake as his Earth-culture tutor, instead of his father, it would be enough at first. It had taken time to learn to respect and love Master Bru Paniego, the southern fight tutor who had been so different from Tizzalurian norms. Smiling, he looked up at Blake.

Blake grinned back and nodded.

"What about the females?" Jake asked. "Do they play these sports, too?"

"Sure. And some of them do it to get rid of excess aggression. But they lack the testosterone. Sometimes they play sports to learn to be more assertive." Blake's grin widened. "Boys are aggressive; girls are assertive."

Jake groaned. Yet another Earth puzzle, girls.

Suddenly, though, this whole thing didn't seem so overwhelming. He tilted his head and looked at Navy Captain Blake Rose. This man had figured out how to combine Risonian and Earthling DNA in a test tube, had implanted the embryo in Dayexi, and had kept track of Jake—his test-tube son—through the years. Blake thought differently than most Earthlings. This discussion, Jake realized, would've been very different from a man who didn't try to think and to evaluate the culture around him. In that regard, Blake was very much like Swann. Both were intelligent leaders who gave Jake a rich heritage. He could never replace Swann but maybe Blake could help Jake navigate through the next few years and help him become comfortable with the Earthling culture.

Jake ran after the brown ball and picked it up. It was a brown globe, like the Moon, no water. Before Jake went down to the blue planet they called Earth, he had a lot to learn.

He threw the ball to Blake and said earnestly, "Teach me how to shoot."

☆ ☆ ☆

In the end, Blake and Jake didn't fish on Saturday morning; instead, they kayaked out of Eagle Harbor, on the eastern shore of Bainbridge Island. Jake had never been in a boat like a kayak before. Long and narrow, it reminded him of a *kvakki*, a Risonian fish that only swam in the northern seas and fed on Risonian's version of plankton.

"Do you want to learn to kayak easily, or do you want to fish?" Dad asked.

"Kayak," Jake answered. The fishing would come after he mastered the boat.

So they left the fishing gear in the car. Dad wore an old Navy wetsuit, but Jake didn't need protection from the cold water. From his old collection of baseball caps, Dad had pulled out a worn brown and yellow hat, and with a raised eyebrow, handed it to Jake.

Hesitantly, Jake said, "San Diego."

Dad grinned. "That's my boy. 1978 San Diego Padres."

Jake put on the cap-of-the-day, silently glad that Dad hadn't noticed the NYPD cap was missing.

The morning was cold with wispy tendrils of fog rising. The harbor glistened like a mirror, reflecting the waning stars and the forest of masts from the sailboats docked at the marina. From somewhere onshore, Jake smelled coffee and bacon. But no one else was out on the water.

Dad slipped into his blue kayak first and paddled out a few strokes, turning expertly to watch Jake.

Jake's stomach felt suddenly empty. He bent and awkwardly put one foot into the red kayak. It rocked and swayed. Lips pressed together, he put his other foot in and awkwardly slipped his feet forward until he was seated. Now, the kayak was stuck on shore, so he grabbed the paddle and shoved at the ground while hitching forward and—suddenly, the lightweight boat was floating on the water.

Heart hammering, Jake dipped the paddle into the water and pulled hard. The boat swung in an awkward circle so fast that only Jake's sense of balance kept him from going over.

"Use both ends of the paddle," Dad called, and then demonstrated, dipping the right side into the water and then the left.

The movement of the paddles was like a figure-8, Jake realized. He readjusted his grip toward the middle of the paddle and tried again. The kayak went skimming across the water. Instead of following his father toward open water, though, he veered right, out of control, toward the inner harbor. Slowly he realized that he was favoring his left arm, pulling too strong on that side. But still, he couldn't settle into a rhythm.

He longed to dive into the water, to swim. That was the problem. To be on an island, surrounded by water, was torture. When Dad had been a boy on this island, the story went that Sir hated it when Dad wanted to stay inside. "Go play outside," Sir ordered.

While on the Moon, Dad had joked. "You're on the computer too much. You're with me too much. I wish I could tell you to go outside and play." But of course, Jake couldn't go outside the domed Moon Base.

Swann had done the same thing. "You can't stay in your room to play video games. Go play in the water."

Now, Jake's orders were always, "Stay out of the water."

If he mastered this kayak, he could at least be on top of the water, closer than anything he'd done since Gulf Shores. He'd be the best kayaker on Bainbridge Island. And if, now and then, he happened to upset his boat and fall into the water—well, accidents happened. Accidents might happen often, he thought, with a grim smile.

That decided, he settled into the rhythm of padding and controlling the flimsy boat. Dad paddled leisurely toward the harbor opening, letting Jake fight his own battle with the kayak. By the time they came out of the harbor into Puget Sound, they were paddling in unison.

"Where will we go?" Jake said, his voice carrying easily across the still water.

Dad pointed to a rocky island. "If we're lucky, there'll be harbor seals on Blakeley Rock."

Distances were deceptive on the water. They paddled steadily for almost an hour before they drew near to the rock. Indeed, sleek, brown figures dotted the rocks.

Several slipped into the water, barely ruffling the surface. Jake laid the paddle across his lap and let both hands drag in the water. He shivered with delight at the touch of brackish water. Puget Sound wasn't as salty as the Gulf of Mexico, but it was still salty. Rubbing his fingers in the water, he felt the difference between the two bodies of water. The Sound was cold enough that humans would need a wetsuit, but it felt balmy to Jake. He'd have to dive two or three hundred feet before the cold affected him.

Jake thought back to his swim with the great shark of the Gulf, the joy of exploring. The hairs on his arm rose, and he longed to plunge into Puget Sound and swim with the harbor seals. How could he stay out of the water?

As if he read Jake's mind, Dad asked softly, "Have you been swimming?"

"No," Jake said. Sadness touched him that Dad had to ask, that Dad didn't trust him. He hesitated, almost ready to tell Dad about the incident in the pool and about Coach Blevins.

But Dad spoke harshly, "Good. Your mom will kill you if anyone finds out who you are."

Jake's lips tightened, and he clenched his jaw. He could tell Dad nothing.

A harbor seal swam closer to Jake's kayak. Jake froze, barely moving, willing the amazing creature to come even closer.

Sleek, brown-freckled fur—it drifted closer.

Its eyes were large, dark pools of black. Softly, it breathed out—Phooo! Phooo! With each breath, its nose closed off completely, like an eyelid opening and closing: underwater, this would keep any water from reaching its lungs. Exactly like the interior nose lids of every Risonian! Jake hadn't known that any Earth creatures so closely mimicked Risonian anatomy.

Jake slowly leaned over and put his hands into the water. He flapped them, trying to send waves that would say, "Friend."

The seal wiggled, sending waves back to Jake. Was it trying to repeat the word, "Friend?" He couldn't be sure. A thrill surged through him because another Earthling sea creature had come to look at him. It was a good omen: Earth's oceans would be a good place for Risonians.

"Do you think I could take it home with me? Would it like the waters of my world?" Jake reached out a hand, hoping to stroke the seal, but abruptly, it dove. Jake watched the dark waters, waiting for it to come up.

Suddenly, from the corner of his eye, Jake saw a kayak paddle flash around and strike Dad's head.

Dad recoiled, and his kayak rocked and flipped upside down. The blue bottom was strangely still.

Shocked, Jake whirled to see someone in a red kayak, but the kayak paddle was now swinging his way. He backpaddled forcefully, frantically wondering if Dad was okay.

He was a powerful enough paddler that within a couple strokes, he was out of range of—it was a woman. Was she crazy?

"Dad!" he called.

And on cue, Dad flipped his kayak upright, blowing and blubbering and gasping for air.

The woman glared from one to the other, "I'll have no poachers on my watch."

"Oh," Jake groaned. She'd heard his last comment and thought he was there to kidnap a seal for some private location or zoo. "You misunderstood."

"I know what I heard. You want one of my seals for your 'world.'" She made air-quotes with her hands.

Dad wiped streaming water from his face and said, "It was hypothetical! I grew up on Bainbridge, and I know better than to harass the seals."

For a long moment, they stared at each other.

The woman took a deep breath, sighed and said, "I'm sorry. It's just that—"

Dad nodded. "You're passionate about protecting the environment. I get it. No harm done." He rubbed the side of his head and added, "But it's a good thing I knew how to right my kayak or you'd have murder on your conscience."

"My name's Bobbie Fleming. I'm a marine biologist for Washington State, and it's my job to monitor the harbor seals, to make sure no one bothers them." Under a red baseball cap—just a generic one, not a team cap—she wore scholarly wire-rimmed glasses, apparently prescription sunglasses. In her leathery, freckled face was written the years spent in the sun and surf. "How could I know if you had guns or not? Poachers are a nasty business. I hit first and ask questions later."

Jake squirmed at the tension between them, remembering Swann's instructions in diplomacy: "When two people are about to fight, change the subject."

Jake's seal still hadn't resurfaced. To deflect the biologist, he asked, "How much do seals weight?"

"150-180 pounds," she said. "Lots of blubber to keep them warm." Gloved hands expertly handled the paddle, and with a quick stroke, she was level with Jake and Dad. Her freckled face still frowned, but she'd lost the intensity of the first moments.

Jake remembered his Risonian tutors lecturing about Earthling creatures: "We Risonians have a specialized myoglobin in our blood, and on Earth, myoglobin is found in harbor seals. Ours is a more efficient molecule and has the ability to warm our bodies without bulky fur like the seal."

Risonian kids were required to study Earth flora and fauna because some of them might actually make it to Earth to live. Jake tried not to think of his friends still on Rison, who would never see an actual harbor seal.

Fleming wagged a finger between Dad and Jake. "Father and son?"

Dad nodded and paddled closer to Jake. "Yes. I'm Navy and just here for the weekend. Jake lives with my parents, Sir and Easter Rose."

Fleming nodded and took off her cap to wipe her brow. In the early morning sun, long blond hair gleamed down her back, and Jake thought again of the mermaid stories. She reached up to stretch, the red cap waving in one hand, and then pulled her hair back through the cap's back and settled the brim to shade her eyes.

Jake had an idea. He nodded his chin toward Blakely Rock. "You come out here often?"

Fleming said simply, "It's my job."

"You ever need help? Someone to come along and—I don't know—take samples or something? Whatever you do?" Jake held his breath, hoping she'd give him a good excuse to come out on the water often.

She held up a yellow dry bag that was clipped to her kayak. In the wetsuit, her body had a lean look to it—as if she clung to her teenage years and wouldn't let them go. Still, he guessed she had to be mid-thirties or older. She reached into a utility belt at the waist of her wet suit and showed Jake a small notebook and pen. "Sure. I take water samples all the time. I have to record exactly when and where I took it, and then quickly get it to an ice chest so organisms can't grow before we test it. You interested in marine biology?"

"Yes, ma'am." That was an understatement. "I'd love to come out and help."

Dad glared at Jake. "Do you think you can do that and keep up with your homework, too?"

"Of course," Jake said. "Not a problem."

He knew that Dad wouldn't forbid him to come out with the scientist, even if he wanted to. Dad and Mom wanted him to fit in with the community, and that required Jake to interact somehow. Jake figured it might as well be on the water.

She shrugged. "It's wet suit weather, anyway." She nodded at Dad, who survived the dunking because of his wet suit. "Where's your wetsuit?"

Thinking fast, Jake said, "I tried it on this morning, and I've outgrown it. We'll order a new one this afternoon."

She nodded. "Saturday mornings work for you? Early?"

Jake grinned at how well this had worked. "6 a.m.?"

Once that was agreed upon, Dad and Jake turned their kayaks back toward Eagle Harbor.

Fleming called after them, "Sorry about the head."

Dad raised a hand in acknowledgment without looking around.

They had just finished strapping the kayaks to the car when Dad's phone rang.

"Yes, sir." Pause. "Yes, sir." Pause. "Right away, sir."

And Jake knew their visit was over.

Driving home, Dad turned on the car heater, so Jake pulled off his jacket. He wondered if Dad felt the awkwardness that had grown between them, too. The Navy would always be Dad's master, and family would always come second.

VOLCANOES

School was exhausting for Jake because he had to be on guard at all times. On Wednesday that week, Jake stood in the cafeteria and scanned the crowd with a frown. He was expected to mingle with the other students, but he still hated making small talk.

He spotted Em across the cafeteria, and she waved him over. With relief, he wound through the crowd to her table. Her hair was twisted and fastened somehow low on her neck, but Jake couldn't see how it stayed in position. Another girl thing to ask Easter.

He plopped his tray beside Em's and straddled the uncomfortable seat. Her friends laughed, and he suddenly realized he was the only boy at the table. She had wanted him to join her, right? Or had she just casually waved? It didn't matter because he still needed information. In Biology, Coach Blevins had emphasized that tomorrow was the deadline to turn in permission slips for the field trip. He needed to know if it was worth worrying about. He bit into his hamburger and looked sideways at her. "What's a field trip? Are we going to visit a field of grass or something?"

Em laughed. "You're so funny. This'll be the best trip of the year for freshmen."

She hadn't answered his question, but he realized he couldn't repeat his question or he'd look really dumb. Instead, he changed tactics. "Why's this one the best?"

"Volcanoes." Em pointed out the cafeteria window toward the mountain in the distance. "Mt. Rainier is an inactive volcano, and we'll get to walk all over it." She held up a thermos of what Jake knew was coffee. "Want some?"

"No, thanks." Jake had decided he didn't like coffee's bitter taste. After binging for a couple weeks, he had cut back on coffee. He picked up the Coke can from his tray and shook it absently. "You ever worry that the volcano might explode?"

"Nah," she said. "It's inactive."

He'd studied Earth's volcanoes, of course, and especially how they differed from Risonian volcanoes. The biggest difference was that Rison had a fixed crust, while Earth's crust was broken into large sections called plates. Plate tectonics, or the science of how Earth's crusts moved around, were odd. The points where the crust plates met were often weaker and that's where magma pushed through the surface to create volcanoes. It created the "Ring of Fire," the volcanoes around the rim of the Pacific Ocean. Jake understood the concept, and he actually admired the scientific study required to come up with the theory. It was just creepy to walk on Earth's crusts that were constantly in motion themselves. The crusts moved, while the Earth rotated on its axis, while it orbited the sun. Stability was an illusion.

Swann had always laughed at him for this aversion. "Rison may have a fixed crust, but Rison also rotates on its axis while orbiting Turco."

Jake opened the soft drink with a pop. Brown foam squirted everywhere, spilling over the can's rim and onto the table. Looking up, he saw Em laughing.

"That's a good one," she said. "Exploding Coke; exploding volcano."

Jake frowned. It was good that he'd made a mess? Was she implying that he'd meant to create an exploding Coke? He searched for a napkin to wipe off his hands, but found none. Even after three years on the Moon, he understood so little of the social aspects of Earth because he'd been the only teen there. Math class or even English class—those were easy. Lunch hour left him exhausted.

He hopped up to grab napkins to mop up the mess. When he sat down to eat again, he found his hamburger bun soaked with Coke, too. He pushed the tray aside and leaned his chin on his hands to study the massive mountain out the window.

The difference between volcanoes on his home planet and Earth meant different geographies. The Hawaiian Island chain was the result of Earth's crust shifting just enough to release enough magma to form islands in a string. The Risonian volcanoes, coming out of a fixed crust, had spewed magma onto the same land for eons, which had created large plateaus, taller than the natural mountains. The largest volcano created the largest southern continent on Rison, and its inhabitants lived at over 10,000 feet above sea level. For a class, Jake had once been required to compare Rison's southern continent to something on Earth. It was like the entire state of Colorado and New Mexico were combined into a single plateau that had been created from one volcano.

"What do I need to bring for the field trip?" Jake asked.

The girls' conversation paused; he realized he'd been ignoring them, and now he sounded like he was butting into their conversation. His head sagged, and he started to apologize. "Sorry—"

But Jillian from civics class said, "It's okay. It can be cold on Mt. Rainier, so wear something warm.

Em added, "Layers. Wear lots of layers, so you can take off things if you get hot."

The girls exploded in laughter, and Em's face turned red.

Now, this, Jake understood. He barely managed to keep a straight face. "When I get hot?"

Before Em could make another comeback and one-up him, he stood and picked up his tray to turn it in. More laughter followed his back. He glanced back to see Em following his progress before she turned back to her friends.

Those rosy brown cheeks—embarrassment suited her, he decided. He smiled to himself. He'd made a good comeback; maybe he was catching on.

Looking up, he paused to stare at the mountains in the distance. From this view, he could see Mt. Rainier, but he knew there were others: Mt. Baker, Mt. Adams, Glacier Peak, Mt. Shuksan, and further south was Mt. St. Helens. Like every other Risonian school child, he'd studied major Earth volcanoes, even spending an entire week on volcanoes of the Cascade Mountain Range. Earth's plates were moving beneath him and magma was moving beneath him. He felt a stirring of excitement; in two days he would get his first up-close look at a real Earth volcano.

THE DRONE

Paradise Jackson Visitor's Center on the south side of Mt. Rainier was indeed a paradise. They say that when pioneer James Longmire's daughter-in-law, Martha, first saw the site, she exclaimed, "Oh, what a paradise!"

Jake had to agree. Spiky evergreens mixed with trees and shrubs that wore dazzling fall foliage. Em explained that the short red trees were mostly vine maples. All Jake knew was that he wished he could paint the landscape. Mt. Rainier towered over them, dark gray rock with drifts of white snow. Swaths of evergreen provided a backdrop for streaks of red, orange, and yellow, and above it all was the intensely blue sky. The colors were so brilliant, so overwhelming.

At the Visitor's Center, they watched a short video on volcanoes—Jake learned nothing new and inwardly chafed at the inadequacy of a couple explanations—then they clambered back on the buses, driving southeast to the trailhead for Snow Lake Trail. The ranger explained that it ran about 2.5 miles along fairly easy trails toward Snow Lake at the base of Unicorn Peak.

One of the things that amazed Jake about living on Earth was that landscapes were always more complicated than you'd expect. Mt. Rainier towered behind them to the north, but it wasn't just one mountain. Instead, it was a series of smaller peaks and valley that together made up a mountain range. The tiptop was Mt. Rainier, but it wasn't just a smooth mountain peak. The topography was irregular and varied. Complicated. Just because you saw one small piece of it, like they'd see Snow Lake today, didn't mean you had really seen Mt. Rainier. To see it and to understand it, you'd have to spend days and days walking all over it.

It would be the same if he went home to Rison. Everyone he met would want to know all about Earth and what it was like. But Jake could only tell them about one beach house outside Gulf Shore, Alabama, and about Bainbridge Island, a small speck of land in Puget Sound. He couldn't tell them about Alaska, or the Pacific Ocean, or Europe, or Australia.

Just like he couldn't tell Earthlings much about the southern seas of Rison, or about Rison's own vast deserts, mountains and jungles. And that was speaking of geography, never mind the different cultures on both planets. You couldn't know an entire planet—that was the incredible tragedy of facing the destruction of Rison. There was so much of Rison that he'd never see, never hear, never touch. And here, he couldn't know Mt. Rainier. He could only know one miniscule patch.

The bus driver, an old guy named Mr. MacDuff, would stay with the bus while everyone else hiked. They all piled out of the bus and stood around waiting while Coach Blevins and Captain Hill consulted with the park ranger. Captain Hill had come along to help chaperone; Jake suspected it was more because of Coach Blevin's possible illness than anything. Jake had looked up Parkinson's and knew it was a progressive disorder. Coach wouldn't be able to hide it for long; his days of teaching and coaching were almost over. Jake recognized, though, that Captain Hill wanted to help his friend whenever he could, and he grudgingly admired that.

Looking around, Jake saw that most students had come prepared for cold and snowshoeing. For Jake, it was a comparatively balmy 50 degrees, and he was glad he had worn layers to take off.

Finally, Park Ranger Jasper Karne took charge. At the trailhead to Snow Lake, he stopped to let everyone gather. Looking out from beneath his wide-brimmed hat, he said, "If you were a ptarmigan, what would you eat in the winter?"

Jake and Em stood close enough to hear the ranger's discussion of the ways different animals survived the winter, but not too close, so they didn't have to participate.

David Gordon answered, "Birds eat berries."

"No," Karne said. "The berries would be ten feet under snow, and the snow's weight would make them mushy, even if you could get to them."

David didn't give up on his quest to be a good ptarmigan, "Pine needles?"

"Yes," Karne said. "And twigs and buds, like willow buds."

Jake barely listened to the ptarmigan conversation. Instead, in his peripheral vision, he watched Captain Hill, who stood near the bus with Coach Blevins. Hill wore camouflage pants and jacket, like half a dozen students. Coach Blevins wore a navy jacket lettered with "SPARTANS," the Bainbridge High School mascot.

Their words were too muffled by distance to understand. Then Coach Blevins pushed up his glasses on his nose and nodded.

The younger man walked to the back of the bus and pulled out a black case that Jake recognized: it held the drone.

Jake rocked from toe to heel, barely controlling his urge to grab the drone and run. He thought: I need to learn Earth curse words. He'd left Rison just as he developed an interest in curse words, so he knew only the most common in Risonian. On the Obama Moon Base, he'd heard the expression, "Cursing like a sailor." But around Jake's father, their commanding officer, the other Navy men had been on best behavior. So despite being the son of a sailor, Jake had heard few curse words. He wanted and needed strong words now.

Ranger Karne had moved on now, starting the hike to Snow Lake. Captain Hill followed behind the group until they came to a fork in the path: he went left, while the group went right. Suspicious, Jake backed up a couple steps, falling behind the group, and then casually strolled away, following Captain Hill. Jake stayed behind a couple hundred yards, making sure to stay hidden behind a tree or shrub. After a quarter mile, Captain Hill went off the trail, following the south shoreline of Bench Lake.

A knot balled in Jake's stomach: the Brown Matter from Blevins's garage was in the drone case. Captain Hill wasn't here just to support his friend; he was doing something with that drone, and he wasn't just playing around.

Jake pulled back a branch to watch Captain Hill pick his way up a slope.

"Where are you going?'

Jake whirled around to see Em, her bright red jacket matching the brilliant vine maples.

"Um, you know, to take care of nature."

Em's face turned red, too, but she shook her head. "No, you're not. You could've done that five minutes ago. You're up to something."

Jake wanted to laugh because she saw through him. He tried to decide how much to tell her, and finally decided on the truth. "You're right. I'm following Captain Hill. He's got a drone, and I want to see what he does with it."

"A drone? No way. I didn't see a drone."

"It's in a black case that Captain Hill had in the back of the bus," Jake said.

Em shrugged. "I saw a black case, but I thought it was supplies. Why's he got a drone?"

Jake shrugged, not worried about whether or not she believed him. "Go back to the group. I'll catch up later." He turned back to the steep path.

"No way," she repeated, but this time, he knew she meant that she wasn't going to let him go alone to see a drone.

They trudged uphill in silence, following a narrow path—not much more than a deer trail—around the edge of the lake. Looking left toward the north, Bench Lake quivered slightly, a light breeze just ruffling its surface. Perfectly reflected in the water were the blue skies and the white-capped peak of Mt. Rainier. They were only halfway up the mountain here, maybe five or six thousand feet above sea level. The peak itself still towered in the distance. This vantage gave a perfect view of the majestic south slopes.

"What's that noise?" Em said.

Jake turned forward again and scanned the area for the source of a loud humming noise. A couple hundred feet away, he spotted the drone laid out on a flat rock by the water. Four black legs forming a quad-copter supported a thick white center; each leg was topped with a spinning rotor.

With a whine, the drone rose straight up, climbing so quickly in elevation that a moment later, Jake wondered if he'd really seen it. While Mt. Rainier's peak stood at over 14,000 feet above sea level, the crater floor was only a climb of around 9000 feet. Captain Hill would be able to see where the drone was going through its tiny webcam, and thus, control it.

Jake almost bent double as his stomach cramped. This was his worst fear: if Captain Hill delivered the Brown Matter to the volcano, somehow managed to dump it into a fumarole or a steam vent—the Earth's core would never be the same.

The Penning Traps used electromagnetic forces to trap the material, essentially a jar without sides. The Brown Matter would need to be in sufficient quantity—a critical mass—to incite the volcano. The amount of Brown Matter to deliver was a crucial, yet delicate calculation.

Jake couldn't let Captain Hill risk that for Earth, like the scientists did on Rison. Brown Matter had the potential to travel through the vent until it reached the heart of the volcano; and from there, it could sink deep into the Earth's core. When Yarborough/Blevins had been doing his research five years ago, volcanologists thought a Penning Trap could operate indefinitely, drawing upon the magma's heat for energy. In the last five years, though, Penning Traps were proven to fail after two or three years. That meant the Brown Matter would be free to go where the magma flowed, which was so unpredictable.

Hill was using old, unsafe technology. Why would he risk it? wondered Jake.

The drone sounded farther away already, but still Jake didn't see Captain Hill. He had to find him and stop the drone; this was a deadly hide-and-seek made harder because Captain Hill wore camouflage and was probably sitting still, concentrating on the drone's screen. Unless he moved and gave himself away, Jake didn't know if he could find the captain in time.

The wind picked up, blowing harder and colder. Jake shivered but wondered if it was from cold or from fear.

Then, Em pointed and whispered, "There."

Captain Hill had climbed an evergreen tree and was sitting on a broad limb, hunched over a screen and using a joystick. The black case lay at the tree's base.

"How'd you see him?" Jake whispered.

She shrugged. "Good eyes. I can always pick out things in the midst of clutter. You ever do 'Where's Waldo?'"

Jake had no idea what she was talking about, but it didn't matter now. "Stay here," Jake ordered Em, and then started to climb. The tree branches were sharp, poking at him through his jacket. Worse, climbing up through the limbs, it was impossible to be quiet.

Captain Hill leaned over his branch, saw Jake, and his eyes went big.

"You can't do this," Jake called out. "You can't dump stuff in a volcano."

"Yeah, kid," Captain Hill said. "What do you know? I'm just playing with a drone." He sat back against the trunk to concentrate on the drone's control screen.

Jake reached for the next branch and pulled himself upward. He climbed steadily for another twenty feet, until Captain Hill was only five feet away.

Glancing down, Captain Hill growled, "Stay away." He shifted his weight, and the sudden movement made a branch swing back and thwack Jake's head, unbalancing him.

Seeing this, Captain Hill shoved against the tree trunk, creating a bigger sway.

Jake's hands slipped, and he fell, crashing through the leafy branches, trying to catch at anything. Irrationally, he thought: Apples! Where are the curse words when I need them?

He grasped branches of needles, but the flimsy branches broke off. He fell again, silent, flailing, trying to grasp anything to stop his rapid fall. He landed on his back—thump!

Em leaned over him, her red jacket filling his vision. "You okay?"

He blinked. He tried to turn his neck, looking right and then left. Curse, curse, curse—the words thumped like the pulse in his head. Such feeble words. "I think so," he murmured.

Behind her, Captain Hill hung by one hand from a branch, and then dropped the last few feet. He dashed downhill.

Jake shoved up, shaking his head gently to dull the pain. "We have to stop him," Jake told Em.

"No. You're hurt." She grabbed his hand and pulled him up. She put her arms around his waist to help him walk.

"No!" Panic threated to overwhelm Jake. "I have to catch him."

Em must've caught something of his desperation because she drew in a shaky breath and opened her mouth to say something—

Turning, stumbling, Jake plunged downhill, following Captain Hill. Em caught at his belt trying to stop him, but missed.

Hill only trotted because he had to stop now and then to look at the drone's control screen. It looked like a tablet computer, but it had hinged sun-shields on the sides and two sturdy antennae at the back. The drone was likely high enough that it could glide for a while without his attention, but Captain Hill couldn't ignore it long, or it would crash.

Throwing caution to the wind, Jake raced pell-mell down the slope, trying to catch up, Em crashing along behind him.

And then, Captain Hill was gone.

Jake pulled up and looked around, trying to spot the captain. Slower now, Jake trotted downward, letting his eyes rove, searching for movement.

There. Behind a boulder.

Realizing he'd been spotted, Captain Hill leapt up and crashed down the slope again, Jake and Em following close on his heels.

They came out of the tree cover at the lake's shoreline. Hill raced toward a tall outcropping of dark gray granite.

Em bent over to catch her breath, but Jake raced toward Captain Hill.

The captain had climbed the ten-foot column of rock and stood fiddling with the drone's control and looking toward the top of Mt. Rainier. "Almost there," he cried.

Jake called, "Stop! You'll make the volcano erupt!"

Captain Hill sneered, "So, the Navy has figured out our plans? So what? Your Dad's a coward, sending a boy to spy on me. Why didn't he come himself? You won't stop me, your Dad won't stop me, and the Navy won't stop me."

Jake climbed the granite column, not knowing how he could stop this crazy soldier, but knowing that Earth's future depended on him.

Reaching the top, Jake peered up at Captain Hill, who was standing spread-legged for stability. Moving the joystick, Hill adjusted the drone's flight. Jake heaved himself up the final inches of rock and charged. He hit Captain Hill squarely on the back, and as they fell, he batted at Captain Hill's hand like an NBA basketball player trying to strip an opponent of the ball. The controller crashed onto the rock and then went flying.

Captain Hill cursed. He was a military man, in his prime; Jake was a teenager who was just getting his full growth. The only reason Jake had escaped from the captain so far was dumb luck. Now, the Captain shoved.

As he went flying, Jake thought: I just need one English curse word. He wished he knew what Hill meant by the words he screamed out now. Jake landed hard onto the gravel beach.

Stunned, he blinked at the blue sky and wondered why Em was screaming.

But there—when he managed to turn his head—five feet away, almost in the water, lay the drone's controller.

Jake rolled over, trying to stand, but only managed to make it to his hands and knees. He crawled toward the controller, watching the images from the webcam. The drone was high up on the mountain, high enough that its webcam only showed snowy slope. Cold lake water seeped into Jake's tennis shoes. He tried to focus on the controls. Could he make the drone crash? Brown Matter was dangerous, but in a remote area like Mt. Rainier, maybe it wouldn't hurt anything—unless it fell into a fumarole.

Suddenly, Jake was shoved from behind, and the controller was snatched from his hands. Nausea welled up, and Jake let his head droop again. When he looked up moments later, Captain Hill was back on top of the granite column, gazing up toward the top of Mt. Rainier.

Jake forced himself to stand, to climb.

Standing near the rock's base, Em called, "Jake are you hurt? Just leave it. Don't let him hurt you again."

She didn't understand; she'd never lived on a dying planet, where you wake up every morning wondering if today was the day that your planet would implode. Mom once said, "You can't live in crisis mode. At some point, you must go into maintenance mode. You just live. Day by day."

He'd never understood that. His last month on Rison before he evacuated had been crisis mode all the way, with every day bringing reports of dormant volcanoes erupting and thousands more dead.

He had to stop Captain Hill and prevent that from happening to Earth, too.

Jake heaved himself back onto the top of the rock, lying flat for a minute, catching his breath. Then he stood. He tried to be light on his feet, tried to keep his knees bent, to be ready for a fight. Instead, he felt sluggish, heavy. He charged. Everything slowed to a crawl. Three steps to reach Captain Hill, who merely sidestepped at the last second. Momentum carrying him onward. Another step. Another. Then thin air. Hanging ten feet above the water. Kicking. He longed for a curse word. Nothing!

Then cold water all around him. Frigid water. Shock!

Momentum carrying him deep, reaching the lake's bottom. It might've killed a human. But Jake wasn't human. His mouth snapped shut. Nose lids shut down so water didn't flood his lungs. His underarm gills opened and shut, switching automatically to water breathing. It happened instantly, without thought, just the normal functioning of his body. And he relaxed. Pure, cold, refreshing ice melt. Luxurious. He hung underwater, just floating.

Above him, though, he saw Captain Hill pumping his arm in a motion that to humans meant, "Victory!"

The Brown Matter was inside Mt. Rainier.

GOING COMMANDO

"Hurry! Keep moving!"

Em raced back to the bus, pushing hard, not letting Jake even take a deep breath. "You'll get hypothermia if we don't get you dry," she insisted.

They stumbled into the parking lot where Mr. MacDuff sat in the driver's seat with strange music coming from a portable speaker. Seeing Jake in wet clothes, the driver jumped into action.

MacDuff started the bus, turned the heater to full blast, and made Jake sit in front of it. Jake wasn't worried. His magma-sapiens body heat was actually drying out his clothes, but he pretended to shiver because it was expected.

The driver called Coach Blevins—and surprisingly, both phones had reception. Blevins charged back from Snow Lake, herding the freshman class with about as much luck as a shepherd with unruly sheep. But when they saw Jake sitting there in damp clothes, the students eagerly offered him odd pieces of clothing. One tall guy had worn jeans and sweat pants over that, so handed Jake the sweats. Another had on three shirts and donated one that smelled strongly of cologne. Dry socks were offered by three kids who had worn multiple pairs.

Fortunately, the driver shooed everyone off the bus, so Jake could at least change in privacy; otherwise, Jake didn't know how he could hide his unusual anatomy. Jake pulled on the sweats, but they were way too long, and the fabric too soft to stay rolled up. Instead, the tall guy came onto the bus and they switched jeans and sweats, Jake using the bus seats to keep his legs hidden. The jeans fit well enough in the waist, but Jake had to roll them up three times.

"Going commando?" joked the tall guy.

No underwear was bad, Jake thought. And then, he pulled on the least smelly pair of socks and vowed to stuff an extra pair in his backpack in case this ever happened again; wearing someone else's sweaty socks was the worst. Throughout all the clothing changes, MacDuff's strange music played, high-pitched and wailing, somehow reminiscent of Risonian opera, Jake thought.

Finally, Jake was in the dry and sitting in front of the bus's heater again. He only lacked shoes.

When kids boarded the bus again, Em was first. She frowned at MacDuff and asked. "What's that music?"

He flushed, jammed buttons on his smart phone, and turned off the portable speaker. "Bagpipes," he said curtly.

Jake nodded to himself. He liked that music; later, he'd look it up and find out more.

Em flopped beside Jake, silent and waiting patiently until the bus was loaded.

Captain Hill boarded last, swaggering down the aisle, slapping hands, and joking.

When Jake had pulled himself out of the frigid lake, Hill had threatened Jake and Em.

"You won't tell anyone about this, will you? Because it's your word against mine. Who will they believe? An officer in the ELLIS Forces or a 9th grader?"

Em furiously protested, "You pushed him."

"So you say." Captain Hill smiled grimly. "I say, he was clumsy and fell. Your Navy Dad may believe you, but he's got no proof."

Jake easily accepted that he couldn't tell anyone, because he didn't want any kind of investigation that would look at him closely. On the way back to the bus, Em tried to protest, but then got wrapped up in making sure Jake didn't get hypothermia. Of course, Jake knew his anatomy wouldn't allow him to get overly chilled, but it was a convenient way to distract Em. He let her fuss and cajole him to hurry.

Still, at the sight of Hill's celebration, Jake's lips tightened, and he sat hunched over, sitting on his hands to keep from standing up and swinging. He had to be patient now until he could tell Dad what had just happened. Only time would tell how bad it would be for Earth.

When the bus finally pulled out of the parking lot, Em leaned toward him and asked in a reasonable voice, "You want to explain what happened up there?"

Jake forced himself to stretch, to lean back. Casually, he let his arm rest along the back of Em's seat. How much would she understand? And what could he say with Coach Blevins sitting just two rows behind them? The truth? Okay, she asked for it. "With the drone, Captain Hill dumped something into a steam vent, a fumarole, on Mt. Rainier."

"Why?" Em asked.

She went for the heart of it. Didn't ask him what was dumped or about the drone or anything. She just wanted to know, "Why?"

He shrugged. "I'm not sure I know all his reasons."

"But you think you know something. Or else you wouldn't have followed him. You wouldn't have tried to stop him."

"I think I know something," he agreed. "But I can't explain here."

Slowly, Em turned so that her feet were in the aisle and her back was toward him. Casually, she scratched her ear and turned her head. Just as casually, she turned back to face the front. Softly, so softly, he almost didn't hear, she said, "Coach is listening to everything you say."

"I know." And sitting in the back of the bus was Captain Hill, with his feet casually propped up on a black case.

"You owe me answers," Em whispered. "Soon."

"Soon," he promised gladly, because it was a good excuse to see her again.

NEED-TO-KNOW

When Jake got home, he wanted to call Mom or Dad immediately but Easter insisted that he take a bath; she still didn't realize how alien his metabolism was, and he still had to pretend to be cold. The hot bath, after the long bus ride to and from Mt. Rainier, made him groggy, so he lay down for a quick nap. When he woke, it was ten p.m., which made it one a.m. in New York City. He should wait till morning to call Mom. He could call Dad any time, day or night, but since Dad was on a secret mission, it'd just be a Navy officer who would relay a message, and there was no guarantee of how fast Dad could answer. No, it was Mom or nothing. And that left him wide-awake to debate as to what to actually tell her.

Did his parents really need to know about the Brown Matter? That was complicated. First, would Brown Matter really affect Earth's core like it had Rison's core? Was it dangerous to use Brown Matter just once, or was it the constant use for a couple decades that caused Rison's core to become unstable? So many questions, so few answers. It'd take a team of scientists years to figure out the answers. Maybe the best course was to wait and see what happened before bothering his mom and worrying her.

Jake shoved back his crumpled sheets. With a sigh, he rose and padded over to his open window to lean out and stare at the stars. High thin clouds blotted out half the night sky. How much longer did Rison have?

Restless, he turned back inside and lay rigid on his bed, staring up at the ceiling. Was he just being selfish? The real reason he didn't want to tell his parents about the day's events was that he wanted to stay here on Bainbridge Island. If he told his mom, he'd have to explain that Coach Blevins was actually the infamous Dr. Yarborough. And that Captain Hill was trying to get a photo of the ambassador's son. That would end with drastic decisions, like moving him to a new location, just when he was starting to settle in and make friends. Like Em.

She'd stayed right with him as they chased Captain Hill, and she'd urged him to get back to the bus quickly. If he'd been human and he really had hypothermia, her instincts were all correct. Beautiful, with that gleaming smile, and steady in an emergency. The more he was around her, the more he liked her.

Jake thought about his Earth culture class, one of the few classes that Swann and his tutor had insisted he attend with others his age. The class had watched a British television show called, "Yes, Prime Minister." One of the hardest things about learning a new language is understanding the slang or metaphors that people used. That show had gone into a funny explanation of "need-to-know." In a complicated play on words, it wound up saying that important people need to know things even when they didn't need to know; otherwise, how would they know if they needed to know?

Mom didn't need-to-know, he decided.

Still, the next morning, Easter insisted that Jake call Mom. She set a plate of blueberry pancakes in front of him and said, "She'll want to hear that you fell into Bench Lake, how it happened, and—most importantly—that you're okay. Best to get it done."

After breakfast Jake put in a vid-call to his Mom and explained that he'd been roughhousing with someone and accidently got pushed into the water. "It was an accident. But Mom, the water was so pure. I'd love a house on a lake like that."

She bought it.

Which scared him. As much as he wanted to not worry his parents, the weight of what Captain Hill might have done—the damage he may have created by trying to awaken Mt. Rainier—was entirely on him to handle. He wanted to be on his own, but now, he was on his own! And he didn't like it.

But he squared his shoulders and told himself, "Need-to-know basis."

THE SEAL PUP

That Saturday, the first weekend in October, Jake set his alarm for 5 a.m. By 6 a.m., he pulled his bicycle up at the harbor to meet the biologist, Bobbie Fleming.

Though it was still dark, the sculling teams were already there, carrying the long, skinny boats into the harbor. The girl's team was efficient, ready for action; the boys huddled in hoodies, with hands wrapped around steaming cups of coffee until the coach got them moving.

Jake had considered joining the boy's sculling team to deflect some of the questions about joining the swim team. He emailed Dad about it, and Dad replied, "Sculling is for people who are tall enough to be basketball stars but are too clumsy, too uncoordinated. You're not tall enough." In spite of Dad's height, Jake still hadn't had the growth spurt that everyone had expected. At 5' 8", he wasn't tall enough to really excel in basketball or sculling.

Meanwhile, though, Jake had asked David Gordon, the team captain, about the sculling team, which resulted in the beginnings of a friendship. After that, he sat with David at lunch, and they hung out some after school.

Bobbie Fleming wasn't at the harbor yet, so Jake went ahead and dragged his kayak out of the storage locker that Sir had rented for him, put on his life jacket, and got ready. When Ms. Fleming drove up a few minutes later, she got out and stretched. Seeing him, she said, "I wondered if you'd be here."

Jake grinned. "I love kayaking."

"Come help me," Ms. Fleming said.

Together, they took her kayak off the top of her car and set it by the water.

Stars still twinkled above Eagle Harbor. With sunrise at 7 a.m., Jake was excited to be on the water while the world woke up. They shoved out onto the water, and Jake relaxed into the task of paddling. Small tendrils of fog drifted up, and it was cold; Jake was glad for his hoodie that covered his head and neck.

Fleming wore a wet suit, complete with booties, a jacket, a stocking cap, and fingerless gloves. She was ready for anything.

"Where's your wetsuit?" Fleming asked. "I thought you were getting one."

"We ordered one," Jake lied. "I've grown two sizes since the last one. I'll be careful today, don't worry."

They paddled quickly out of the harbor and on to Blakely Rock. Harbor seals barked noisily, throwing back their heads in agitation. A large male barked almost without stopping, a harsh cry that echoed across the water. Pups huddled close to their mothers.

Fleming raised a hand, signaling to Jake to slow down. Opening a dry bag, she pulled out binoculars and scanned the rocks. She pointed toward the west end of the island. "There. That's what has them upset." Her own voice was tinged with anger.

Jake saw a seal nosing a pup that was motionless. Sick? Or dead?

Fleming paddled silently, drawing closer to the mother and pup. Over the calm water, her voice carried easily, "It's alive. I saw it move."

She pulled a cell phone from her dry bag and punched in numbers. "Jeremy, I've got a sick harbor seal pup. Can you meet us at Eagle Harbor?"

When she hung up, she told Jake: "The vet will meet us. We've just got to take the pup back to the harbor."

Jake raised an eyebrow. "How do we do that?"

"I'll carry it," she said. Her mouth was set in determination, as if she was a she-bear ready to fight for her own cub.

The problem, of course, was the mother harbor seal. Her dark eyes followed Fleming's movements, and even when Fleming's kayak bumped against the rocky shore, the mother didn't back off.

Fleming crooned, maybe a different language or maybe just nonsense sounds. It reminded Jake of Em's singing, except Fleming's voice was deeper. The seal seemed to tilt its head and listen before it wagged its massive head from side to side. It was almost as though they were having a conversation, and the mother was saying, "No."

But Fleming wasn't one to take no for an answer. She crooned again, her voice insistent. Jake was surprised when the mother seal backed up slightly.

Carefully, Fleming rose out of the kayak and stepped toward the pup. The mother seal backed farther away, but barked furiously.

"It's okay," Fleming said. "I'm here to help." She warbled again in that strange way.

The mother seal stopped barking and just watched Fleming intently.

The scientist turned the baby seal over and laid a hand on its chest. "It's alive, but really sick."

The sunrise now lit the horizon, and wan rays of light spilled over. The island, the rocks, the other seals barking, the mother seal watching—everything was in sharp focus in the sudden sunrise. In the distance, Mt. Rainier filled the skyline, and a twinge of worry sucked at Jake. Was the Brown Matter going to affect the volcano or not? He hated this waiting game to see what, if anything, came of Captain Hill's actions.

Fleming worked both arms under the pup and stood awkwardly, the baby seal's weight making her stagger on the uneven rocks. She eventually lined up the pup along the kayak's hull and held it there while slipping into her seat. The pup slid from side to side but finally it was stable enough for Fleming to shove off.

It was almost impossible for Fleming to paddle, though, Jake saw that immediately. She had to hold the pup on the kayak with one hand—fortunately it wasn't moving much, or it would fall for sure—and try to paddle one-handed.

"Do you have a rope?" Jake asked. "I could tow you."

Fleming's teeth were clenched, intent on her awkward task. "Can't get to it. I'll make it."

She paddled for half an hour, until they were near Eagle Harbor, then called to Jake, "I need to rest. Slow down a minute."

She was breathing hard with the extra effort.

Back paddling, Jake circled her. "Is there anything I can do?"

Suddenly, Jake's kayak rocked. Whirling around, he saw a couple harbor seals that had followed them. They dove and came up under him, rocking his kayak again and almost upsetting it. Seals surrounded both kayaks now, clearly protesting that Fleming had taken the pup away.

She started crooning something again—it must be a different language, Jake decided. It didn't make sense, though, because the seals wouldn't understand a human language.

A group of seals dove suddenly, creating a wave that hit Jake's kayak. He capsized.

Jake hadn't been strapped in, so he plunged into the waters of Puget Sound.

Cold. Not as pure as the snow-fed Bench Lake, but still clean.

Somehow familiar. Yet still foreign. Definitely not the warm waters of the Gulf.

Jake felt his gills working even through the thick fabric of his hoodie, and his magma-sapiens blood responding to the cold, warming him up.

Sounds. Thrumming of boat motors, the barks of the seals. And under those the deeper sounds of an ocean: very low frequency sounds of some leviathan of the deep, and a slow, steady thumping from the north. Mechanical or organic? He had no idea. He wanted to stay underwater and investigate each of the sounds, but his life jacket popped him up.

Breaking the surface, Jake heard Fleming screaming, "Jake! Are you OK? Jake!"

"Fine," he called.

"No!" The panic in her voice was clear. "You'll get hypothermia. You don't have a wet suit, and you won't last ten minutes."

The harbor seals were still swimming in and around them. As best he could, he flapped his arms and sent a message of reassurance, "We're going to help the baby. It's OK. We'll bring him back as soon as he's well."

He didn't know if the waves he created in the water said what he wanted, but the great shark in the Gulf had seemed to understand his intentions anyway. A seal—he thought it was the mother seal—barked at him.

He flapped his hand at her again. "Help. We help."

"Jake!" Fleming's voice was frantic.

He had to calm her down, too. "I'll swim, and that will warm me up," he said in the most calming voice he could muster. "You hold the pup, and I'll pull us in."

With powerful strokes, he grabbed the rope of his kayak and hers. He wished he had on shorts so his legs would mesh to form a powerful tail, but even if that was possible, he couldn't take that chance with others watching. Instead, he flutter-kicked. Slowly, the seals fell back from them, except the mother, who swam just off Jake's side.

Jake gloated in the feel of the water. Kicking, he swam faster than he should, but it felt so right to be in the water and swimming that he couldn't make himself slow down.

They rounded the edge of the harbor and came into sight of the dock. Scullers were still there, and Fleming took one hand off the baby seal to wave and yell, "Help!"

Instantly, one of the boats shoved off and came rowing toward them. Jake saw that it was led by David, the sculling captain. "What happened?" he called.

Fleming answered, "The seal pup is sick. But the other seals dumped Jake's kayak. You've got to get him out of the water before he gets hypothermia."

David went into action. "Jake, grab onto the end of the scull."

Jake held on to the scull with one hand while still holding the ropes of the kayaks in the other. David roared a rapid rhythm for the rowers, and they skimmed over the harbor waters to shore. Jake grinned at the speed and wondered if this was what it felt like to water ski. That was one thing he definitely had to try soon.

A girl from the sculling team ran over and helped Fleming get the pup to shore while David grabbed Jake and raced him to a nearby shed. Ms. Fleming had her cell phone out and yelled to Jake, "I'll call your grandparents to come and get you."

He nodded agreement.

Once again, Jake had to wear someone else's clothing. David shoved him inside the shed and threw him extra clothes donated by the scullers. Jake toweled off roughly with one sweatshirt, and then put on a dry sweatshirt. He worried about keeping his arms tight against his body to hide his gills. But David made it easy by flapping his long arms at the others, shooing them away, and then turning his own back to Jake. Jake even managed to get on someone else's jeans without anyone seeing his Velcro legs.

When he was dressed—again without dry shoes, just in borrowed, smelly socks—David turned back. "Dr. Fleming is worried that you might have hypothermia."

"I swam hard. That kept me warm," Jake said.

David raised an eyebrow, but repeated the words, expanding them even more. "You swam really hard because you knew the danger. You weren't out that far, either. Just lucky."

"Yes, lucky. I swam hard, and it wasn't that far." He nodded to David, grateful for his help.

David kept repeating that to every adult who showed up. "Really lucky that they weren't out very far."

Fleming frowned, and said, "We were pretty far out."

But then, the veterinarian drove up, and she concentrated on the sick pup.

Jake went to squat beside them.

"I'll give it an antibiotic shot and hope that works," the vet said. "I've been seeing several sick seals lately. Don't know what is happening."

"Will it be OK?" Jake asked. He shook his head to one side, making warm water leak out of his ear. He almost said, "You need an anti-*umjaadi*." But he stopped himself in time.

He sat back, unbalanced and landed on his butt in the gravel. What was he thinking? *Umjaadi* was a Risonian organism. The closest relative on Earth was maybe a prion, or a misfolded protein, like the one that caused "Mad Cow Disease." People got Mad Cow Disease by eating affected meat. If Puget Sound had *umjaadi,* when a person immersed in the water, the *umjaadi* could enter through the eye, nose, or mouth.

Something about the water of Puget Sound, he realized, felt vaguely familiar. *Umjaadi* didn't infect Risonians, it just gave a certain—not texture, not taste, not smell—maybe it was a tang, a sharpness, a different combination of texture, taste and smell to their oceans on Rison. But *umjaadis* were light-years away from Puget Sound.

Fleming's voice rose in anger, "You have to do something. I told that mother seal we'd save her baby."

The vet said in a calming voice, "An antibiotic is our best chance." He stuck a syringe into a bottle of medicine to draw out medicine, pulled up a pinch of fur, and injected the pup.

From the water came a barking. The mother seal.

Fleming stood and walked knee deep into the water, protected by her wet suit and boots. "It's OK," she called. "We'll bring it back to you."

Bark! Bark!

Fleming waded further out, and her voice came sweetly, crooning again in that strange way, until the barking stopped.

"Jake! Are you OK?"

Jake rose at the sound of Easter's voice and went to reassure his grandmother that all was well. But he was sure that he was telling a lie. Something was very wrong with Puget Sound.

FERRY RIDE

It was a week of worry. Jake waited for Mt. Rainier to explode. Or, perhaps there would be a massive fish kill in Puget Sound. Maybe the paparazzi would finally find him, and his photo would go worldwide. Instead, the week dragged by, slow minute by slow minute.

Finally, Friday afternoon arrived. He was scheduled to visit Sir's dental office in Seattle. One problem of being Risonian on Earth is that he had to get his teeth pulled constantly: Risonians teeth grow rapidly, and an adult Risonian sheds teeth about every 2-3 weeks. If Jake let that happen on Earth, people could start to notice. He went to Sir's dental office a couple times a month to take care of it.

After school he walked quickly to the ferry station. With a sense of adventure, Jake followed the queue of people to board the afternoon ferry. It was his first time to cross Puget Sound by himself; Easter had always gone with him, but she was busy today, and he had insisted that he could do it himself. He climbed the steps to the upper deck and found a seat outside facing Mt. Rainier. It was cold and windy, but Jake loved the open air. He shrank into his hoodie and stuffed his hands into the hoodie's front pocket. Slowly, the ferry chugged away from Bainbridge Island and headed toward Seattle. Jake slouched, pulling his hoodie down to meet his sunglasses and closed his eyes.

"Look!"

Jake opened his eyes and jerked upright. "What?"

White smoke—clearly, it WAS smoke, not just a cloud—rose straight up from Mt. Rainier's crater. It didn't drift around; it was pouring out of the crater fast enough to rise quickly, making a thin column of smoke.

Jake tried to take it in, tried to understand.

"The volcano is going to explode!" someone yelled.

Now, the upper decks were crowded with people who lined the rails, cell phones in hand, snapping pictures and videos to send out to friends. Within minutes, the world would turn its focus to Mt. Rainier. And if Captain Hill or his associates blamed the Risonians—

Quickly, Jake shoved aside a kid, snapped his own picture, and sent it to his mother along with a text: They will blame us.

She didn't answer.

He sent it to his Dad. They will blame us!

He didn't answer.

People were hugging each other and crying: "The end of the world."

No, Jake thought perversely. It was Rison that was dying, not Earth, and no one cared about that. Maybe this is a good thing. Maybe the panic at their own world dying would give them sympathy for Risonians. But no, if they blamed the "Sharks," it would only make things much worse.

The wind whipped through coats, sweaters, jackets, and hoodies, penetrating and chilling everyone to their core. While they were trapped on the ferry, the crowd had remained calm. As the ferry pulled into the dock, though, people rushed down the stairs toward the exit, which was blocked off with a chain until the ferry was fully docked. In front of Jake, a small woman held the hand of a tiny girl in a pink jacket.

"Hey! Stop pushing," the woman cried.

But the crowd pressed closer and closer to the exit. They were still five or ten feet from the dock, but the pack wanted off the ferry.

The waiting area might easily hold a hundred people, and on a normal day, people waited patiently for the docking. This time, panic drove them, and they packed closer and closer.

Someone shoved hard from behind, and like dominoes in a row, people floundered. The small woman stumbled. Her daughter slipped out of her mother's hands and fell, her pigtails flying. She wailed, "Mom!"

Jake's heart went cold.

The crowd tried again to surge forward, and the girl wailed again, "Mom!"

Franticly, Jake wiggled past a fat man and scooped up the girl. He braced his legs wide trying to create a small space for the woman. She looked up, panic in her eyes. She wore a perfume so strong that even out here in the open, it made Jake cough.

She hissed a warning: "When the gate opens, they'll stampede."

"This way." Jake sidestepped, trying to reach the edge of the mass of people, while making sure the woman could move, too. The girl clung to him, eyes wide, her hands pinching his ears; he barely noticed.

Bump. The ferry barely touched the dock with a gentle touch.

Looking down at the girl, her dark eyes were filled with tears, and she was shivering. Awkwardly, with one hand, Jake buttoned her coat and tried to reassure her. "It's okay." Her mother's scent clung to the child, but at least on the girl, the smell was a muted floral.

The officials had barely opened the gate when the mob surged. Jake clung to the rail for support and fought to stand upright. The child gripped his shirt collar and moaned. Somehow, he managed to keep their eddy calm, to keep the woman protected, standing upright. Ten feet in front of them, the fat man—the one he'd pushed past earlier—swayed, and then toppled, falling slowly. Immediately, the man roared like a mad bull and swept his arms and elbows around like a longhorn steer to clear a space, standing clumsily—but standing—before the hoard of frightened people swept him to the gangplank and down to shore. If it had been the child who fell—Jake couldn't think of it.

Only when the crowd had thinned did Jake hand the girl to her mother. She stroked the child's dark head. Jake realized he'd buttoned the jacket wrong, putting the second button through the first buttonhole, making it lopsided. Face somber, the mother looked up quickly and mumbled, "Thank you." Turning, she scurried off the boat and rushed up the hill without looking back.

Everything now seemed lopsided. Jake had hoped that Mt. Rainier would stay dormant, that the Brown Matter would have no effect. Instead, the laws of physics were universal, operating the same for Earth and Risonian volcanoes. It was probably time to talk to Mom and Dad. But Jake quaked at the thought. They were going to be furious.

SMOKING VOLCANO

When he arrived at Sir's dental office, Jake rapped on the reception window and waved at the receptionist, Marisa. She was in her mid-twenties, freckle-faced, and had—of course—a perfect smile. When Jake had first met her, he was surprised that she worked all day in an office because she seemed so athletic. But she'd explained, "I always knew what I wanted to do: give people a smile."

She meant it literally; as in give them a mouth of perfect looking teeth. "I wish I could do stand-up comedy," she said. "I really don't have much of a sense of humor, though. So maybe I can make sure that when something strikes them as funny, they aren't ashamed to open their mouths."

Jake pulled open the reception window.

"You're here again?" Marisa's forehead wrinkled in confusion. She often looked this way because she was curious about everything, and she often asked about things she didn't understand.

Jake said, "Just my molars again. They're aching, and Sir said he'd just take a look."

"He's with a patient," Marisa answered his unspoken question. "About 30 minutes."

Jake turned away, but Marisa called, "Hey! I hear you've been talking to Em a lot. I kinda look out for her since Mom and Dad are traveling, and I don't like her going home to an empty house. I'm glad she has swim team till late. But then, I'm always a little scared about her safety walking home alone. She says you've stayed and walked with her this week. Thanks."

Jake blushed. He wasn't thinking about Em's safety when he walked her home! "Yeah, no problem."

Marisa smiled and said, "Hope that tooth isn't too bad." And then she turned back to her computer.

Jake sat and flipped uneasily through magazines. Marisa clearly suspected something because Jake was showing up here too often. He'd only lived with Sir for six weeks and this was his third time in. Yet, when he smiled, no teeth problems were evident. They'd have to do this at home, he realized. He couldn't keep coming here even if it was easier for Sir. He yawned, leaned back, stretched out his legs, and tried to nap. The TV in the reception room, though, suddenly flashed a picture of Mt. Rainier smoking. He leaned forward to catch what it said, but the volume was low.

He tapped on the window. "Can you turn the TV up?"

Marisa came out to the waiting room with a remote control and turned up the volume. Together, they stared at the footage of the smoking Mt. Rainier.

Marisa nodded at the TV. "You just came over on the ferry. Did you see it?"

"It was eerie." Jake shivered at the memory of the mob stampeding. "And people on the ferry went crazy."

Marisa sat down and leaned forward to watch the TV. "I would hate to be trapped on a ferry when the volcano blew. I bet they were frantic to get off."

"It was dangerous." Jake shuddered at the memory of the mob stampeding. "They almost trampled a little girl." He felt his earlobes, still sore from the girl grabbing them. "I held her until the crowd passed." He was babbling. Until this moment, he hadn't realized how scared he'd been.

"Ma'am?"

That was the last patient of the day, and Marisa went around the door to her desk to check out the patient.

Moments later, Marisa led Jake back to Sir's examining room.

"Did you hear about Mt. Rainier? It's smoking," Jake asked his grandfather.

Sir patted his dental chair. "No. But you can't talk right now. You can tell me about it on the way home."

Marisa was finishing up the accounting so she could drop checks off at the bank. Because she lived on the island, she'd take the ferry back with them. She had a tiny efficiency apartment, but when her parents were gone on business, she stayed at the family house with Em.

Sir's assistant was already gone for the day, so they were alone in the exam room with no one to see what Sir was doing in Jake's mouth.

"Open wide," Sir said.

Risonian teeth grew in a very different manner than humans. Like a lemon shark on Earth, a Risonian's teeth grew in a circular fashion, and grew so fast that they lost two or three teeth a month. It happened naturally, and strictly speaking, they didn't need a dentist; however, Mom and Dad both thought it better if Sir pulled Jake's teeth regularly.

He had two teeth to be pulled, very loose, side-by-side; in 10 minutes flat, Sir was finished and packed up to catch the ferry back to Bainbridge.

Locking the door to the dentist office, Sir asked, "Now, what's this about Mt. Rainier?"

Marisa chimed in, "It's all over the TV and radio. Do you think it will really explode, and the city will be covered in ash like Pompeii?"

Jake knew that Pompeii was a famous Earth volcano that erupted somewhere over in the Mediterranean Sea, in Italy or someplace like that. It was famous because centuries later, scientists excavated the site and found people who had little or no warning about the volcano; they had been buried in ash where they had been cooking supper or walking through a street, like Jake and Sir and Marisa were walking now through the streets of Seattle.

"You worry too much," Sir said. "We've talked about this before. The biggest danger in Seattle is from lahars, or mudflows."

"My parents have a cabin near Mt. Rainier. They've gone to Japan for ten days of meetings about imports and just emailed me that they had seen the reports of the mountain smoking. They want me to go and get any valuables from the cabin that I can carry from there. They've got some expensive paintings and works of art they brought back from different travels."

Sir frowned. "When will you do that?"

"Will you go with me?" Marisa asked hopefully. "I don't want to go alone."

Sir winced, but said, "Of course. We'll go tomorrow, Saturday. Easter will want to help, too."

"I'll come, too," Jake said.

"Sure," Marisa answered. "And my sister will come."

Surprisingly, the ferry ride was pretty normal except for a few rows of people standing quietly on the south side of the ferry, staring at the smoking mountain. At least there wasn't panic like earlier.

Later, at home, Sir, Easter and Jake talked about Mt. Rainier again.

"I wonder," Jake said, "if Risonian scientists would be able to stop Mt. Rainier from exploding."

Sir bit into a pizza slice and mumbled, "No. That's how Rison got into so much trouble."

Jake eyed the sausage and green peppers pizza. He and Dad preferred pepperoni and pineapple, but Easter said, "Gross." So, they got this instead.

"We've learned so much about volcanoes," Jake said "We know more about planetary cores than anyone. We might be able to help."

"Or you might make it worse than ever," Easter said.

"Is Earth my home now?" Jake asked. "If so, shouldn't I try to protect it?"

Sir and Easter looked at each other, and Jake cringed at the flash of sympathy they exchanged. Easter reached a hand over to cover his hand. "You know that Earth is your home now. You'll never go back to Rison."

He looked at her hand freckled with age spots. If he lived long enough to be considered old, it would be on Earth. Easter thought she understood what he was going through, the anguish of losing his planet. But there was no way she could understand. He couldn't even explain a simple thing like a fruit to her. How did you describe that in English? Impossible. He withdrew his hand and pushed back his plate. Homesickness overwhelmed him: he longed to go fishing with Swann, to swim with his friends, to hug his pet *kriga*, Bell. Instead, he got sausage and green pepper pizza.

"May I be excused?" he said formally.

Easter came around to his chair and enveloped him in her strong arms. She said nothing, for there was nothing to be said. But Jake was grateful for this old lady who somehow knew that sometimes grandsons just needed a hug from their grandmother.

ALONG THE COWLITZ RIVER

Sir, Easter, and Jake picked up Marisa and Em early that morning. Jake supposed that he knew Marisa and Em were sisters, but he hadn't really remembered that they were both adopted until Em climbed into the van and sat in the back seat beside Easter, who had insisted Jake take the front seat. The Tullis sisters looked nothing alike. Marisa was short, freckled and athletic while Em had a darker complexion and long, straight hair. After studying the internment of Japanese-Americans, Jake had paid attention to how Americans described the different races on Earth: Asian, African American or black, and so on. He realized now that Em was Asian American, but couldn't say from what Asian country her ancestors had come.

Three hours later, stepping out of Sir's van, Jake was struck by the beauty of the Tullis's A-frame cabin and the surrounding area. Below them lay the wide Cowlitz River, flanked by tall evergreens. Large, smooth stones littered the streambed, but of course, it was the hulking volcanic peak to the north that dominated the landscape. Jake knew that to the southwest lay Mt. St. Helens, even if they couldn't see it from here. They were surrounded by active volcanoes, and he suddenly realized that he could hear them. Risonians could hear lower frequency sounds than humans. For example, in the ocean, he could easily hear the songs of whales, while humans needed special microphones to translate those sounds into frequency ranges they could hear.

The volcanoes were singing: magma vibrated - whine, hiss, whoosh and chug-chug. Here, the sounds were faint, inconstant, but it still felt oddly comforting, like being home on Rison. The song of the volcanoes was the background noise of his home planet.

The Tullis cabin was about ten miles south of the Paradise Visitor's Center, where Jake's class had been last week, just outside Packwood, Washington. Lovely, quiet, and spacious—the cabin would be utterly destroyed in any explosion of Mt. Rainier because the lahars would follow the Cowlitz River bed. Volcanologists predicted the cabin could be hit by a 20-600 foot high wall of mud traveling up to 60 mph, a massive lahar. That's why Em and Marisa's parents were so worried. They had to clear out everything valuable.

"Yes, 600 feet tall is possible," Sir explained, "depending on how Mt. Rainier blows."

Jake thought it was crazy to build in such a place; but then, Killia, the capital of Tizzalura, was built on a plateau of volcanic rock and would eventually be destroyed when their volcano erupted. So far, the volcanic activity had been south of the city, but it was just a matter of time. He supposed that no matter where you built a house, some natural disaster was possible, from tornadoes to earthquakes to floods to volcanic eruptions. You just learned to deal with the dangers in your area of your planet.

"How long have you had this cabin?" Easter asked. "It's beautiful."

Marisa stretched after the long car ride, pulled a rubber band from her hair, and shook it out. "My parents bought it about fifteen years ago. We love it because our nearest neighbor is half a mile away. We played in that river growing up, right Em?"

Em flashed a glare at Marisa, and then waved at the river. "Sometimes, we see elk crossing the river."

But when they looked toward the river now, the sight of the smoking mountain was impossible to avoid; on the light breeze came the faint smell of sulfur. This wasn't a day for play, but for caution. They should work fast and get out of there.

A man was working his way along the riverbank toward them. He looked up and waved.

Marisa broke into a smile and jogged down to the river to meet him.

"Who is it?" Jake asked Em.

She frowned. "Cyrus Hill. He's been calling Marisa all week, and she told him that we'd be here. His family has a cabin half a mile upstream. This is where they met."

Grimly, Jake watched Captain Hill climb up the riverbank. Captain Hill stopped to give Marisa a hand up a steep part, and then kept hold of her hand; their arms swung in unison. Marisa glowed under his attention.

When Captain Hill and Marisa came up, Captain Hill stopped short. "You didn't tell me the Roses were coming."

Marisa looked slightly embarrassed. "Oh, Sir and Easter were glad to come and help, and I felt safer with them along. I think you've met their grandson? This is Jake."

"We've met," Hill and Jake said in unison.

Jake remembered the insane dash around Bench Lake and the struggle for the drone's controls. But no one else knew about all of that except Em. Sir didn't know that Captain Hill was the soldier who came to their beach house in Gulf Shores. If Dad had known that Captain Hill had a Bainbridge Island connection, he might've given Sir his name. But as far as Sir knew, the soldier in Alabama was just an anti-Shark extremist.

Em stepped forward and said, "Marisa, there's something you should know about Cy."

Marisa gave a short laugh, waving her hand dismissively. "Cy's already told me about it. He said you two went off at the freshman trip to Mt. Rainier. And you two were roughhousing and fell into Bench Lake. And he's the one who caught you and got you in trouble."

"That's not how it happened," Jake said.

Em glared at her sister, but was silent.

Now, Easter turned from the van and said, "Then what did happen?"

Jake was caught in the middle of the truth and the lies he'd told. He couldn't explain everything to Easter and Sir. But Marisa had the story wrong, too, from Captain Hill's lies. Anger tore at him, and he hesitated, not sure what to say. In this anyway, Captain Hill was right: who would take the word of a 9th grader over the word of an ELLIS Forces officer?

"Jake?" Easter said quietly. "What happened on the field trip?"

"Nothing." Jake looked down and shook his head. "I told you about it. Just messing around."

"Good," Marisa said. "Because I don't care if you two get along or not. Today, all I care about it getting Mom and Dad's art work out of danger. We can all work together, right?"

"Don't worry," Em said. "We'll do our part." She was still in a glaring contest with Marisa. The sisters were mad, and Jake thought it went a lot deeper than today's problems.

Meanwhile, Jake glared at Hill, who calmly stared back. A truce, then, thought Jake grimly. That was fine with him. With a shrug, he turned to the van and helped pull out huge rolls of bubble packing material.

Marisa ordered everyone around for the rest of the morning: she walked through each room and stuck a piece of blue painter's tape on items that she wanted to remove—and there were a lot. The Tullis family ran an Asian import company. For the tourist trade, they brought back trinkets such as Chinese yo-yos, cheap chopsticks, and inexpensive replicas of the Great Wall. But they also had a quirky sense of color and art and bought quality for their personal collection: jade statues, carved teak platters, delicate watercolors, and much more. Everything had to be bubble-wrapped and stacked near the kitchen door.

Easter said, "Don't start packing it in the car until it's all wrapped. That way, we'll put the heavy stuff on the bottom and lightweight on top."

What with Marisa and Easter's organization skills, the small crew divided up the task of packing efficiently. Jake and Em were assigned the task of wrapping things in the living room, which suited Jake just fine. Marisa and Captain Hill took the loft, while Easter and Sir took the bedrooms.

Jake and Em worked efficiently for a while, saying little, just letting their stack of bubble-wrapped items grow.

Em moved to the shelves beside the fireplace and started wrapping carved jade figures. She stopped, though, when she came to the middle shelf, picked up one of the figurines, and brought it to show Jake. Holding out a five-inch tall horse, she said, "Look. It's my favorite. Mom and Dad brought it back from a trip to China and let me name it."

He took the horse from her and let his hand hold hers while he turned the green horse over to examine it in the light streaming in a window.

They were standing close now, and Jake bent his knees to bring himself to a level where he could look at her long dark eyelashes. Jake raised an eyebrow and nodded at the jade horse.

Em blushed, turning a rosy pink. "I just named it Beauty. I know, a kind of plain name for something so pretty."

The sunlight made Em's hair gleam like polished ebony, and Jake couldn't look away. With a husky voice, he said, "Beauty would be a good name for you."

Her dark eyes widened; her faint orange-spicy perfume filled him with a longing. He leaned closer, and she didn't back off.

This was it, he thought. Just like in the movies, he was going to kiss her. It would be his first kiss of a human girl, heck, of any girl, since he'd never kissed a Risonian girl, either. He bent to her, clumsy, unsure—

"Em, how much more do you have to wrap?"

Em jerked back and turned to the trinkets on the cocktail table.

Marisa stood in the doorway. Behind her, Captain Hill towered over Marisa, and he was glaring at Jake.

Guiltily, Jake turned to the bubble wrap and cut a small strip to wrap around Em's jade horse.

"Almost done," Em said. "Just the jade figures to finish."

Was she breathless? Jake wondered. Had she wanted that kiss as much as he did? But this wasn't the time or place. Soon, he promised himself, soon.

They worked hard, and by mid-afternoon, it was all done, and the van was packed to the ceiling

"I brought a picnic," Easter said. Sir carried in a basket, and she pulled out sandwiches, chips, plates, forks and drinks. Jake didn't want to be around Captain Hill, though, so he asked Easter for a couple sandwiches and drinks and pulled Em down to the shore. They sat cross-legged on large boulders and chatted while they ate, the previous tension between them gone.

"Hey, Beauty, do we have time for a walk?" Jake joked.

Em grinned. "If you call me Beauty, I might have to call you Beast."

Jake frowned. She was probably talking about a folk tale or something, and it was probably a good thing, but Beast didn't sound as good as Beauty. On the other hand, he thought philosophically, it was better than Shark and Mermaid.

She stood and strolled along the streambed, leading the way around a bend. He followed a couple steps behind where he could watch her graceful walk.

When they rounded the bend, she pointed. "That's Captain Hill's cabin. Marisa met him one day when she was wading barefoot in the river. Her feet had gotten so cold that she fell and he picked her up and carried her back to shore. Rescued her."

Jake studied the Hill's cabin. Unlike the Tullis's A-frame cabin, this was a regular log cabin, with two stories. Cabins in this area were very expensive. Idly, Jake wondered what Hill's parents did for a living.

"I'd like some answers, you know," Em said quietly. She nodded up toward Mt. Rainier. "Is it smoking because of what Captain Hill did, because of that drone and what was in it?"

"I don't know," Jake said.

"Don't tell me that! You tried to stop Cy; you know something."

Jake was quiet, watching the smoke rise into the dazzling blue sky. Earth's blue sky was the result of the earth's atmosphere and how it scattered light. Rison's sky with its slightly different atmosphere shaded more toward blue-purple. How could Jake explain everything to Em? She wouldn't understand.

"Well," she demanded. "I've been patient, and I've kept it secret. But you owe me some answers."

"I really don't know what Captain Hill did; I only have suspicions."

Em's lips tightened, and she had her hands on her hips in a cheerleader stance that meant she was ticked off. "So?" she said. "You suspect what?"

His own fists tightened from tension. If only he could tell her. But the life of every Risonian depended on him keeping his mouth shut. He couldn't tell her anything; he regretted that she'd been there to see him try to stop the drone.

"Captain Hill is blaming all this on the Sharks—the Risonians. I've seen him on TV news talk shows," Em insisted. "Is he right?"

This time, Jake got mad. "First you say that Captain Hill put something in the volcano. And now, you say that the

Sharks caused this. How can it be both of those at the same time?"

Em sighed in exasperation. "Of course, it can't be both. So help me out here."

"The Brown Matter may have caused the mountain to wake-up, yes. If that's the cause, it's Captain Hill's fault. If."

Em sucked in a sharp breath. "Brown Matter?"

Jake whirled away and started walking back to the Tullis cabin, furious with himself. Em hadn't suspected Brown Matter, and now he'd slipped up and mentioned it, and she'd never let it go.

Em trotted alongside him, trying to keep up with his longer stride. "Jake, listen. Are you saying Captain Hill put Brown Matter into the volcano? We have to tell someone."

Jake stopped abruptly and turned to her. "Let's get this straight. I don't know what Captain Hill did that day. I don't know if it was Brown Matter or just—well, just sugar. But HE dumped something into the volcano. If anyone gets blamed, it should be ELLIS Forces. But I'm not saying another thing."

Without waiting for an answer, he strode away, reached the steep bank, where he started to climb. A clatter of gravel rushed down on him and Jake looked up. Captain Hill stood above him, scowling. Jake glared back.

Hill bent to scramble down the stream bank and past Jake without saying a word. Jake heaved a deep sigh, barely controlling his anger against the man. He finished the climb and went to lean against the van. When everyone was ready to leave a few minutes later, he climbed into the front seat of the van without looking back to see where Em sat. He leaned against the van's window and closed his eyes, pretending to sleep. But all he could think was that when he got home, he would have to look up the story of Beauty and the Beast.

STATESMAN VS. POLITICIAN

Mt. Rainier started smoking on October 10, and it smoked all that month. Surprisingly, life went on. Jake got up, went to school, came home, slept, and then got up the next morning to repeat the process. Like on Rison, one quickly got used to living in the shadow of a volcano.

After the trip to the Tullis cabin and their argument, Em avoided him. It was easy to do, what with her swim team and work at the coffee shop. That made the civics and biology classes even more important for Jake. They were the only times when he could watch and listen to her, and maybe even talk to her.

In civics class, they were covering American politics.

"Would you vote for a politician or for a statesman?" Coach Blevins challenged.

David shrugged. "What's the difference?"

"A statesman does what's best for the country; a politician does what's best for himself, which may or may not be good for the country," Coach Blevins said. He rolled a marker between his palms.

"You imply that it's bad to look out for yourself," Jake said.

"Is it?" Coach Blevins said.

The arguments swirled for a few minutes, and then Coach Blevins raised his hands for silence. "Let's do a test," he said.

Coach Blevins set up two old Coke bottles, the old glass kind with a narrow neck. He looked around. "Jake and David come and try this."

"I'll give you each ten glass marbles. You must close your eyes, and without looking, see how many you can drop into the Coke bottle."

Immediately, Jake's competitive streak surfaced: he wanted to win. He stood over the Coke bottle so that the tips of his shoes just brushed it.

"Ready? Go."

Jake didn't hesitate: he positioned his arms with elbows out, centering his hands right over his feet. He let the first marble drop. It bounced noisily on the floor, and the students roared in laughter. It was soon too noisy to monitor his progress with sound. He'd either get his marbles in the jar or not. Quickly, he dropped his next nine marbles. When done, he raised his hands in surrender and looked. Zero. He had zero marbles in his jar!

David had two. He won.

Blevins said, "Sit. And let's talk about what just happened."

A girl raised her hand, "David cheated. His eyes were open a little."

Blevins nodded, and a grim smile played across his face. "Yes. And in fact, that is the test. We didn't blindfold either one. We just asked them to keep their eyes shut. So who won? Jake got zero marbles in his jar; obviously he kept his eyes shut. David, however, got two marbles in his jar because he did open his eyes. Who wins?"

Jillian said, "Jake. He followed the rules."

Em said, "David. He got results."

Blevins spread out his arms and said, "Politician or statesman?"

Jake frowned. "It's not that easy!" Swann was a statesman. He was working for the good of Rison, for the good of the whole planet. But what if they allowed the Southern hot heads to rule, and they attacked Earth and forced them to yield the oceans to Rison? Surely, they were desperate enough, and generations from now, they would be praised for making the choices that let their species survive.

What did it matter if a person acted on his moral principles such as "Do not cheat"? Did the stakes matter?

But look who was talking! Blevins had cheated on his research papers by not citing the Risonian scientists. What had he accomplished?

"Does it matter," Jake asked, "if you get caught cheating?"

"Did David cheat? Some would say the end justifies the means," Blevins said.

"He broke the rules. Let's call that cheating. Does cheating matter? Should you break rules any time you want, if it gives you some advantage?" Jake said.

Em glared at him, "Maybe results are what matter the most."

Blevins said, "Would you vote for a politician or for a statesman?"

Jake realized that Blevins wasn't going to answer. He was enjoying setting up the moral question, then letting them struggle with it. In his previous life as a volcanologist, Blevins had acted like a politician—and suffered the consequences. Pragmatic, he didn't care what rules he broke if he came out ahead.

Jake wished again that he'd been able to see the aged-up photo that Captain Hill had of him. Jake had recognized Coach Blevins from the old photos—even with the nose job—but that was because he had found that old black-and-white photo at Blevins's house, and that had given him context. For Blevins to recognize Jake, though, would be harder because of two things: Jake had grown from a child to a teenager, and the context was all wrong. They expected the Ambassador's son to be in some fancy school, or in New York.

But it was only a matter of time.

Sooner or later, paparazzi or not, Coach Blevins would look at Jake and know the truth. And when he did, there'd be no chance to explain anything. Blevins would act like a politician, at best. At worst—well, maybe it was time to transfer out of Blevins' class. It meant no classes with Em, but stories about Beauty and the Beast didn't always end happily.

SCIENCE PROJECT

If civics class left them arguing about statesmen and politicians, Biology class threw Jake and Em together.

"You must do a research project with a partner. Something about animals and ecosystems, preferably something in the Pacific Northwest," Coach Blevins said. He paired off students and told Jake, "You're new on the Island, so I'll put you with Em, who's lived here all her life."

Jake slouched in the too-small desk chair and doodled on his paper while Em verbally went through some options. She'd pulled a desk over but made sure it was far enough away so they wouldn't touch.

While she talked, Em stared out the window. "We could do something, you know, on how salmon find their way back to their home streams. Or something. But I don't know how you'd research that." She shrugged. "Or something about lung capacity of swimmers versus non-swimmers."

"Swimmers?"

Glancing at him, Em returned to gazing out the window. She nodded solemnly. "Humans are animals. And the Pacific Northwest is our ecosystem."

Jake grimaced at the bad joke but said nothing else, just doodled on his paper. She was supposed to think of something, not him. That's what Blevins had said.

"Cloning?" Em asked. "Although, I don't know what we could do on that because it's so complicated. Maybe we could clone a grasshopper or something simple. Maybe a flat worm, what do they call them? Planaria?"

Jake started drawing a happy face, over and over, cloning the thing across his paper. In all the discussion of how to survive their planet's implosion, cloning was one thing Risonians discussed widely. The idea was that each person who was evacuated from Rison would bring along the cell tissue from a hundred other people, and when the time was right, they could clone that person. The arguments never worked, though, because of the environment versus genetics debate. Just because you had the ability to clone someone didn't mean they'd turn out to be the same person because they'd grow up on Earth instead of Rison. That environment would create a very different Risonian.

They weren't getting very far in choosing a research topic. His mind wandered: tomorrow was Saturday, and he'd be out on the water with Bobbie Fleming, and wouldn't have to worry about class for a while and—that was it!

Leaning forward, Jake explained to Em about meeting the wildlife biologist and the sick harbor seal pup. "We can talk to the vet," he said, "and see what he found out. Even if it's just one pup, maybe there's something that would work for this project. I bet he took blood samples and stuff."

"Wow, good idea." Then, as if she remembered she was supposed to be mad at him, she sobered. "Let me ask Coach Blevins if that's okay." She stood and went to the front of the class to talk to the Coach.

She came back, nodded curtly, and stared out the window again. "He says okay."

Jake ran a hand through his hair. "Well, um. I don't know the vet's name. Dr. Fleming talked to him. I could call her, but it would be better if we went tomorrow morning and talked to her in person. We need her permission, too. If this idea doesn't work, maybe she'll have another idea."

"Sure," Em said.

"I'll bike around to your house at 5:45."

"A.M.?"

"Yes."

"You've got to be kidding," Em groaned.

□ ☆ ☆

Before Jake met Em the next morning, he stopped at a coffee shop and bought her a venti latte with one sugar and a touch of cream, just the way she liked it.

Jake rang the doorbell and waited, latte in hand.

When Em answered the door, though, she just frowned at him.

"What?" he asked.

"My stomach is upset. I don't need coffee. You drink it."

"You coming? Or are you sick?" Jake tried to pat her back in sympathy, but she shrank back.

"Coming," she said. "I just don't want to eat or drink much right now."

When they arrived at the marina, the tide was out, leaving a large boat beached, leaning now against the concrete dock, protected by several bumper floats. The boat's owners were probably scraping the hull because turquoise paint gleamed in a couple streaks, but the rest of the boat was covered with barnacles. Jake and Em parked their bikes and stretched.

The sculling crews were just pulling up, getting ready for practice—crazy on a Saturday morning, Jake thought, but they were doing well in competition this year and wanted to keep their season going.

David called a hello to Jake, so Jake went to help carry some oars while David and another guy carried their scull to the water's edge. David straightened, looking like a pocketknife unfolding, suddenly doubling his height. "What are you doing for Halloween tonight?"

"Nothing," Jake said.

"Come over. A few of the guys and I aren't doing trick-or-treating, but we're listening to 'War of the Worlds.'"

"Interesting," Jake said. In Earth Culture class, his Risonian teachers discussed the famous 1938 radio drama that scared half the population of the United States into believing that aliens were really invading. Anything that culturally touched on how humans treated or viewed aliens had been presented in his Risonian class. But Jake had never heard the actual radio drama, had only heard of it. "Are you listening to the whole thing?"

David grinned. "The You-Tube video is an hour long. We'll have snacks and stuff."

"Sure. Sounds like fun," Jake said.

Em was talking to the girl's sculling team when Fleming drove up. Jake trotted over to help Fleming with the kayak and explained the biology project.

"I'll call the vet," Fleming said, "when we get back. If he agrees, I'll cooperate with you. Who's your partner for the research project?"

Jake gestured to the group of girls. "Em Tullis."

Fleming's brow furrowed. "Emmeline Tullis?" She turned to the car and undid the strap of the kayak. Suddenly, though, she stopped. "You know what? I'm not feeling very good; my stomach is queasy. I think I'll pass on the trip out to Blakely Rock this morning." She pulled the kayak's straps, cinching it tight again.

Em said, "I'm not feeling very good, either."

Fleming whirled around with a startled look. "What's wrong?" she said sharply.

Jake watched the two of them. Fleming looked upset, while Em looked curious.

"Upset stomach, too." Em held out her hand. "By the way, I'm Em Tullis. I've heard of you, but we've never met."

Fleming quickly shook Em's hand, and then ducked her head, pulled off her wire rim glasses, polished them on the hem of her t-shirt and put them on again. She tilted her head. "Well, I'm leaving."

Jake looked from Fleming to Em and back again. Something about the way they tilted their heads was similar, almost as if they were related or something. But Em was adopted from someplace in California, if he remembered right.

"Do you want to go home, too?" He wanted to feel her forehead and cheeks to see if she ran a temperature. But he didn't think she'd allow him to touch her.

"Yeah, I better," Em said. "But you go on out and check on the harbor seals." She turned to Fleming and asked, "Could I get a ride?"

Fleming's brows furrowed and for a moment, Jake thought she'd say no. But she nodded reluctantly. "Sure. Put your bike in the back.

While Em wheeled her bike to Fleming's car, Fleming turned to Jake: "Here's the phone number for Jeremy Prism, the vet. Call him and explain your project. Tell him it's okay with me, but to call me if he has questions."

She got in the car and stared straight ahead, like Em was invisible. Jake didn't know what was going on, but she didn't seem to like Em at all. Wouldn't have had anything to do with her, except Em was sick and asked directly for a ride, and she couldn't avoid a direct request like that.

KILLING EARTH

On Monday morning, Jake walked deliberately down the noisy school hallway and stopped in the doorway of the counselor's office. After Friday, he had worried all weekend that eventually Coach Blevins would recognize him. It was time to get out of his classes.

"Excuse me," he said.

"You need something?" the secretary said.

"Yes. Could I see the counselor or get an appointment to see him?"

"Wait here."

She disappeared through a back doorway, and Jake plopped his backpack onto an empty chair. He couldn't seem to sit still, though. He rolled his feet from toe to heel, stretching, and then back heel to toe. Toe, heel. Heel, toe.

"You can see him now," the secretary said.

Jake had met Mr. Cuvier the first day of school when he got his schedule. His office looked about the same with jumbled shelves of books; the desk, however, looked almost empty now that school had started and schedules were worked out. Mr. Cuvier stretched out his legs, leaned back in his chair and put his hands behind his neck. "Have a seat. What's up?"

Cuvier's massive work boots were scuffed and the shoestrings were half-raveled out. They were a working man's boots. Jake had heard that Cuvier owned a small farm with goats, U-pick strawberries, and blueberries. In fact, he had a side contract with the school to provide them with goat's milk for students who were allergic to cow's milk.

Jake sat and hooked his legs around the chair legs. "I'd like to change classes, please."

Cuvier's eyebrows went up in a question.

"Well, I'm just not getting along well in civics class with Mr.—with Coach Blevins."

"Why not?"

"I don't know. He wants me on swim team, and I don't want to do it. Always talking about Risonians too, calling them Sharks. I just don't feel comfortable in that class." There. That should do it, Jake thought. He didn't have to be any more specific than that.

Cuvier stared at him for a slow minute, and then leaned forward to rise to his full height. He wore a plaid flannel shirt and jeans that gave him a casual, laid-back look. Calmly, he said, "Wait here."

He left Jake alone in his office.

He's probably just getting the right forms to make this switch, Jake thought. Nervously, he stood again and held onto the back of his chair to do a lunge that stretched out his hamstrings. He knew he should just sit still, but he had worried all weekend. He had to get out of Blevins's class!

Jake smelled something odd. Looking around, on a side table he saw a shallow bowl with small wrapped packages. He picked one up and smelled it. The label said, "Goat Milk Soap, made on Bainbridge Island by the Cuvier Farms." Each bar of soap smelled different, and after sampling a few, Jake's nose was confused.

"He's in here." Cuvier entered, and behind him was Coach Blevins.

Shocked, Jake let the soap bar drop. It hit the edge of the shallow bowl and flipped the bowl over, spilling soap bars across the room.

"Oh! Sorry!"

Face blazing in embarrassment, Jake crawled around grabbing soaps until they were all safely in the bowl again. Then he stood awkwardly and looked from the counselor to the civics teacher.

"Sit," Cuvier said.

Jake sat. This was an ambush, but he had to see it through.

Blevins had a puzzled look on his face, "Why do you want out of my class?"

Jake said nothing.

Cuvier said, "Answer him."

So, Jake repeated what he'd told Cuvier, since Cuvier had probably already told Blevins. "I don't want to be on swim team, and you won't stop asking. And you're always talking about Risonians, too, calling them Sharks. I just don't feel comfortable."

Blevins's dark brown eyes opened wider and his nostrils flared. "Look—I teach a fair class. Sure, I talk about my political opinions because it's a civics class. And sure, you're entitled to your own opinions. Just like I'm entitled to my opinions. I'm a fair teacher, though. I'll never give you a grade based on your politics."

It was good to know that Blevins still had some morality. He tried to be fair in the classroom, at least in his own eyes. But Jake couldn't risk being around him day after day. Of course, getting his personal attention right now was dangerous, too.

Jake gathered his courage and asked, "Why do you hate the Risonians so much?"

"Can't say Sharks, can you?" Blevins shot back.

"It's not a good name for them," Jake insisted. "They aren't anything like Sharks."

"And how do you know that?" Blevins narrowed his eyes.

Jake looked away and self-consciously scratched his ear to keep his hand away from his nose with its alien flaps that were designed to shut out the water. "I don't, of course."

"But I do." Blevins's voice was hard now, bitter. "I've dealt with them. They're trying to kill the Earth, to invade, to get us off guard before—" With an effort, he stopped. Nostrils flaring, he said, "I'm just trying to protect my students."

Jake balled up his hands in frustration and literally bit his tongue to keep from saying anything else.

"Sorry," Coach Blevins said in a cold, but calm voice. "You're not getting out of my class that easily." He stood and stomped out.

Curvier shrugged. "There you have it."

Jake stood stiffly, too. "If my grandmother came in to talk with you—"

"She'd get the same answer," Cuvier said. "But you can take Easter a sample of my soap. Been trying to get her to try it for a long time."

Angry, embarrassed, defeated—Jake just wanted to get out of there. He took a step, turned back, grabbed his backpack and—

"Stop."

Jake stopped in mid-stride and spun back, ready to fight.

But the counselor merely held out a hall pass.

Grabbing it, Jake stomped out. The hallways were eerily silent, waiting for the next bell to disgorge students from classrooms. At his locker, Jake put away books he didn't need. Suddenly emotions flooded through him, and he sank to the floor with his back to the lockers and put his head between his legs. For a long minute he was overwhelmed with a jumble of emotions: anger, fear, hope, frustration. Everyone here on Bainbridge Island was against the Risonians.

The alone-ness of it all struck him with a force. He was unique, the only creature ever born who was half-Risonian, half-human. He was born different, and it would never change for him. He'd always be alone. He wanted to bang the lockers, to kick them, to smash something hard—or to be smashed by it. He just didn't want to be alone any longer.

Slowly, though, the emotions passed, and he was left just tired. Coach Blevins's words came back to him. "They are killing the Earth."

He means Mt. Rainier, Jake thought. But what if he was right, just in a different way. Something about the waters of Puget Sound made him think of *umjaadis*. What if somehow, someway—as impossible as it sounded—a Risonian had released *umjaadi* into the waters? It was possible that the *umjaadi* would love the salinity of the Earth's oceans. If it started living and growing in Earth's oceans, what damage would it do?

Jake decided that he had to investigate. He had to swim in Puget Sound and try to figure out what was happening. It would be his own private biology research project, at least until he knew that it wouldn't betray the Risonian cause.

EAVESDROPPING

Later, walking to the cafeteria for lunch, David caught up with him, slapped him on the back and asked, "Hey! Why were you late to first-period?"

Jake smiled. Gordon was becoming a good friend, and Jake liked that.

"I was in the counselor's office," Jake said. "Trying to get my schedule changed so I didn't have to have Blevins for a teacher."

"They wouldn't let you change?"

"Nope. Ambushed me. Cuvier brought in Blevins, and I had to say things directly to him. Embarrassing."

David whistled. "Wow, that's bad."

Jake nodded. "He didn't like it, at all. Called me a Shark Lover." They stopped at Jake's locker long enough for him to throw his backpack inside, and then at David's locker a few steps farther on.

"He's been on your case since you came."

"Yeah. I would've asked for a different class a lot earlier, except—"

"Em?"

"That obvious?" Jake's face flamed.

"You just watch her all the time." He looked at Jake sideways, started to say something, but stopped. He nodded his chin.

Slowly, Jake pivoted.

Em's locker was near enough to David's that she'd just heard everything. She was blushing.

Jake's heart leapt up. She wasn't frowning.

David gave him a small shove toward her. Throwing a smile back at him, Jake took another step closer and said casually, "Going to lunch? Mind if I walk with you."

Em looked at him sideways and smiled. "Please yourself."

Behind them, David burst out laughing, but Jake didn't care. He was going to get to eat lunch with Em. After all the tension between them for the past week, this was a pleasant change. The day wasn't totally lost.

DIVE, YOUNG MAN, DIVE

After supper, Jake decided it was time to investigate the steady thumping sound that he heard toward the north each time he was in Puget Sound. It wasn't a natural sound, and he thought he should recognize it, but he couldn't quite place it. And besides, he was still suspicious about what was causing the harbor seals to be sick. He needed to spend some time in Puget Sound to see if he could figure out anything.

He told Sir and Easter, "I'm going to walk along the beach to David Gordon's house and visit a while. I'll be back later."

"Great," Easter said. "Glad you're making friends."

The early November wind off the water was cold. Jake wore his swim trunks and a rash guard shirt under sweat pants and a hoodie, along with lightweight, waterproofed tennis shoes. It was just 6 pm, but the sky had already gone from twilight to full dark; across the water, Seattle's skyline glittered. And beyond that, a steady stream of smoke poured from Mt. Rainier.

At the water's edge, Jake pulled up the sweatpants and let the elastic bottom hold it above his knees so he could wade, picking his way among the rocks till the shoreline curved west into Murden Cove. The land started to rise, leaving a narrow beach that would vary in width as the tide rose and fell. Here and there were wooden stairs from a house or public access to the beach from the road above. If he was really going to David's house, he should leave the shoreline and find the road that paralleled the water. Instead, he stayed at the water's edge until he found a couple large boulders that would act as landmarks when he came back to claim his clothes.

With only the constellations as witnesses, he stripped off his sweats, hoodie and shoes, walked into the water till it was waist-high, and dove.

The shock of hitting the cold water lasted only a moment before his body adapted: his nose flaps shut down, his gills opened and took over his breathing, and the villi on his legs meshed. Instantly, he was transformed from a land to a water creature. For a moment, he reveled in feeling like himself for a change; he'd almost forgotten how it felt to be fully Risonian.

Jake followed the sloping sea floor downward in a leisurely swim. After weeks on land, it was a joy to be weightless in the water again. In the dim light, he found himself at the edge of an underwater shelf, a cliff. He waved his hands in circles and fluttered his feet, his villi unlocking automatically several inches to adjust to the movement. He hovered and studied the drop. The deeper he went, the darker it would be. The thumping sound definitely came from somewhere down there, though.

With a joyous abandon, he let the thumps pull him deeper; he spread his arms and dove.

On Earth, he'd read about skydiving, or jumping out of an airplane with just a parachute, but the feeling of free-fall and the thrill of skydiving couldn't be better than this. He fell quickly, steadily, yet at every moment, he knew he was in control. He tucked his head and pulled up his feet to do an aerial-like somersault; he un-Velcroed his legs so he could spread both arms and legs wide to slow down. He somersaulted; he stopped; he hovered. Abruptly, he Velcroed his legs, pulled them in, and wrapped his arms them. He plummeted like a huge rock. To slow, he opened his arms and spread his unVelcroed legs wide. Spread-eagled, he hung suspended upside down, looking upward. Currents washed over him, colder water pouring off the shelf above in a sort of underwater waterfall; but it was a slow-moving current and he drifted easily, watching the distant surface.

Gently, he did a slow barrel roll, turning to face down, and then completing the roll to look upward again. With the deepening of night, the darkness had grown, and he barely saw the surface.

He paused.

That wasn't right. The light was brighter below him than above him. Probably a bioluminescence of some kind. Lazily, he did half of a barrel roll and floated, looking downward.

Jake wavered, caught in limbo between two worlds, the air and the sea, each hiding its own secrets. Below him the diffused glow grew brighter; it was definitely not bioluminescence. And now that he paid attention, the thumping was louder, filling him, beating against him gently, calling to him, "Come down, come down."

It was like he stood at the center of time, watching it unwind.

He let it uncurl for a heartbeat, a heartbeat, and half a heartbeat.

Then, he pulled his body back into a line and down he went, like a straight arrow, shooting directly for the light and the thumping.

The water temperature grew colder and colder. Jake guessed he was 150 feet deep and going deeper. His Risonian metabolism responded though, keeping him at a comfortable warmth, giving him the liberty of swimming even deeper.

As he drew closer to the light, he realized that it was coming from structures. Definitely manmade structures. On one side, it looked very much like a Risonian building with windows open to the sea. Especially in old villages or towns on Rison, like Koloman or Danot in the Southern Sea, houses were open to allow ocean currents to flow through them. And why not? In Easter's house, he might open his windows to let the ocean breeze blow through.

But on the other end were structures that looked like submersible-buildings. They weren't submarines, probably because subs are too small. Instead, it was—

Jake shivered in fear. And anticipation.

Jake had been on Earth for over three months now and had heard that thumping sound before. He'd heard it when he had kayaked with Ms. Fleming and fallen into the Sound. He had heard it, but he hadn't heard it. He hadn't connected it. Anger at his foolishness surged through him. That sound was a common tool on Rison that allowed people to navigate the dark depths of the sea; it was a homing beacon.

This was a tiny bit of Rison transplanted to a tiny bit of Earth. A beginning.

Jake swam cautiously now, on the lookout; he didn't want to trip any warning system and alert the inhabitants that he was here. For there were definitely inhabitants. Even from this distance, some of the windows showed blurry figures that moved around. Humans or Risonians? It could be either. Or both.

Jake swam slower and slower, his shock growing. This wasn't just an underwater habitat; it was a small village. The center was a circular structure, large and sturdy; circular structures were more stable underwater because of the steady pressures of the water around them. From the center, three tubes ran sideways creating hallways to three other sections.

The first large pod was dotted with smaller windows, probably living quarters. A second pod had large windows but it was dark, work areas Jake guessed. It would be lit up during the day. Jake realized the third pod was separated by airlocks that the first two lacked. It would be a saturation diving lab, then, for humans.

At this depth, a human would need to decompress for hours before going back up to the surface. Jake did a rapid calculation and thought it would likely be 2 1/2 or 3 days of decompression. The problem with humans at this depth was the formation of gas bubbles in the body. Air on the surface was composed of oxygen and nitrogen, with traces of other gases. At ocean depths, the gases are under pressure and are forced into the body's cells. But as the diver rises, the pressure lessens and the gas expands.

One fisherman described it like this: fish have a swim bladder, a structure that holds gas and helps give them buoyancy which lets them swim easily. If you take a deep-sea fish and travel toward the surface, the swim bladder can expand to seven times its normal size, which crushes the other organs in the fish's body.

If a single gas bubble expanded seven times, it could cause great pain in a human's body. That's exactly what happens; the Bends or Decompression Sickness (DCS) can be painful, or it can affect the human's brain making it sleepy or incoherent. It can create rashes, cause paralysis or even death. Jake didn't like the way Navy men talked about it: "bends" for joint or skeletal pain, "chokes" for breathing problems, and "staggers" for neurological problems. Bends, chokes, and staggers. Scary.

Jake swam around the dormitory pod, staying low below the edge of the windows. No sense in getting caught. But the temptation to see who was living here was great.

Immediately, the lights went off, except one—it was like someone had called, "Lights Out."

Jake crept close, swimming up the curved wall. Someone was leaning against the window, though. He stopped just in time.

SEASTEAD

Jake backed away far enough from the windows so that no light fell on him. Those inside couldn't see him, but he was still close enough to see them.

The door opened, and a figure strode in.

Startled, Jake recognized the man as Commander Gordon. Risonian military had different ranks than the U.S. Navy, of course. Jake and Dad had once sat down and created a chart that showed comparable duties, and Gordon's rank on Rison equaled Dad's rank as Commander.

This was a Risonian military installation. A Seastead.

The impact of this hit Jake full force. As Risonian ambassador, his mom had been pushing for diplomatic permission to install an experimental station. Officially, the answer was a resounding no. But apparently, someone had said yes. Because getting this kind of an installation built and functional meant lots of work, and possibly lots of work that the public might see; that meant lots of public relations work to make it look like something else.

The door opened again. Jake froze in shock. Walking into Commander Gordon's room in this illegal Seastead was his friend from school. David.

Looking from David to Commander Gordon, Jake realized they were father and son. That's why David had looked so familiar, yet so different.

That meant—

A quiver ran down Jake's spine. In civics class, they'd discussed Sleeper Cells and how enemies infiltrated a country and acted just like they were normal folk. That is, until they were needed. David was like that. He was a daily spy, coming to Bainbridge High School and pretending to be a normal kid. If the press ever learned about this Seastead, it would be a disaster for Risonian public relations.

And yet Jake understood why they so desperately needed this experimental station. When they did get official permission, they couldn't afford any disasters; everything had to run smoothly from Day One. This was probably experimental in the purest sense of the word, including problems or even disasters.

Now David and his Dad hugged; they turned to bunks, and the light went out. It was late and Jake needed to get back before Sir and Easter worried. Jake wanted to laugh at the irony of this evening: he'd visited David's "house," after all.

Swimming upward, Jake thought about his strange friendship with David Gordon. He'd been helpful, without Jake ever knowing why. When Jake had fallen into Puget Sound and pulled Ms. Fleming's kayak back to shore, it'd been David who told people that Jake had only been in the water a few minutes. He'd smoothed out things without anyone noticing. That meant—David knew who Jake's parents were! He was a fellow Risonian. All this time, Jake could've had a Risonian friend and just didn't know it. But, Wow! David played it well. Even Jake hadn't suspected that he was Risonian. He wondered if David had plastic surgery on his nose or something. Or if he'd learned how to hold his nose membranes open all the time.

Jake had to think about what this all meant. Rison had—with or without permission—already created a Seastead on Earth. Were there more Seasteads in different places around the globe? Or was this the only one?

His mother had to know. And that hurt. Like Dad, who was under orders not to share his activities, Mom was probably ordered to keep him out of the loop. But it hurt that both parents had secrets—important, life-changing and world-changing secrets—but told him nothing. Instead, they had commanded him to disappear, to be silent, to hide. He wasn't a coward! He could take the pressure. But they didn't believe that. Jake longed for a way to show them that he was part of this fight and not just an innocent bystander.

But the Seastead installation meant something even deeper. Jake had to think this through. He'd always told himself that someday he'd go back to Rison and see Swann and his friends and his home and—but no. Rison had at least one Seastead installation on Earth. This plan—evacuate as many Risonians as possible and establish a new home on Earth—was the only feasible plan they had. They had considered invading, of course, just taking the planet by force. But that wasn't the Risonian way, any more than it would be an Earthling strategy if humans had to leave their planet. Risonians had morals just like humans had morals.

The fact remained: there was no fallback plan; for twenty years they had fought against this alternative and looked for other planets, other options. Their starships had scoured the universe for a new home. They had satellites similar to Earth's Kepler Space Observatory that hunted for habitable planets. But in the star systems they could reach, no other planet could sustain them. Only Earth was a water planet like theirs; only Earth had acceptable temperature ranges and atmosphere. It was Earth. Or nothing.

Earth either accepted them, or it was xenocide, the death of an entire race. Seastead confirmed that.

So, perhaps it was time for Jake to accept Earth.

THE FULLEX INCIDENT

The next morning, Easter was glued to the morning TV programs, as usual. She flipped from station to station, sampling the news stories. She particularly loved the stories about a woman's 100th birthday, or a boy whose dog rescued him, or an adopted kid who is reunited with a birth mother. Sappy stories were like candy for Easter.

Jake poured a bowl of cereal and milk, and then ate it hunched over his tablet while scrolling through news feeds and wishing his parents would let him set up social media accounts.

Easter watched a touching video of a military man coming home and crying when he saw his wife.

"You aren't still homesick, are you?" Easter asked casually.

Suddenly, Jake was homesick. A flood of memories crashed over him: Swann racing him through the South Seas near the resort of N'Drew; watching the Gripla Volcano erupt at sunset; eating *wolkev*, his favorite Risonian pastry, often served at breakfast. It required Risonian spices and the sweet *wolkev* fruit; where would they find that on Earth? Did his Mom even have a *wolkev* recipe? Could they bring seeds of the fruit to plant here on Earth or would that disturb the ecosystem?

"I'm okay," he managed to mumble.

Easter flipped channels again, just in time for them to both hear a news anchor say: "This just in: the Risonian spaceship Fullex has been shot down."

Jake spun in his chair to stare at the TV.

The anchor continued, her face grave: "A Risonian spaceship, full of 500 refugees, including an estimated 100 children, has been shot down by the European Union."

All dead. No survivors.

Fullex. In Risonian, it meant "Peace."

Jake was stunned. He dropped his spoon into his cereal, and it splattered milk. Dumbly, he saw the milk droplets land on the table and pool up. A white drop of cow milk. They didn't have cows on Rison. What did that matter? He asked himself stupidly. Vaporized. 500 fellow Risonians were just—gone.

He wondered if he had known anyone on the flight. 500 Risonians out of a planet of millions. Likely, they'd come from the Bo-See Coalition of countries in the southern hemisphere, because they disagreed with the Chancellor Quad-de and Tizzalura on negotiating with Earth. Bo-See had pushed for a different ambassador, a different strategy. They had probably just decided to launch their own ship. The chance that he personally knew anyone was slim. And yet, he was nauseous, sickened by this waste of life. Risonians only wanted a new start, a new home, and for that hope, they had been shot out of the sky.

The head of the European Union was on the TV now: "We regret the loss of life, but they were warned not to violate Earth's air space. The U.S. wasn't going to take action, so we had to."

On Rison, it was Tizzalura vs. the Bo-See. On Earth, it was the U.S. vs. the European Union. That was too simplistic a description on both planets, but the results were clear: politics had killed those 500 Risonians.

Then it was Mom talking on the TV, tears running down her cheeks, her hair mussed, her lips trembling, her voice a high wail: "We come in peace. We come in peace. We come in peace."

She was so shaken that she could say nothing else. The camera and lighting was angled up from below her chin, so you could see her nose membranes quivering. Mom had never looked so alien. Or so forlorn. The Face of Rison.

Easter came over and hugged Jake. He clung to her, not conscious of anything except the smell of coffee and bacon from Easter. And he longed for the sweet taste of *wolkev*.

EARTHQUAKES

After the news of the Fullex explosion, Jake was too shaken to go to school. He stayed home and watched the news reports pour in. But interest in the Risonian tragedy flagged quickly, and by noon, the news programs were back to Mt. Rainier. He should've turned it off, but now he was as obsessive as Easter, flipping from station to station.

Mt. Rainier might blow. How many ways, Jake wondered, could you say that? The news programs were incredibly inventive:

Helicopter shots into the crater.

Reports on the history of Mt. Rainier, with a recap of the "paradise" statement from early explorers.

Interviews with those in the lahar's path, like the Tullis's and Hill's cabins.

Rehash of the Mt. St. Helen eruption and a comparison of that mountain to Mt. Rainier.

Comparisons of a possible eruption of Mt. Rainier to the Big 3: Vesuvius, Pompeii and Krakatoa.

Comparisons of Mt. Rainier to any other famous volcano eruption.

Interviews with volcanologists, each repeating the other, but claiming exclusive information.

Scientists talking about the increasing temperature of the fumarole gases.

Scientists holding their noses and talking about the increasing presence of sulfur dioxide in the fumarole gases.

Interviews with wackos who predicted the end-of-the-world.

Jake thought the wacko interviews were particularly ironic, since it almost was the end of Rison. Predict that Rison was about to be blown to bits, and you'd be right.

Missing from every news program was a comparison of Mt. Rainier to volcanoes on Rison. ELLIS Forces were hinting that the fault lay with the Risonians, but without specifics, it was just a rumor. And Jake guessed that they wouldn't admit—if they even knew—that their Captain had sent a drone full of Brown Matter into Mt. Rainier's crater. That wouldn't play well in the press.

But in the midst of it all, there was no denying that Mt. Rainier was still smoking. And now, there were earthquakes. Minor tremors, something locals might actually ignore, except—there was that smoking volcano. It was impossible to ignore the increasing instability of the ground they walked upon. He suspected that if he were closer to Mt. Rainier, he'd hear the magma songs even louder now.

Three times that week, small earthquakes struck. Once while in civics class, which, of course, prompted Coach Blevins to rant and rave about Risonians. The second time was while Jake was cooking with Easter. She took it calmly enough, stopping only to close her eyes and offer up a silent prayer.

The third time, Jake was walking with Em, which he did regularly now.

Jake met her after school and took her backpack. She resisted for a second, but he held up a hand to stop her. That was enough; she handed over her backpack and smiled shyly at him. Now, shouldering both backpacks, he began to walk Em over to the Aquatic Center.

Suddenly, the ground jolted and Em stumbled. One leg slid left and she fell, catching herself on her forearms so that her face didn't smash into the ground. Just as quickly, the Earth settled. The whole thing took just three seconds.

When she rose, Em's face was dark. "If you don't tell some official what happened on the field trip, I will," she threatened.

"No," Jake said. After the spaceship was shot down earlier that week, there was no way he was going to do anything that might point suspicion to Risonians.

Em flipped her black braid behind her back and said to the sky, "I've already talked to Marisa and told her about Captain Hill and the drone. She didn't believe me until she talked to him. He said that the Sharks had already put Brown Matter into Mt. Rainier, and was trying something to counteract it. Is that true?"

"No," Jake's panic turned to fury. He let both packs fall to the ground and stood rigid, trying to control his anger.

"Hey! Don't drop my pack like that!"

Em snatched up her backpack and flailed around trying to get both her gym bag and backpack settled on her own shoulders.

Grudgingly, her awkwardness loosened his anger. He wanted to stay angry at Captain Hill, but how could he do that when he was around Em? She was too charming, too—practically perfect.

She leaned to one side to keep the backpack in position, and the gym bag hung almost to the ground. Even awkward, though, she was so lovely. "Captain Hill also says that the Sharks are poisoning Puget Sound."

Jake sucked in a breath. "What?"

"He says that's why the harbor seals are sick."

Through gritted teeth, he asked, "You believe him?"

Em sighed deeply. "I don't know what to believe. What did I see at that mountain lake? You and Captain Hill fought, but over what? I don't have enough information and neither of you is giving me more."

Frustrated, Jake said, "I don't have enough information, either."

Then, lips compressed, he turned and stalked away. Saying it out loud had made him realize the truth of it: his parents told him nothing. There was a Seastead under his nose and no one thought to tell him about it. Okay. He'd go and find more information. And when he had the information, he'd tell Em everything.

SHARK SPIES

Across the parking lot, Jake saw David and Jillian. Okay. David was Risonian and lived in Seastead. Suddenly, he saw Jillian with new eyes and frowned. Was she Risonian, too? Did David have a partner-in-crime after all? Her face was long and narrow, but she didn't have nose wrinkles. But then, neither did David. Did they both get a nose job?

Angry with Em, Captain Hill, and pretty much the whole planet of Earth, Jake decided to follow the two potential spies. They were a block ahead, and he kept that distance as he followed. He'd watched enough spy movies while on the Moon Base, though; he crossed to the opposite side of the street, so he wouldn't be noticed as easily.

David and Jillian walked slowly, talking and laughing. It was a lovely mid-November day with clear blue skies. They turned onto a street that led down to Murden Cove. A couple blocks later, Jillian unlocked the door to a large house, and the two slipped inside.

Jake walked around the house, and at the back, the house sat right on the water. A dock led down to a fancy fishing shack painted forest green. Outside hung a couple cheap fishing poles and nets to scoop up fish. A white Styrofoam ring hung next to them, proclaiming, "Save the Whales."

The back door opened.

Quickly, Jake pressed against the sidewall and sank to a deep crouch, making himself as small as possible.

David and Jillian emerged.

Jake could barely stop himself from whistling. In her bikini, Jillian was stunning. She was tall for a girl, blond hair halfway down her back. Walking to the fishing shack, her hips swung and entranced, Jake thought about the Earth folk tales of mermaids again. If Jillian was caught and accused of being Risonian, she could probably use that as an excuse: "I'm a mermaid, sir." And any young police officer would want to believe her.

But it was all wrong. You didn't wear a bikini this time of year to go swimming. Unless you were a Risonian female.

To be fair, there was an unusual fence alongside the dock that blocked any view of the shack and dock from the street. David and Jillian probably felt safe from any onlookers. Isolated, the house sat at the end of the road, off a little bit from the others.

Sneaking to the shoreline, Jake shed his shoes and jacket and wished he had swim trunks to wear. He strode into the water and swam quietly under the dock, taking care not to splash, until he was almost under David and Jillian and could hear them talking.

Apparently, Jillian was mad. "Are we a sleeper cell?"

"Of course," David said reasonably

"But that's awful," Jillian wailed. "Sleepers are despicable, because they have divided loyalties. You think they are just normal Americans and then you discover, what? They're evil aliens? That's us, David! Don't you see how awful it is? We're Americans! How can we be a sleeper cell, too?"

"You think that's awful? Earth just blew up the Fullex and my aunt is dead. That's despicable. Earth isn't allowing Risonians to come here, so they'll just stand aside and watch genocide. No, a xenocide, the death of a whole planet. That's what's despicable."

Jake was surprised at David's vehemence, but he understood it. The Fullex incident had hit him hard, too.

"But we shouldn't be surprised," Jillian said sadly, her anger suddenly gone. "They can't even save the whales. Or the tigers. Or a thousand other species. They can't share Earth even with the species who are supposed to be here. We're crazy to think they'll let us crowd up their planet."

"So," David said, "as a sleeper cell, we're important. We will do what we can to smooth things over so Risonians can come here. And if we fail, if the planet is destroyed, at least a few of us have survived. A remnant."

Jillian said through clenched teeth, "I know. You're right. We need to be here. But geez. We are a sleeper cell."

By now, they were inside the green building. A door above creaked open, and Jake realized that a stairway led down to the water from inside the building. Of course. That was how they secretly came and went in all kinds of weather. Their only mistake today was to change clothes in the house, instead of in the shed.

David changed the topic. "Seastead should try to stop Mt. Rainier from blowing."

"We don't have the right equipment," Jillian said.

Jake sank low into the water, letting his gills take over his breathing. He only tried to keep his head high enough to listen to their conversation. Jake wondered if it was true that the Risonians didn't have the right equipment to control Mt. Rainier. Surely by now, Dolk's antigravity work had been turned into fully developed protocols. Stefan and Mai-ron Dolk, his best friend and his friend's father, and had been dead for five years now, so that was enough time to try it out and perfect it, right?

David laughed. "We won't solve this now. Let's go home. I think the cook is making *wolkev* for supper."

Wolkev? Instantly, Jake's mouth watered. It was another good reason to sneak into Seastead!

Without looking around, David and Jillian splashed into deeper water and dove.

Jake had escaped their notice, but he forced himself to count to 100 before he followed. After all, he had a homing beacon to guide him.

THE MOON POOL

A stiff breeze blew the surface of Puget Sound into white caps, but diving underwater, Jake soon left behind the layers affected by wind. Puget Sound's waters felt clean, in spite of the sick seals. His legs automatically Velcroed together so that a few powerful thrusts carried him deep enough to see Jillian and David at the edge of the underwater cliff. They dove in unison.

Jake hovered a few feet away from the cliff's edge, giving them a few minutes to get ahead of him. Finally, he stood on the edge himself, listened to the homing beacon thrumming from below, and dove. This time, Jake didn't play; he clasped his hands to his legs and dropped headfirst like a rock plummeting toward Seastead.

As the lights of Seastead grew near, Jake did a spread-eagle and slowed to hover while watching the dark figures of David and Jillian. Surprisingly, they dove underneath a pod. Looking through huge windows, Jake realized the pod had a moon pool; the air pressure inside the pod would keep water from coming inside. It was like pushing a glass upside down into a bucket of water; the water wouldn't go inside the glass because the air pressure kept it out. Open access like this made sense, but somehow, he'd expected them to go through an airlock.

Jake watched the two teens pull themselves out of the water, grab golden-colored chamois cloths to dry off, and then go into separate rooms, probably changing rooms.

It was time to decide. Was he going in or not?

For Jake, the biggest question was what Seastead intended to do about Mt. Rainier. Would they use Risonian technology to stop the volcano from erupting? From David and Jillian's conversation on the surface, he guessed that they planned to do nothing but wait and see what happened. But Earth couldn't wait. He needed to see what equipment Seastead had and try to figure out how to get something over to Mt. Rainier in time to stop an eruption.

Jake grinned. If he could find the kitchen and steal a *wolkev* pastry, he'd do that, too. He hadn't eaten anything since lunch, and his stomach was an empty pit.

He waited, looking at his waterproof watch and forcing himself to wait for five minutes. He must not get caught.

Finally, Jake moved to the edge of the chamber, ducked down under the chamber wall, and swam up until his face broke the surface of the moon pool. Glancing around, he saw no one. He realized he'd been worried, too, about some alarm going off. But all was silent.

Jake heaved up onto the side of the pool and grabbed a chamois cloth from the nearby hooks to towel off. He tiptoed to the changing room where he'd seen David enter and slid around a corner. Instantly, a light came on. Motion-activated, Jake guessed. That meant David was long gone, which was good. The room was lined with lockers, plastic cubicles that held random pieces of clothing. Some lockers had padlocks—there was always someone less trusting than others. Jake didn't have to change clothes because he'd stay warm no matter what. But his underwear would drip water up and down hallways if he didn't.

With a thumping heart, he rummaged through three lockers before he found a pair of shorts and shirt that fit. The t-shirt had a photo of a dog wearing a brown hood and robe, and said, "Adorable, I am. Give me treats you must." Apparently some alien here liked "Star Wars" too much.

At the far end of the room was a door. It could lead to anywhere. Jake hesitated, worried about the unknown. But in the end, he shrugged. He had to risk it.

The shiny metal doorknob was warm. Jake clung to it for a moment, telling himself to calm down. He took deep breaths, but something was different about the air here. He could breathe, but it was felt odd.

He steeled himself, pulled the door open an inch, and peered out. The view to the right was clear, but in order to be able to see toward the left, he'd have to open the door wider.

Go for it, he told himself. Jake jerked the door open wide and stepped into the corridor, right into the arms of Commander Gordon.

"Jake Rose, I presume," said Gordon. His voice squeaked, high-pitched and unnatural.

Instantly, Jake understood. Seastead was using the famous Tri-mix gas mixture of helium, oxygen, and nitrogen. It was easier for humans to breathe this mixture and caused fewer problems with decompression issues, fewer cases of the bends, chokes and staggers. But the side effect was a high-pitched voice that sounded like the classic Earthling Donald Duck cartoons. The addition of helium was the problem: because it's a lighter weight gas, sound waves travel differently than in the regular mix of atmosphere, so the sound changed.

Behind him, squeaked another voice, "I'm sorry."

Jake spun to see David blocking the doorway back into the changing room.

He was caught.

David went on, "I wanted to tell you a hundred times, but I had orders."

Bitterly, Jake said, "Yeah. I know about orders." His voice was a disconcerting squeak, too.

"This way," Commander Gordon said and gestured to the corridor behind him.

Jake followed him until they stopped just before entering the airlock to a different chamber. Commander Gordon pulled out a key and opened a door to the right. He stood aside and motioned for Jake to enter.

As Jake passed, Gordon said angrily—or as angrily as he could when sounding like a cartoon duck, "You've ruined everything that your mother has worked for her entire life."

Taken aback by the anger, Jake stepped inside, away from the Commander.

The door slammed behind him. The lock turned with a click.

Jake was a prisoner in Seastead.

THE COMMANDERS

Jake's prison room was a small bedroom or stateroom, like what you would expect on a submarine. A bed dropped down from the wall to fill half the width of the room. On the other wall was a tiny drop-down desk, a chair and empty storage, including a long cavity for clothing; the rest of the wall was drawers. Everything was a tan plastic, plain and boring. At the back was a tiny bathroom. No window. He wondered if this was indeed a prison room or just a regular bedroom.

For a time, he sat on the chair and waited. He set the timer on his watch so it would keep track of how long he'd been in here. Surely, someone would come back and question him soon. But after a while, he grew tired of waiting. He pulled down the bunk and sank back with his hands behind his head. How long would they make him cool off?

His stomach grumbled.

Stoically, he waited, eventually closing his eyes.

The next morning, Jake woke early, his empty stomach rumbling. According to his timer, he'd been a prisoner for sixteen hours. Sir and Easter must be going crazy by now.

A knock startled him, and he sat straight up. Before he could react further, a Risonian soldier shouldered his way in, and with one hand expertly undid a knob, which dropped the desktop. He set a covered tray there. Just as abruptly, he left, saying nothing.

Jake hopped out of bed and padded barefoot the two steps to the desk. Lifting the lid, he stared. Pastries. Leaning closer, he drew in a deep breath. Sweet, tangy. *Wolkev*!

Hungrily, Jake pulled up the chair and bit into a pastry. The fruit was obviously canned, not fresh, but it was *wolkev*. He tried to compare it to Earth fruits. Perhaps it was the consistency of a banana, but it was red, and juicier like a raspberry, but not as sour, and no seeds. It was no good making comparisons like this, he decided. You had to add too many qualifiers to get it right, and by then, it was a worthless comparison. *Wolkev*s were just *wolkev*s, the breakfast of his childhood. He nibbled, savoring the bites. He burped. It wasn't such a bad thing to be locked up by Risonians, he decided.

Abruptly again, the door opened, and the soldier motioned for him to follow.

Jake followed, still barefoot. In the middle of the corridor, the soldier opened a room and gestured for Jake to enter. It was a conference room with a small table.

"Sit," squeaked the soldier.

He left and locked the door behind him.

To the side, Jake found another table with refreshments and filled a plate with another round of *wolkev* pastries. Intent on his food, he didn't look around when the door opened again, until Commander Gordon said, "Good morning."

Jake turned to wave at him, but stopped short, speechless. Standing beside the Commander was Dad!

When had they notified his Dad, and how did they get him to come down this quickly?

Commander Rose nodded to his son, but let Gordon take the lead.

"Jake, you realize you are trespassing by being here?" said Commander Gordon. He was trying to sound stern, but the duck-like squeaky voice made him sound ridiculous.

"Trespassing? You have illegally created and hidden an entire Seastead, and you're going to talk to me about trespassing?" Jake almost laughed at his own voice. This would take some getting used to, but it was kind of fun.

Gordon raised an eyebrow and turned to Jake's Dad. "He's not a child. I didn't think we'd be able to intimidate him that easily."

They were testing him? No, he wasn't a child. Growing up on a dying planet, the stepson of the Chancellor—he'd never been allowed to be a child.

"Dad, why'd you come down here?" Jake asked.

Commander Rose looked startled, then laughed and said to Gordon, "He doesn't know."

"Know what?" Jake demanded.

Dad cleared his throat and straightened his uniform. "Seastead is my post, my assignment. I am the Navy liaison with Seastead."

Jake leaned his chair back on its legs and stared. "You've been posted here for the last month? And you didn't tell me?"

"Orders," said his Dad shortly.

Jake ducked his head and let his chair slam down on the floor—an action he knew his father hated. "You didn't trust me."

"Jake, it was my duty. I was ordered to not tell anyone—especially my family."

"Does Mom know?"

"Well, yes."

Jake's chest tightened, like someone was squeezing this lousy thin air out of his lungs. Bitterly, he thought, this is what betrayal feels like.

Dad pulled up a chair to the table and said, "She's the Risonian ambassador. Of course she knows that her people have set up a Seastead. She's part of the reason the Navy chose me for this assignment."

That sounded reasonable, Jake thought. But he still felt betrayed; neither parent trusted him.

"The question is what to do with you now?" Gordon said.

"David and Jillian go to school," Jake said with a shrug.

"Yes." Commander Gordon drew up his own chair. "My family and the Lusk family moved here fourteen years ago. While my wife stayed here, I traveled back and forth to Rison, serving in the space fleet until Seastead opened three years ago, when I accepted the position as Director here. Jillian's father died two years ago, but her Mom still runs the bookstore on Bainbridge Island. That means David and Jillian have been raised on Earth since birth. In all ways except anatomy, they are Americans. Yet, they understand what is at stake for Rison and their race."

"What's at stake? Everyone knows that, especially after the Fullex was blown up!"

The room was silent, like the air had frozen. Jake looked from Dad to Gordon, wondering what he was missing.

Dad shook his head and looked down. "Commander Gordon's sister was on that flight. She was the Tizzalurian ambassador to the Bo-See Coalition. She hoped to help negotiate their landing on Earth."

Horror hit Jake like he'd been physically slapped. He'd been glad that he hadn't known anyone on the ship. And then he felt guilty that he had so easily shrugged off its destruction.

He hadn't known Gordon's sister, of course, but even one real connection made it more awful. "I'm so sorry," he stammered.

Gordon nodded stiffly, sitting ramrod straight. His nose membranes flared, and his hands clenched into fists. But he said nothing. Visibly, he drew a breath and came back to the situation. "The question is what to do with you now."

Jake realized that this was a crucial question. As the Ambassador's son, he was going to be watched more carefully; in fact, the paparazzi were offered lots of money to take a single photo of him. And no one even suspected that he was half-human. The uproar over that issue alone could easily derail the entire process of finding a place on Earth for Risonians.

"I know what's at stake," he said solemnly. "I would never tell anyone about Seastead."

"How did you find us?" Gordon asked.

"A harbor seal brought me here."

"What? How?"

Jake explained about the sick pup and how he'd crudely talked to the seal. That meant he had to back up and explain about talking to the Great White shark in the Gulf of Mexico—which brought a sharp look of disapproval from his father. But he said nothing, just motioned for Jake to continue his story.

"The Earth sea creatures don't understand everything I try to tell them," he said. "It's like a different dialect or something. But they understand some of it. After I helped the seal, I noticed a thumping in the water. I didn't recognize it as a homing beacon because it was so out of place. But it made me curious enough to investigate and eventually led me here." He stopped and remembered the seal pup. "I think," he said slowly, "something is making the harbor seals sick."

Gordon wasn't distracted by this; he kept the same line of questioning. "When'd you find us?"

"Two days ago."

"Why didn't you try to sneak in then?"

Jake leaned forward and said earnestly, "As I came up on Seastead, there were lots of lights on; then, everything went dark except in one window. I watched. It was your room, sir. And I saw David. I had to think."

Gordon nodded. "That explains part of it. You followed David and Jillian down here last night. Right?"

"Yes, at first. But then the beacon brought me down all the way."

Gordon frowned. "Who've you told about Seastead?"

Jake leaned back and crossed his arms. The question hurt; they really didn't trust him. "No one."

"Easter? Sir?" Dad asked.

Jake shook his head. "No one. I knew this was special, and I wanted to investigate, but I knew I could never tell anyone about it. But I bet Easter and Sir are worried that I didn't come home last night."

"No," Dad said. "David called and asked permission for you to spend the night with him. Your grandmother was impressed that he called, not you. She already likes David. And it's a good thing that it's Saturday, so you don't have to go home till much later. By then, I'll call Easter and ask about you and get excited that you're making new friends."

Jake glared at Dad. No trust at all.

Well, it went both ways. Where was Dad when Captain Hill was bullying him at the coffee shop? Where was Dad when Captain Hill dropped Brown Matter in the crater of Mt. Rainier?

"You ever get the photo I sent you of Mt. Rainier smoking?" Jake asked.

"What? Oh. Yes, I got it. Wi-Fi reception is good here."

Jake took a deep breath. "I know why the volcano is smoking. Brown Matter.

He had their attention now, he thought.

Dad jerked upright, standing to place his palms face down on the table and lean toward Jake.

"What've you done?" Gordon cried.

If Jake had been mad that they didn't trust him, he was absolutely furious now. What had he done? "What? You think I'm an idiot?"

Through gritted teeth, he told about meeting Captain Hill in the coffee shop. Finally, he thought, I have Dad's attention. He told about breaking into Blevins's house—and Dad couldn't sit still. He jumped up to pace the tiny room, fists clenched and barely controlling himself. But his father's eyes got big and thoughtful when he explained that Blevins was Yarborough, the Canadian volcanologist who had plagiarized.

"He has a photo of me when I was only seven," he said.

"This is bad," Dad said.

"It's worse." Jake explained about Captain Hill using a drone to deliver Brown Matter to Mt. Rainier.

Gordon shook his head. "We were wrong. We should've brought you in from the start. Too many things have happened to you, and we knew none of it. That's dangerous." He hesitated, but grudgingly added, "You've handled yourself well."

Dad looked at Gordon, "Can you do anything about Mt. Rainier? Will the Brown Matter make it erupt?"

Jake stood and walked to the window; his bare feet should've been cold on the plastic floor, but he found it a comfortable temperature. He pressed his face against the window and tried to peer outside. He thought a shape—a shark?—drifted by. It was large, maybe a six-gill or seven-gill shark, both common in Puget Sound in deeper waters. A shark. That was appropriate.

Behind him, Gordon and Dad were throwing out ways they could potentially stop the volcano from erupting.

Over his shoulder, Jake called, "Why don't you just use the Dolk's TAG-GIMS?"

They continued talking as if they hadn't heard him.

Dad said to Gordon, "There's nothing we can do?"

Jake turned around and raised his voice louder, "Use Dolk's TAG-GIMS."

Gordon looked up and frowned. "What're you talking about?"

"You know. Dr. Dolk's invention creating anti-gravity. Mai-Ron Dolk. Why don't you use that?"

Gordon and Dad looked at him blankly.

Finally, Gordon said, "I've no idea what you're talking about."

So, Jake sat down and told them.

TWO FRIENDS

Four years earlier.

The last day before Stefon Dolk, Jake's best friend, left for the southern continent dawned with a purple glow. Stefon and Jake yawned. They'd stayed up all night, playing the latest version of DinoGrad, a video game where they fought dinosaurs similar to those that had roamed Earth in ancient times. The game had become wildly popular in the last few months. Media commentators explained that Risonians were still struggling with the idea of moving to Earth and wanted to take out their anger in a video game. Jake just knew the game was fun.

After being up all night, they were famished and went to find Stefon's dad. Mai-Ron Dolk's laboratory was a mess, as usual. Mai-Ron was small and wiry, and often underestimated. A mistake. His understanding of volcanoes was incredibly rich; the man was—literally—a genius. He backed that up with the ability to make theory practical by building equipment that no one else thought of. But he couldn't keep files in order. Except his volcano research. He had one briefcase, one computer, and one suitcase where he kept all his volcano papers, databases, and blueprints of equipment. They were his life.

"Stefon, we go in an hour. Are you packed?"

Stefon nodded. He was a head taller than Jake, and very skinny. When they swam, he usually wore a shirt and trunks so no one would see his ribs. And he hated the fight floor because he was required to go shirtless. During training, Stefon usually beat Jake. But on the fight floor, Stefon could never relax, which gave Jake the edge he needed to win the trophies.

"Sir," Jake asked again. "Why do you have to go for the whole summer?"

Mai-Ron reached out to rub Jake's hair, but Jake ducked away. Mai-Ron always tried that, but Jake had finally figured out he could move fast enough to avoid the gesture.

Mai-Ron patted his computer and his equipment box. "I think I've got this volcano problem figured out."

"He's been working on it all his life," Stefon said honestly. He walked toward the door. "He tells me that all the time."

Jake went to the open case and looked at the equipment. Living with Swann Quad-de, he'd seen lots of volcano equipment. Lying inside the case were just a couple square packets. Jake picked up one—it felt much lighter than he expected. "What's so different about this?"

Mai-Ron pushed up his glasses and scratched his nose. "Everything. We've been looking at this the wrong way. The Brown Matter changes to Red Matter, which is creating a black hole at the center of our planet, right?"

Jake nodded. "Yes and some scientists think we should use Brown Antimatter."

"It's a good theory." Mai-Ron nodded and paced back and forth. Talking about scientific theories got him excited now. "Everyone knows that when matter and antimatter collide, there'll be an explosion. But how big of an explosion? If one nanogram, or one billionth of a gram, of matter and antimatter collided, it would give off enough energy to boil a teakettle of water. The Brown Antimatter would need to be in sufficient quantity to counter-act the Brown Matter in the volcano, but not create an explosion the size of a nuclear bomb. It's been tricky figuring out how to deploy the exact amount needed."

"What's the answer?" Jake said. The fabric of the square packet was slick in his hands.

"We're thinking of it all wrong," Mai-Ron said. "A black hole is just an extreme case of concentrated matter where gravitational forces become enormous. Instead of focusing on what caused the black hole, I started thinking about black holes. Can anything escape a black hole?"

Jake shrugged, "Theoretically, no."

"Wrong," Mai-Ron said. "What you need is a Gravity Lens with a negative index of refraction."

"What?"

Mai-ron took off his glasses and held them out. "Look. We focus light rays, one type of electromagnetic waves with pieces of glass. But optics is limited by the wavelength of light. If we want to look at smaller things, we use an electron microscope, which is limited by the wavelength of electron movement. Gravity has even smaller wavelengths, so to focus it with a lens, we need an ultra-thin material."

Jake nodded. "Okay. That sounds reasonable."

Mai-ron put his glasses back on and took the packet from Jake. He opened one corner of the package and pointed. "This is a Gravity Lens that I made last year when I was in space. It's a 3-D nano-printed tungsten meta-surface. Across the surface, the gravity refraction index is a gradient and produces an anti-gravity effect."

Jake stared in awe. "You made an anti-gravity thing?"

Mai-ron chuckled. "Thing? It's a tungsten anti-gravity gradient-index meta-surface, or a TAG-GIMS. The tungsten will withstand the temperatures in the volcano. The pouch will burn up and the TAG-GIMS will unfurl or unfold, creating enough anti-gravity to slow the encroaching black hole."

"Is it working right now?" Jake backed away from the pouch.

"Barely. When it's folded, it's about 1-millioneth the size unfolded. Only the top layer is interacting with gravity, so it might seem a little lightweight, that's all. That's why I had to make it in space and fold it before I brought it back to Rison."

"So, you can escape a black hole?"

"Hmmm," Mai-ron said. "Probably not escape. But used early enough, we might slow collapse of matter into the black hole."

Jake caught his breath. "You can stop the planet's implosion?"

Mai-ron's eyes were shining with unshed tears. "We're going to the Kalaptia Volcano to try it out."

"That's in the Holla Sea, in the southern hemisphere?" Jake didn't want his friend to be so far away all summer.

Mai-Ron nodded and put the cylinder back in his case. "Yes. They are predicting that Kalaptia will erupt this summer, and I want to try to stop it."

"And if it works?"

"There's hope for Rison." Mai-Ron's forehead wrinkled, and he picked up a second packet. "I meant to take this extra TAG-GIMS to my lab and leave it in the safe there. I don't know if I have time now."

Jake held out a hand and shrugged. "I'll keep one for you. I have a strong-box."

Mai-Ron looked uncertain, but then he looked at the time display and sighed. "We'll miss the shuttle if I take time to go by the lab." He tapped a finger on the packet. "You'll take care of it?"

"Of course," Jake said.

Mai-Ron and Stefon dropped Jake off an hour later at his house and left for the airport.

Later, Jake heard the devastating news. The Dolks had arrived at Ocarina, a small town near Kalaptia Volcano, too late. It had just exploded, and the ash created the normal lightning storms. A stray thunderbolt hit their vehicle, and it rolled and crashed, killing everyone, including Mai-ron and Stefon. Just a freak accident.

▯ ☆ ☆

Gordon leaned across the table, "You never told anyone about Dolk's TAG-GIMS?"

"I was nine years old, and I'd just lost my best friend." Sometimes, the ache of that loss still weighed Jake down. Stefon had always wanted to see Earth and if things had worked out differently, he would've been with Jake when he stepped foot on Earth. "When I did think about it, I assumed he'd told other scientists. I didn't want them to take the TAG-GIMS away from me because it was—" He cleared his throat, the emotions raw even after so many years. "Well, it was the last thing Mai-ron ever gave me."

"I've never heard of Dolk's anti-gravity thing," Gordon said.

Jake wanted to smile at calling Dolk's invention, "a thing." Instead, his forehead wrinkled. "You're kidding. The other volcanologist didn't know what he was working on?"

"No." Gordon dropped his head into his hand. "If he had a new theory, it died with him."

Heart thumping wildly, Jake shook his head. "No, it didn't."

Gordon lifted his head, and Dad stared.

"I kept the TAG-GIMS. Someday, I had planned to figure out if it really did create anti-gravity. It was a sentimental thing—"

Gordon stammered. "Wh-wh-where is it?"

"In my room at Sir and Easter's house. In my strong-box."

"Dolk's ideas are five years old," Gordon said. "Surely someone else has done something similar."

Dad opened his arms wide and said, "Maybe. Maybe not. We have to retrieve that—what did you call it? A TAG-GIMS—and study Dolk's theory to see if there's anything useful there. Think of all the time wasted."

Jake looked from Gordon to Dad.

"We need to get Dayexi here," Dad rose and went to lean his head against the window. "In three days."

"What is going on?" Jake asked.

"It takes me almost three days to decompress to get out of here." Dad pounded softly on the window.

So that's why Dad came so seldom. Once he came down to Seastead, he stayed long enough to make it worthwhile, usually a couple weeks.

"Can't she come down to Seastead? She's dying to see it," Gordon said.

"Absolutely not!"

"You're right, of course." Gordon sighed. "We can't risk it. I'll find a quiet place in the Seattle area and make sure it's secure."

Dad nodded. "I'll call and make sure she's here in three days."

Thrilled, Jake realized that he'd get to see his mom soon. "So what now?" he asked.

Gordon took charge. "I'll take you back to your house and meet Sir and Easter. After all, I am David's father. In fact, he can go with us."

"And I'll give you Dolk's TAG-GIMS?"

"Yes."

Jake whispered. "Will this really make a difference? Will it save Rison?"

"Dolk was a genius. But still, his theories are five years out of date. And Rison's core—it's so unstable. It may be too late." Gordon said.

"But Mt. Rainier," Jake pleaded. "You can reverse the Brown Matter there?"

"If Dolk really figured out something, then—we have a chance. And that's more than I thought we had when we first heard what Captain Hill had done."

THE GLOBES

While Gordon went to find David and get things set for going back to shore, Dad asked, "Would you like to see my room here?"

He's trying to make up for not telling me about Seastead, Jake thought. But he was curious to see more of the installation. Still barefoot, he padded behind Dad to his cabin.

Dad's room had bookshelves—real paper books—scattered among *umjaadi* globes. He'd had the Risonian water globes on the Moon Base, too, but it looked like he had even more.

"You've never told me why you have so many," Jake said.

Dad smiled sadly. "They remind me of Dayexi." Dad took the *umjaadi* globe from Jake and held it up. "She gave me the first one fifteen years ago. Let me tell you the story."

☆ ☆ ☆

I was on the first envoy to Rison, a medical officer, the Navy's expert on comparative anatomy. Your mom and her family volunteered to be examined by humans: your grandparents, Jasa and Chan, and their daughter, Dayexi. We needed a family like that for genetic studies. Swann was there, too, wanting to protect them all, but he had to stand aside and let me do the anatomical examinations and tests.

After the initial examinations, Dayexi invited me to swim in the Risonian pool. We swam and played around some. And then we argued—it was a little thing, nothing important—and then to show that she wasn't really angry, she dove.

You have to understand: it was one of the first times for me to see a Risonian in action in the water. She dove and let me watch her legs Velcro together and then swim like she had a tail. I'd done the anatomical studies, and even seen the villi work on the examining table. But to see it in the water and the effect it had on her swimming—well, it was something to see.

To demonstrate her gills, Dayexi sat on the pool's floor for a long time, water-breathing. Just letting me observe, to see for myself that she was—well, alien.

But I didn't see her as alien. To me, she's always been a beautiful and fascinating mermaid.

All over the pool's floor were *umjaadi* globes with bioluminescent starfish. The pool glowed with life and with possibilities. Watching her, anything was possible that night.

Anyway. When she finally surfaced, she carried this *umjaadi* globe and handed it to me. A peace offering. She called it a Glow Star.

Of course, she had to show me how to shake it to activate the bioluminescence.

She said, "Keep it. To remember this day."

I've kept it. And every time I see another *umjaadi* globe, I'm a sucker. I have to buy it. Please, don't tell her I have so many.

□ ☆ ☆

Jake lay back on Dad's bed, his eyes blurry, and thought about the young Navy officer, so anxious to learn about Risonians. Falling in love with Dayexi, it must have been the best time of his life. Dad loved Mom.

And Mom loved Dad.

It shouldn't work. It left behind Mom's life with Swann Quad-de on Rison. It left behind the physical differences in the species. It left behind the struggle of Earthlings to protect themselves and the struggle of Risonians to find a refuge from their own foolishness. It shouldn't work.

Yet, here he was. Proof that it did work.

CONTAGIOUS?

To leave Seastead, Dad had to decompress for three days or risk the bends, chokes and staggers. Meanwhile, Mom had important meetings set up that she couldn't cancel. They had finally arranged for a face-to-face meeting for the next Sunday.

That week of waiting was somber as reports came in from volcanologists studying Mt. Rainier: the crater was bulging at the rate of a meter a day. The temperature of the gases coming from fumarole increased daily, and the amount of sulfur dioxide increased, too.

And, worst of all, the pristine glacier streams and frigid mountain lakes and ponds around Mt. Rainier turned deadly. The newspapers ran stories like, "Stink Killing Fish on Mt. Rainier." One lake had a massive fish kill, with fish floating on top of the calm waters: rainbow trout, bull trout, dolly varden, whitefish, and salmon. Scientists warned that gases were seeping into lake waters and releasing chemicals that had strange effects.

There could be just one conclusion: Mt. Rainier was getting ready to explode.

"The mountain is rotten," warned volcanologists. "The snowcapped peak is sitting on soft, muddy slopes. When it explodes, the lahars, or mud slides, will be the biggest in centuries."

People from the Mt. Rainier area responded by evacuating, streams of cars clogging the streets, loaded down with every possession they could cram into vehicles. Many of the students and faculty at Bainbridge High had relatives or friends moving in with them until the situation calmed. It was a somber week.

Jake was nervous, ready to charge to the mountain and use Dolk's TAG-GIMS, confident that Mai-Ron's theories would be effective in containing the effects of the Brown Matter. But no decisions could be made till Sunday when Mom would arrive. Gordon and his crew spent the week studying Mai-Ron's gravity lens and trying to put his theories into a context that made sense.

It might have been a hard week of waiting, except for Em.

Till now, Jake had hung back with Em, thinking that an interstellar love story was impossible. But his parents had made it work. Sure, he was the product of a test tube and wouldn't have been alive without his father's skills in the lab. But here he was, half-Risonian and half-human. That meant it might be possible to fall head over heels in love with Em—and expect it to work.

At some point he'd have to tell her his background, but that was years in the future. At fifteen Earth-years-old, neither of them was ready for anything serious yet. But he might reasonably expect her to be his girlfriend. Right?

On Monday morning, Jake showed up at Em's door before school. She was grabbing her bags and books and trying to tie her tennis shoes all at the same time.

Stepping inside, Jake smiled at her. "That's why you need me around. To help you carry books and bags."

She blushed, clung to her gym bag, and frowned. "I do fine by myself."

Jake stepped closer and put a hand on her shoulder. "Of course, you do. But you'll do even better with me along."

For a moment, they stared at each other, until a slow smile spread across her face.

"You're right," she said. "You might just make life easier. Certainly, it's more interesting with you around."

She bowed slightly to heave her backpack off her shoulder and then held it up for him. He slung it across his left shoulder. Using his best manners, he opened the front door and let her walk through before closing it gently behind them, turning to watch her amble down the front path.

We're going together, he thought. He felt his face warm with a blush. But he didn't back off. It was nice to have a girlfriend, even if she was a human.

Every day that week, he walked her to school; after school, he walked her to the Aquatic Center, where he sat and watched her practice her backstroke, freestyle, butterfly and breast strokes. The state swim meet was next Monday, and she had qualified in backstroke and IM. She was ferocious in her practices, pushing herself hard.

Jake was determined to see Em every day, even Saturday and Sunday. It had been a while since Jake thought about the harbor seals, but it was almost time to turn in the science research paper that he and Em were working on together. He called Dr. Fleming, and she said to meet her at the harbor on Saturday morning, and they'd kayak out to check on the seals.

But Em didn't want to kayak. "With the state meet on Monday, we don't have any practices this weekend. But I want to do something fun. I haven't done any open water swimming in a while. What if I bring my wetsuit and swim while you kayak out to the pup?"

At his skeptical look, she added, "I'll just play around. I won't work hard."

"A change of pace would be good," Jake agreed.

By now, Seattle's days were down to less than ten hours of sunlight; sunrise wasn't till 7:15 or so. It was still dark when Jake stopped by Em's house, and they biked to the harbor. Bobbie Fleming was there before them, but she was talking to a tall man with straight blond hair. So Jake and Em locked up the bikes and pulled his kayak out of storage.

Bobbie and the man were arguing as they came up, and they barely glanced at the teens.

"The question is, why are they sick?" the man said. "And if it spreads to us—"

Embarrassed, Jake said, "Are we interrupting something? Should we—"

"No, it's fine." Fleming said shortly. She pushed up her glasses frame and frowned at the man. "We're finished."

She glared at the man, who glared back.

Their straight blond hair, the way they both stood so straight-backed, and the matching wire-rim glasses, made Jake ask, "Are you related?"

"Brother and sister," the man said. "I'm Dr. Maximillian Bari. I work at the hospital, the human hospital; I'm not a vet." He took off his wire-rim glasses and rubbed them clean in a gesture that Jake had seen Dr. Fleming do many times.

Em said, "You're the new GP, the general practitioner doctor. Right? I think we're switching over to you."

Suddenly, Fleming looked at Jake and Em and backed up a step. If possible, her frown deepened.

"Yes," Dr. Bari said. "Dr. Josiah Smith retired, and I bought out his practice."

Jake frowned. "Is it contagious? What the harbor seals have? Will people get it, too?"

Fleming and Bari both shook their heads, like they were twins moving in sync. It's almost eerie, Jake thought. He tried again, "You said, 'if it spreads to us.' Can humans get whatever it is?" Ironic question, Jake thought, since I'm not human. If Dr. Bari said, yes, then Jake figured he'd have to carry the question one life form farther and ask if it would affect Risonians.

"Ah," Dr. Bari said. "Well, that's a good question. Not likely. I told Bobbie that I'd look at the veterinarian's lab work, but it's just not likely. Few diseases cross from aquatic life to humans."

Fleming took a deep breath and obviously changed the subject. "How's the science report coming along? Need anything else?"

"We just need a final check of the pup," Em said. "We've got the vet report and stuff, and it's almost written. We just wanted one more look."

"Let's go out, then," Fleming said. To her brother, she said, "I'll talk to you later."

He nodded and strode off, walking toward the marina.

Em disappeared into the girl's bathroom and reappeared encased in a wet suit. Jake raised an eyebrow at the strange color. It was mottled shades of blue-green, with shades ranging from very light to dark.

"It's shark resistant," Em explained. "It's sort of like camo gear, except it's camo designed especially for the water."

It would be hard to see in the water, Jake decided. The colors would blend and give Em an "invisibility cloak." Jake watched her walk toward the water, awed by her athlete's build. If her racing suit showed off her muscled shoulders, this wetsuit showed off her long legs. He whistled, and when she turned, he called, "We'll be back soon."

She nodded, adjusted her mask and walked into the water. She began a lazy crawl—lazy for her, anyway.

Jake and Fleming pushed off kayaks, paddling swiftly to Blakely Rock. Early morning on the water was still one of his favorite times because it was so calm. Except for the splash of his paddle dipping into the water, few sounds broke the tranquility of Puget Sound.

Blakely Rock was silent, too. No seals.

Slowly, the two kayaks circled the tiny island—really just an outcropping of rock.

Jake said, "Nothing."

Fleming nodded but pulled binoculars from her ever-present dry bag. She scanned the shore and suddenly froze.

"There," she said.

She paddled straight for a large boulder and pulled her kayak onshore. Bending, she touched—

—the pup was dead.

Ashes and nails filled Jake's heart. They should've come out sooner to check on the pup, or the vet should have kept it longer until he was sure the pup would live. What was wrong with it? Had *umjaadi* killed the pup?

The carcass was fresh. Only a few crabs had found it.

From her kayak, Fleming retrieved a white kitchen-sized trash bag and tugged the pup's body inside. This time, because the pup wasn't squirming with life, she tied it to the front of her kayak where it would stay dry.

Jake wondered about the other seals. The mother seal, was she okay, or was she sick, too?

Somberly, they paddled back to the harbor. Jake wanted to explain about *umjaadi* to Fleming and have the veterinarian check for the organisms. But he couldn't.

At the harbor, Em came dripping out of the water to greet them, and she was just as horrified as Jake and Fleming over the pup's death. "Why did the vet send it back?"

Fleming said grimly, "I don't know. He'll do a post-mortem, and then we'll know more."

Jake kicked at the gravel. The post-mortem would be pointless if the vet didn't know to look for *umjaadi*.

It made the research report difficult to wrap up. Jake and Em spent the evening finishing the project with no choice but to leave it open-ended.

Em assured Jake, "Coach Blevins will understand."

Jake nodded. Mom would be here tomorrow, though, and this was one more thing they had to discuss. One more thing for which Seastead might have to answer.

AN EARLY THANKSGIVING

Early Sunday morning, Sir dropped Jake off at a house the Risonian Embassy had rented on the Hood Canal, right on the water. Dad was waiting for him, along with several Risonian military guards, including Commander Gordon. Dad and Jake paced the beach, waiting for Mom.

Finally, a dark SUV drove up, and they hurried to meet her. When Mom stepped out of the car, Dad pulled her into his arms. They stood for a moment, just holding each other. Embarrassed, Jake turned away, but Mom was already searching for him among the officials and guards and grabbed him from behind in a bear hug. Seaweed perfume, he thought affectionately. No one on Earth smelled quite like his mom.

But the situation was too urgent to linger; they strode quickly into the house.

Mom's voice dripped with regret and reproach, "If only you'd told us about Mai-Ron's theories."

"I thought you knew." Jake had been over this with Dad and Commander Gordon, so he expected it. "I was just a kid, and my best friend was dead. I didn't know I was the only one who knew anything."

"Mai-Ron always kept his research close to the chest," she said and cupped her own hands to her chest. But when she opened them, it was with an empty gesture.

The commanders showed her the photos of Captain Hill and Yarborough-Greg Blevins, and Mom remembered the Yarborough incident perfectly. Jake explained about Captain Hill deploying the Brown Matter.

"A stupid way to get revenge," Mom said. "Risking your own planet just to justify your wacky friend's theories. Doesn't he know the meaning of the word, 'theory'?"

Ignoring her righteous indignation, Dad rose to pace, "The question is, what now? Do we test Dolk's TAG-GIMS on Rison? Or do we test it on Mt. Rainier?"

"Both," Mom said with decision. "Rison is likely too far gone for it to matter, but we have to try. Mt. Rainier is the first place anyone has used Brown Matter on an Earth volcano, so we have to contain it before it goes any further."

"What if Dolk's theories are wrong, or his invention doesn't work?" Commander Gordon said.

Both Dad and Mom rounded on him, and Gordon stepped back, almost stumbling over the massive leather couch.

"It could be wrong," Gordon insisted. "Volcanic theories have come and gone for years. Why should Dolk's theory be any better?"

"Because he was Mai-Ron Dolk, of course," Mom said. As if she realized how illogical that was, she threw up her hands in disgust. With a sigh, she said, "You're right. Dolk could be wrong but it's something that no one else has ever tried. We know that nothing else will help Mt. Rainier. This is our only chance."

Jake shook his head. "No. We could do nothing. Maybe it will only smoke and never blow."

But he thought about the week of escalation: bulging crater, dead fish, lakes gone crazy, rising temperatures of fumarole gases, and more sulfur dioxide in the gases. It was getting worse, not better.

Dad sat down and hung his head. "If it blows—"

"—it will affect too many people," Mom finished.

They were all silent for a few moments. Outside, the sunlight glittered off Hood Canal. It was cold, but beautiful. A perfect fall day. Captain Hill was forcing them into decisions they didn't want to make. Earth, the blue planet, was balanced upon the head of a pin, and the wind from a butterfly's wing could unbalance it.

Reluctantly, Jake said, "Let me tell you about a seal pup that we've been studying." He didn't want to deliver yet another unpleasant detail, but they had to know. He explained the pup's death and his suspicion that it was *umjaadi*.

Mom looked sharply at Commander Gordon. "Is he right? Did someone break an *umjaadi* globe?"

Gordon rubbed his hands wearily over his face. "Yes." He suddenly looked older.

"And you didn't report it?" she demanded.

"It was done. We couldn't undo it."

And that was the problem: as careful as any Earthling or Risonian would be, it was inevitable that there would be a cross-contamination. That had been the concern of the early contacts. It was Orson Welles' "War of the Worlds."

In the end, the discussion went nowhere. The *umjaadi* would either cause problems or not. If and when it did—as Jake suspected with the seal pup—they would try to respond. Dad would make sure the Navy quietly got tissue samples from the seal pup, and that was all they could do for now.

Later, after all the discussions, Jake went outside to walk along the beach, and he was pleased when Mom joined him. Walking along the shore, he suddenly saw a three-foot long fish swimming up into the shallows. Mom put a hand on his shoulder, and together they watched the insistent salmon wriggle up a tiny rivulet that led inland. The water was so shallow that it barely came halfway up the fish's sides. Maybe somewhere the rivulet would open up into a larger stream, but here, it looked like the fish was going nowhere. It would never make it home. Maybe, Jake thought, Risonians were closer kindred to this salmon than to sharks. The salmon was just seeking its home waters so it could spawn, so it could make sure its species survived. That's all the Risonians wanted: survival of their species.

☐ ✰ ✰

The photographer jammed the monopod that supported his heavy lens into the sandy shore. The ambassador from Rison was across a shallow strip of water. If he got any closer, they'd spot him. It had to be from here. He'd seen her disappear into the house, and if she went in, she'd have to come out sometime. He shivered in the cold breeze and pulled his sock cap closer over his ears.

Then, he got lucky. The teen who'd gone into the house came out. He looked to be the right age to be the Ambassador's son. He didn't know the other men, probably a bodyguard and officials who were plotting with her.

And from a side door, the she-Shark joined the boy. This had better be her son, the photographer thought. His car needed engine work, and he needed the bonus money offered by the National Enquirer. They stopped, and she put a hand on his shoulder. Amazingly, they were facing his camera; it was his chance.

The camera's motor whirred, taking dozens of photos in just a few seconds. Quickly, he flipped on the camera's monitor and scrolled through the photos. They weren't great. The subjects were too far away, and the light was already failing. Not what he had hoped for, but maybe good enough? In a few frames, the boy's face was dimly visible.

He snapped again, but this time the boy and woman were headed away from him, and he only got a silhouette against the bright sky. The first set of photographs would have to do. He wondered how much the press would pay for the photos. He hoped for enough to fix his car and pay rent for the month, or even a couple months.

☆ ☆ ☆

When Jake and Mom returned to the house, Dad met them at the door.

"I have a surprise," he said.

Sir and Easter came out of the kitchen, both wearing pink aprons. On Easter, it looked fine, but Sir's face was as pink as the apron because of the heat in the kitchen.

Dad beamed. "Since Dayexi won't be here next week, we are having Thanksgiving dinner tonight."

At the offer of food, Jake lifted his head and sniffed. Something smelled great.

Easter said, "We'll eat in about thirty minutes. The bread is almost done."

Mom stepped forward, and in her best ambassador manners, she took Easter's hands in hers. "Thank you for such a warm welcome."

But Easter pulled her into a hug, and then pushed her back to stare straight into her face. "You're the only girl Blake ever brought home to meet us, which makes you special. And your son is a pure joy. He's so much like Blake at that age. Stubborn and proud."

Mom blinked back tears, and her mouth quivered.

Jake watched in amazement. This old couple had welcomed them with open arms. Mom and Jake didn't deserve such hospitality. Dad stepped in and pulled everyone into a group hug. And when they pulled apart, everyone blinked back tears, even Sir.

Sir cleared his throat. "I better carve the turkey."

And Jake's first Thanksgiving on Earth was full of good food, laughter and gratitude.

THE STATE SWIM MEET

Late on Sunday night, Jake asked the thing he'd been dreading, but had to ask. "Em, my, um, my girlfriend. She's in a swim meet tomorrow. It's the state championships. Can we go watch?"

Dad shook his head, but Mom nodded. "I want to meet Em."

"Won't someone recognize you?" Dad said.

She grinned. "You leave that to me. I'll go incognito."

Early the next morning, she came downstairs transformed. She had shed her ambassadorial pantsuit and pulled on a pair of worn jeans. Her hair pulled back into a ponytail that she tucked through the back of one of Dad's old collection of hats. Since he'd visited Jake, Dad had taken five or six caps with him, and every day he wore a different one. He must have brought this one with him. It was a burgundy cap with gold letters that said "Florida State."

"Where'd you get this one?" she teased Dad.

"I went to a junior national qualifying meet for backstroke. I didn't do very well, only 57th in the country. But I exchanged baseball caps with a guy there. He was getting a swimming scholarship to the University of Utah, so he was willing to switch for other Pac 10 caps. I gave him an Oregon Ducks cap."

"Ducks, bears, cardinals—your Earth tradition of mascots is still strange to me. Why would anyone want to be called a Duck? Quack, quack." Mom shook her head and tied the laces on some running shoes. Then she stood and twirled around. Her Bainbridge High sweatshirt hid her figure, and the cap shaded her face.

Jake barely knew her. "Where, oh where, has the Face of Rison gone?"

Dad, Jake and Mom grinned at each other.

"Let's go to this swim meet and watch Em," Mom said.

The King County Aquatic Center was packed. Because they arrived at 9 a.m., early enough to watch the warm-ups, they had their choice of seats. Jake led the way, climbing bleachers to the top row, and sat next to a beam that supported the roof for added shadows. With animated gestures, Dad explained how the swim meet worked to Mom.

Meanwhile, Jake trotted down to talk to Em. He found her on the Bainbridge High team bench, hunched over with a towel around her neck and her face in her hands.

Concern shot through Jake. "You okay?"

She shook her head. "So tired."

"Let me get you a power bar. You just need some quick energy."

She dipped her nose toward a half-eaten power bar on the bench beside her. "Not hungry."

This really worried Jake. Em ate five or six power bars a day sometimes. "Coffee? Gator-Ade?"

"Ugh." Em shivered.

Gently, Jake touched her forehead, her neck. "You're hot. I think."

"Mom took my temperature this morning. Said I was okay."

Jake shook his head. If this wasn't the state meet, she should just sit out because she obviously felt really bad. But she'd worked so hard to be a contender in the backstroke and IM.

"Can you lay down or something? In between events?"

"Coach is letting me sit out the warm-up." She tried to smile and nodded toward the pool where her teammates were lazily swimming laps. She shrugged. "It's the state meet. I can't sit it out."

Jake felt awkward, unsure of what he could do to help. Finally, he just told her his news. "Um. My mom is here today."

Em tried to sit upright and scan the audience. "Where?"

"Up there with Dad." He waved toward the top row. He sighed in relief: from here, they were hard to see. They'd be safe today watching the meet.

Em rolled her head, stretching out her neck muscles, and then swung her arms in wide arcs. "I'll try to give her a good show."

"I'll talk to you later, then. Just rest in between!"

He trotted back up the bleachers to Mom and Dad, worry dogging his steps.

The morning rolled by slowly, event after event. Em's first event, backstroke, was scheduled for 10:15, but as usual, the meet was already behind by then. Every time he looked down, Em was asleep on the bench. Apparently Coach had also decided that she needed rest. About 10 am, though, he woke her. She seemed to have more energy, and he saw her eat a power bar and drink orange juice. She even smiled and joked with a couple other swimmers before she slipped into the water about 11 a.m. for the 100-meter backstroke, or four lengths of the pool.

Dad was still in teacher mode, excited to explain everything to Mom: "Watch this stroke, how the legs do a strong flutter kick. Velcro legs wouldn't work for this one."

Mom wouldn't let him win the point, though. "Even with a flutter kick, most ten-year old Risonians would out swim even the best Earth swimmers here."

Jake was glad this was the girl's state meet, not the boys. He'd be too jealous to watch a boy's meet. I could take on anyone for any stroke, he thought. It'd be too easy. Since it was the girls' meet, he just relaxed and leaned forward to watch.

At the starting gun, Em shot forward, taking the early lead. She wore Bainbridge High's robin's-egg-blue cap, so she was easy to track in the third lane. Even though she was a freshman, she was expected to do well.

When they flipped, Em still held the lead, but a red capped swimmer had done a better underwater flip-turn and now led. Em needed to concentrate on doing a cleaner turn. Red and blue caps came out of the second turns, neck and neck. But this time, Jake thought Em was aware of the red-cap because her strokes came faster. She churned water. At the flags above the lane, she took two more powerful strokes, rolled to her belly, flipped, and dolphin kicked out of the turn. She was behind, maybe a third of a body length. One of Em's strengths was her uncanny ability to sense where her opponents were; Jake expected her to break open.

Em poured on the speed, churning water faster than ever, arms wind-milling backwards smoothly, like a well-oiled machine until—

—about halfway across, she suddenly slowed.

Em kept going, but her stroke speed was noticeably slower. She struggled to kick. Red cap tagged the wall. In the far lane, a green cap tagged. Em settled for third place.

Jake ached for her. Em had worked so hard for this meet and now, because she was sick, she had ended up with only bronze when she should've had gold.

Em waved the coach over, and he hauled her out of the water.

That's what worried Jake the most. She didn't have the strength to pull herself out of the water. And once she was on the side of the pool, she curled into a fetal position. Even from the top of the bleachers, Jake saw that Em was shivering.

He jumped up and called over his shoulder to his parents, "I'll be back."

Jogging down the steps, Jake watched Mrs. Tullis and Marisa rush to Em's side. They pulled her upright, supporting her under her arms. Marisa wrapped a huge beach towel around Em's shoulders, and they staggered into the dressing room.

Alarmed, Jake dodged through the onlookers and would've pushed into the girl's dressing room if necessary to find out what was happening. Instead, Mr. Tullis paced in front of the door, waiting himself.

Jake demanded, "Is Em OK?" He was breathing hard with worry.

"No," Mr. Tullis said. "We're taking her to the ER."

JUST FRIENDS

The hospital door swung open, and Dr. Bari stepped in. Following him was a nurse in plain blue scrubs who carried a tablet computer; she wore dark curls in a long ponytail. Jake sat in a chair holding Em's hand; her eyes were closed, and she was half asleep.

Dr. Bari stepped immediately to the sink to wash and dry his hands while the nurse opened the tablet and activated a wireless keyboard. Dr. Bari turned to Mrs. Tullis and Marisa and explained the test results while the nurse took notes.

"She's anemic," Dr. Bari announced. "We'll have to figure out what is causing it, but for short-term, we can do a transfusion."

Mrs. Tullis nodded. "Will this help her feel stronger?"

"She'll be better within 24 hours," Dr. Bari said.

He sounded confident, but as Jake watched, his stomach knotted with worry. Dr. Bari leaned over Em and studied her face. But he didn't touch her. Dr. Bari just nodded to Mrs. Tullis, stepped back to the sink, and washed his hands again—even though he'd touched nothing—and left. All that washing of hands—something was wrong.

Jake decided to follow Dr. Bari. "I'll be back in a few minutes," he told Em. "Just want to get some coffee."

"Triple-shot venti," Em murmured and tried to smile.

"You want something?" Jake asked with concern.

Em gave a small head shake and closed her eyes.

"I'll be right back," Jake murmured.

He followed Dr. Bari through the hallways to a small chapel in a corner of the third floor. Dr. Bari pushed open the swinging doors and strode inside. Before the doors swung shut, Jake saw him looking around. Quietly, Jake cracked open the door and slipped inside. When his eyes adjusted to the dark, he saw Dr. Bari sitting beside Bobbie Fleming on a front pew. Jake sat on the last row of pews and scooted all the way over to the wall to stay as unobtrusive as possible. The room was so small that he'd be able to hear any conversation except whispers.

Fleming stood suddenly, and said in a low intense voice, said, "You've got to do something or she'll get sicker. And if that happens, I'll never forgive you." She strode angrily down the aisle toward the door.

Jake bent his head as if in prayer. Fleming passed his row without a glance.

She was followed a moment later by Dr. Bari. Stealing a sidelong glance, Jake was surprised that Dr. Bari's face was a thunderstorm.

What was going on? Clearly this had to do with Em, but why was Fleming interested? At the harbor, she'd acted as if she didn't like Em. She had only reluctantly given Em a ride home. And why was Dr. Bari involved? Jake needed to know more—much more. Maybe later when he had a computer he could research Fleming like he had Yarborough/Blevins. He wondered what he'd find. But for now, he needed to get back to Em.

When Jake returned to Em's room—holding a cup of awful-tasting coffee from the vending machine—a nurse in purple scrubs was hanging a bag of dark blood over Em. As soon as the transfusion was set up, Em dozed off.

Dad and Mom strolled in a few minutes later.

After introductions, Dad asked Mrs. Tullis, "Would you and Marisa like to go get something to eat? We'll stay here till you get back."

With a grateful nod, Mrs. Tullis accepted, "We won't be gone even 30 minutes."

"Take your time," Dad said.

After they left, Mom leaned against the windowsill, as far from Em as she could get, and asked, "You like this girl?"

"I am an Earthling now. Right? I have to live here, so of course, I'm going to have Earthling friends."

"But that doesn't mean you get to marry an Earthling." Mom's face settled into a frown. "Just remember that. Friends, okay. But don't let it go deeper than that. When Rison evacuates, we'll need everyone to intermarry so we have enough of a gene pool to keep the population healthy."

Dad cleared his throat. "We've talked about this. We don't know if Jake can even have children. Often times hybrids—"

Jake finished it, "—hybrids are sterile. I know."

Pacing, Mom repeated, "I forbid you to fall in love with Em."

Jake stood and leaned over Em's pillow to push a strand of hair off her face, which was almost as white as her pillow. He hoped the transfusion would be enough; she was so very pale.

To Mom, he said, "She's just a friend."

"Friend?" Mom said.

Jake stared at Em. Even asleep and even sick, she charmed him as surely as a mermaid had ever charmed a sailor. Yet, to calm his mother, he said, "She's one of the first girls I met here. It was just easy to pick her up."

Mom nodded. "Okay. Just don't fall for her."

"I'd never fall for her." He said it almost scornfully, trying to convince his mother to stay out of his business. If he didn't, then he'd get questioned about Em every time they talked.

Em's eyes popped open.

Oh. Jake swallowed hard. How much had Em heard?

"Em! You're awake. How are you feeling?" he asked guiltily.

She just stared at him with cold, accusing eyes.

TRIPLE-SHOT VENTI

The bells on the coffee shop door jangled. Jake led the way to the counter and ordered for Mom. "She wants to try a triple-shot venti. Dad and I will take the same."

The store manager's eyebrows shot up. "You've never tried one? Ready to stay awake for a while?"

Mom shrugged. "Jake tells me you make great Earth muffins, too."

Ken put three muffins on plates and handed them a tray with the coffee and pastries. It was Tuesday, the week of Thanksgiving, and Mom would go back to New York that afternoon because she'd been absent from the Risonian Embassy for far too long. When she got back, she'd contact Swann Quad-de on Rison, and they'd talk about Dolk's TAG-GIMS.

For Jake, his mother's visit was way too short. Mom had watched Em swim but had barely talked with her because Em had been so sick. How much of their conservation had Em heard the day before? She was too sick for Jake to try to explain what he had said—why he had said it, to keep his mother off his back. But it chaffed not to clear up everything with her. Not to apologize. For he had betrayed her by allowing his mother to goad him into lying, to say that he'd never fall for Em. In fact, he'd fallen for Em the first time he saw her in this coffee shop. And fallen hard.

Defiantly, he picked up one of the painted coffee cups and told Ken, "Add this in, too."

At the table, he pushed it across to Mom. "You know, Em works here. She paints these coffee cups and sells them for extra cash. I want you to have this to remind you of your trip here."

Mom turned the cup around, studying the painted Seattle skyline.

"Great, isn't it?" Jake said.

Mom sipped her triple-shot and said diplomatically, "Seattle has been interesting."

Jake wasn't going to let her ignore Em. He'd tried to shrug Em off once, and he'd never do that again. "See how Em uses a really fine paintbrush to get details?"

"Details. Yes. There are lots of details to consider when you think about Seattle."

"Em got all the landmarks onto the cup. See? That's the Space Needle."

"Space. Earthlings have always liked the idea of space. But the reality is far different from their ideas."

In disgust, Jake snapped, "Mom, do you have to be a diplomat all the time?"

Mom leaned forward, her voice low and intense. "Of course I have to be a diplomat all the time. For my entire life, all I've known is a planet that's dying. I've given up everything to work for the survival of our people." She reached over and squeezed Dad's hand. "Everything." She repeated fiercely, "Everything."

Dad turned her hand around and held it gently. Softly, he whispered, "Dayexi."

She looked up, her eyes brimming with tears. "What?" she asked angrily.

"Not everything." Dad held her gaze with his own. "We have Jake. And now, we have the possibility of more."

Mom's lips compressed into a frown.

"Yes," Dad said. "Give him hope."

Breathing rapidly, Mom closed her eyes. "Em is nice," she whispered.

Jake's own eyes filled with tears. More than Dad even, Jake knew at what cost Dayexi was here on Earth. His entire life, he'd watched Swann and Dayexi fight for the Risonian people, both on Rison and on Earth. Their sacrifices of time and effort, the arguments with the southern Bo-See delegations, the desperate sleepless nights, the angry tirades at each other over strategy, the ever-present tension of an overwhelming tragedy about to literally explode in their faces. The only surprise was that neither had broken. Truly, Mom was the Face of Rison.

For Mom to step back now—to give him hope—perhaps, it was the biggest miracle of all.

He repeated, "Em is nice."

But Mom was Mom, and she couldn't let the moment drag on. She opened her eyes, straightened in her chair, withdrew her hand from Dad's and picked up her Earth muffin to nibble. "Strange combination, this bread," she said, deliberately turning the conversation neutral. "Sweet, vegetables, nuts—everything rolled into one. Not to my taste."

Dad looked like he wanted to say more, but in the end, he took his cue from Mom and asked, "How's the coffee? Need some cream? Sugar?"

"Thanks," Mom said. "But coffee should be straight up, not doctored. I like the flavor of coffee by itself, not blended into some mix of milk and sugar."

"Caffeine is helpful, whether it's doctored or not," Jake said. "Helps me stay alert. How's caffeine affect you, Mom?"

She smiled at Dad and put a hand over his hand. "Not much. I'm so different from you and your Dad."

Dad grunted. "I'll be up all night anyway, getting back to work, and catching up."

"Wish I could see your office," she said wistfully. She pushed a stray curl behind her ear.

Dad nodded and blinked. "Someday things will get easier."

"When?" Mom's voice was more plaintive than Jake had ever heard. "The press is against us. The U.S. Congress is against us, as are the governments of almost every other nation. The U.N. is against us. And every day we delay—"

She broke off because, well—they all knew the situation.

Despair washed over Jake. He would never see Rison again. For all he knew, he'd never see his mother again, not with that bull's eye painted on the Face of Rison. He was tired of waiting for things to happen; he was tired of hiding here on Bainbridge Island. He couldn't do this much longer.

REVENGE

Reluctantly, Dayexi left Blake and Jake at the coffee shop. Her bodyguard, the Risonian Colonel Lett, had pulled up a few moments ago to pick her up. He opened the back door for her and then jumped into the driver's seat of the SUV. He held himself tall and straight, a military man to his core. Like the Earth military, the Risonian military enforced a strict set of personal and professional habits: short hair, crisp uniforms, and well-oiled weaponry. Lett's dark hair was close cropped, his blue eyes alert for any danger. Trained in hand-to-hand combat—he was always a champion on the fight floor—he'd been Dayexi's bodyguard for a decade. As they drove away, Dayexi turned and waved at Blake and Jake until they turned the corner. Blinking back tears, she turned forward and closed her eyes, trying to find a place of peace within. But calm eluded her.

Colonel Lett drove the SUV onto the Bainbridge ferry to Seattle and parked. Without speaking, Dayexi and Lett climbed out of the car and climbed the steps to the top floor of the ferry, where they sat on benches and stared at Mt. Rainier. From the peak, smoke billowed upward, still streaming almost straight up. Trembling in the cold wind, she remembered the first time she'd seen a similar signature smoke trail from a volcano. The Ja-ram Volcano, on the western edge of Tizzalura, had been treated with Brown Matter, and it did this for three years before settling down again. She wondered if Ja-Ram had exploded yet in the new set of eruptions reported from Rison; there were too many explosions to keep straight any more.

"Too cold?" Colonel Lett asked in concern.

She nodded and let herself be led inside to sit at a padded booth; large picture windows still provided a view of the smoking volcano, but it was comforting to be out of the wind. Lett brought her a cup of coffee, and she pressed her face against the cold window, blinking back tears at leaving Jake behind yet again.

By the time the ferry docked on the other side of Puget Sound, they were back in their SUV. Lett drove off the ferry and followed the signs for the airport. Traffic was light. They'd only gone a few blocks, though, when Colonel Lett glanced at the rear-view mirror and said sharply, "Someone is following us."

Dayexi turned in time to see an old SUV zoom toward them. It slammed into the corner of their bumper, expertly spinning them 360 degrees. Dayexi's head jerked back against the headrest. The whiplash sent crippling pain up and down her spine, so that all she could do was hold herself rigidly still.

Her door jerked open. Hands unbuckled her seat belt and hauled her out.

Blinking, her vision blurred from pain, but she recognized the man from photos: Captain Cyrus Hill. In the front seat, Colonel Lett had struck the steering wheel, and he was slumped over it, moaning.

Since Lett was injured, Captain Hill ignored him; instead, he pulled Dayexi toward his vehicle, her heels dragging on the pavement.

By now, though, the Colonel had recovered enough to push his way out of the SUV, make a stumbling charge, and tackle Captain Hill. Dayexi fell roughly while the men rolled on the shoulder of the road for a moment. She wanted to stand and help, but dizziness washed over her. When she lifted her head, Captain Hill sat astride the Colonel, pummeling his face.

But this was a seasoned soldier, one of Tizzalura's best. He heaved upward and flipped Captain Hill over his head. The rogue ELLIS Forces officer landed with a thud on his back, but instantly rolled, a good strategy since the Colonel was already up and aiming a kick at Captain Hill's head.

Meanwhile, Dayexi tried to stand, unsteady, having to stop and balance herself a couple times before finally pushing upright. She, too, had been trained in hand-to-hand combat. Watching the men maneuver, she looked for an opening.

Captain Hill stepped closer to Colonel Lett and raised his fists in a boxer's stance. Colonel Lett aimed a kick at Captain Hill's face, but as his leg came around, Captain Hill caught his heel and thrust upward. Lett tumbled askew. If he hadn't been injured already in the car wreck, he would've caught himself and recovered quickly. Now, though, he lay still.

Dayexi stepped in behind Captain Hill and stomped on the back of his knee, making him fall forward. But Captain Hill caught his fall, spun, and whipped his leg around to knock her off her feet. She fell heavily, dizziness washing over her again.

Rough hands jerked her up, dragged her, and shoved her in the back seat of Captain Hill's car. Head still spinning, she couldn't fight. Using plastic zip-ties, Hill strapped her hands and feet, and then buckled her seat belt, immobilizing her. He cut off any screams by slapping a strip of silver tape onto her mouth.

Captain Hill returned a moment later with an unconscious Colonel Lett. Again, he tied hands and feet, buckled the man into the back seat, and taped his mouth. Lett's head slumped awkwardly, and Dayexi could only hope that he was still alive.

Now, Captain Hill looked straight at her.

She could only raise an eyebrow in question: Why?

He understood. Eyes glaring, Captain Hill spit out the words. "Killing you is too easy; I want you to suffer. You'll die here on Earth, all alone, in a volcanic eruption created by your technology. They'll find your body with incriminating evidence and blame the Sharks for the eruption; that will seal the fate of your people. YOU will be responsible for killing all of Rison. And Swann Quad-de will finally know our wrath."

THE BABY SHARK

Wednesday morning dawned grey and foggy. Jake had stayed up late with Dad the night before, rehashing everything and deciding nothing. Dad had left at dawn to report back for duty. He'd meet with officials all morning and go back to Seastead that evening. Sir and Easter insisted that Jake go to school for half a day before it let out for Thanksgiving holiday. That afternoon, they argued, Jake could take an afternoon ferry across to see Em in the hospital. Groggy and anxious to be anywhere but school, he pushed into the dark hallways.

He missed going by Em's house; he missed listening to her chatter as they walked to school; he missed the excitement of brushing her hand when he took her gym bag. He groaned. How much had she heard in the hospital? He had to talk to her soon.

Walking into civics class, he cringed at the sight of Coach Blevins. Jake expected Coach to dissect the girl's state swim meet. Jake and his family had left early to follow Em to the hospital, so they hadn't seen the final results. But the TV news had reported that Bainbridge High had come in second by only one point. Coach would spend the entire class period complaining. Jake steeled himself to stay calm when Coach griped about Em's performance.

Instead, Coach was passing out a stack of newspapers with a huge grin. Handing a newspaper to Jake, Coach said, "Exciting news. They got him."

"Who?" asked David Gordon.

"The Risonian ambassador's kid. They got a photo of the She-Shark and the Baby-Shark."

Across the room, newspapers rustled.

Bernie, the class nerd, called, "Jake, this looks like you." He held up a paper and glanced from the front page to Jake and back again.

Jake grabbed the paper away and shook away the cobwebs in his head. The picture was poor, blurry at best. It showed a woman and a teenage boy, that much was clear. Jake recognized the house on Hood Canal where he'd been with his parents that weekend. With a sinking heart, realized that it was indeed a photo of him.

In a too loud, sarcastic voice, Jillian said, "I could take a better photo with my cell phone. This is so blurry, you can't tell a thing."

Jake appreciated Jillian's attempts to throw off the others. Maybe it would work.

But Coach Blevins walked toward Jake, the newspaper in hand.

Coach held the paper up to Jake's face, while Jake cringed. He couldn't look away, or Blevins would really get suspicious. Besides, it was an awful photo. The Ambassador was recognizable, just because you knew it was her. But the kid was a blur, half hidden beside her. Still it was a photo of Jake, and he was furious that the photographer had gotten that close to them.

Blevins's dark eyes were wrinkled, but his stare was intense. Suddenly, he sucked in a breath. "Stay after class. We'll talk."

The rest of class was a blur. When the bell rang, David stopped to murmur, "You need me to stay with you?"

Jake shook his head, no. Even if Coach discovered Jake's identity, they still needed to protect the identities of David and Jillian.

"I'll wait outside," David said.

Jake stayed in his seat until the room was empty. Blevins pulled a student's desk around to face Jake and sat heavily. For a moment, he looked back and forth between the newspaper and Jake. Finally, he said, "I know you. You've always looked familiar. You were there the day I went to beg your father to not ruin my life. You came up out of the water."

Jake shivered. This was the worst that could happen. He played the only card he could. "And I know that you're Yarborough. You've had plastic surgery, and you've buried yourself here on this island, but the world will still remember who you are."

It was a standoff. They both had information that the other wanted to remain quiet. Or so Jake hoped.

But Blevins just smiled, showing his teeth. "It doesn't matter now. Mt. Rainier will be the end of Risonian's hope." He added under his breath, "And of that She-Shark."

"What does that mean?" Bewildered, he demanded, "Did Captain Hill do something to her?"

"You don't know, do you?" Coach Blevins said.

Jake gripped the desk so hard that his knuckles turned white. Tersely, he shook his head.

His voice quavering with controlled anger, Coach Blevins said, "After Swann Quad-de made such a big stink about my research papers, I had to go into hiding." He gestured to his face. "I had a nose job done. Grew a mustache. Threw away my contacts and used heavy glasses. But the worst was changing my name. I was raised to be proud to be a Yarborough. Raised my son that way, too."

Jake studied the Coach's face and thought about the man in the black-and-white photo shaking Swann's hand. That had been a happy and confident man. The man in front of him was bitter and angry.

But Coach wasn't finished. Now his voice was softer. "Cyrus Yarborough is my son's name. But after that mess with Rison and changing my face and identity, well—Captain Cyrus Hill is my son." Coach stood taller, his face hardening into a defiant glare. "Hill was my wife's maiden name. My son—Cyrus—he's ashamed of the Yarborough name. Ashamed." He ran a hand across his face. "When I had the nose job, we went to our cabin on the upper peninsula of Michigan and stayed there while I recovered. For a month, every time he looked at my new face, my son cried. The last day, he told me he was changing his name to Hill and joining ELLIS."

Jake stared in sudden understanding, and he froze, fear gripping him hard. "Oh." It explained Hill's anger and desire for revenge.

"Yes. Oh," sneered Coach Blevins. Eyes wide, his lips twisted in a cruel smirk, Blevins looked half-crazy. He spat out the words: "When's the last time you heard from your mother?"

"What does that mean?" Jake shoved back his chair so violently that it tipped and fell with a loud bang. Jake's insides quivered in fear. What had this man and his son done?

Coach Blevins rose sedately, turned his back on Jake, marched out the door and into the teacher's lounge across the hallway, where Jake couldn't follow.

As his words sank in, Jake's stomach turned cold and hard.

Mom had told him over and over, "Think before you act."

Not this time. He turned and ran.

CHASE

It was dusk when Dad's SUV spun gravel and jerked to a stop in front of Captain Hill's family cabin on the Cowlitz River. Jake and Dad were desperate: Mom had to be here.

Jake, David, Dad and Commander Gordon had talked it over and over, and this was the only logical explanation. Mom had never made it back to NYC; once they realized she was missing, the Embassy was frantic with worry because there had been so many death threats. Dad had thought she was just busy and didn't have time to call him; the Embassy thought she was stealing an extra day or two of family time for Thanksgiving. Instead, Dad's Navy sources finally talked to the police and found a report of the Embassy's SUV abandoned not far from the airport. When Jake reported what Coach Blevins said, they surmised that Mom had been brought here to the Hill's cabin. The Gordons would investigate other angles while Jake and Dad drove frantically to Mt. Rainier

At the last minute, Gordon said, "Blake, you've got to take the TAG-GIMS and a drone. If everything works out, you'll need to try to deploy it."

"You've studied it long enough? You have all the info you need to replicate it?"

Gordon nodded, "And improve on it. We just need to know if it will work."

Dad held out a hand for the lightweight package. Grimly, he said, "It had better work."

Then Dad and Jake sped toward Mt. Rainier, breaking almost every speed limit in sight. Mom might not even be there, but it was their best guess. It was a gamble that Jake hoped worked out.

Jumping out, Jake wanted to run around the cabin to the front door that opened on the river's side and charge in. But Dad put a finger to his lip and motioned him to stay back. Instead, they crept along the cabin's south wall, skirting the stone fireplace, and Dad peered around. He nodded at Jake, and they walked quietly toward the steps in the middle of the porch. At the far end, Captain Hill sat slumped in a rocking chair, apparently napping.

Dad waved his hands toward the door, so Jake tiptoed toward it.

But Captain Hill either woke up or hadn't been napping. He bellowed, "Stop!" Jerking up out of the chair, he started for them.

Without hesitation, Dad charged into Captain Hill, and they crashed against the railings. Captain Hill cried out and shoved Dad backward into the cabin's wall. Dad shook his head, bent low and charged again, this time getting under Captain Hill and throwing him off the porch.

Pretty evenly matched, Jake thought. He wasn't needed, so he turned back to the doorknob, which opened smoothly.

Inside, he found a light switch and had to pause to let his eyes adjust. The cabin was neat and clean, if a bit sterile. It was furnished as you might expect for a log cabin, with leather couches and stuffed deer or elk heads on every wall. Downstairs was a big open room for the kitchen and living room. Jake jerked open doors: a bathroom, a closet, and a pantry. No hidden rooms or doors to a basement. He raced upstairs, taking the steps two or three at a time. Three bedrooms. Empty closets. No one under the beds.

Mom wasn't here!

Where had he taken her? His heart pounded with anxiety and fear. Had Hill hurt her?

Jake raced downstairs and burst out the door, just as Dad slammed into an SUV, probably Captain Hill's vehicle. Dad arched his back and instinctively reached around for his spine.

Captain Hill stood back and taunted, "You won't find her. She's here to get what she deserves."

Jake gritted his teeth and felt the anger burn in his gut. This man, this human, this stupid Earthling—where was Mom?

Captain Hill put his hands up like a boxer and threw a punch toward Dad's face. Still weak from being slammed around, Dad barely managed to raise an arm in self-defense.

Jake looked around for a weapon, something, anything. A fallen branch caught his eye. Snatching it up, he darted toward Captain Hill and crashed it over his head. Captain Hill staggered back, shook his head and looked around. Seeing Jake,

Captain Hill must have decided he didn't like the two-against-one odds. Suddenly, he darted toward the river.

Jake rushed to Dad, "You okay?"

Dad wiped the back of his hand across his mouth. It was bloody.

"Okay," he mumbled. "You find Mom?"

Jake shook his head. "Not in there."

Dad nodded and straightened, his face streaked with dirt and blood, but his eyes glinting with anger. "Where'd he go?"

By now, Captain Hill had clambered down the riverbank and stood looking back at them from the water's edge. He turned and raced south along the riverbank. His khaki camouflage was harder to track than Jake would've believed; it was only because he was in motion that Jake could follow Captain Hill's progress at all.

Dad nodded toward the river. They scrambled through the weeds and slid down the bank. Running was awkward because, although the stones were polished smooth by the water, they were uneven sizes, a jumble. Ahead, Captain Hill stumbled and fell. He stood, grabbing his right knee, and hobbled onward, but slower, so that Jake gained ground.

Dad stopped and leaned his hands on his knees, panting and breathing heavily. "Go on! Catch him! I'm coming!"

Jake concentrated on his footing, glancing up now and then. Captain Hill was heading toward a shallow ford, and Jake thought he might be able to catch him before he got there.

Still limping, Captain Hill sped toward the shallows.

Jake put on a burst of speed, afraid that he'd fall but determined to catch Captain Hill and make him tell where he'd stashed Mom.

Captain Hill splashed into the water, and Jake leapt for him, catching his back and knocking them both into the stream. Cold water made Jake catch his breath, but he had no time to worry about water temperature. Captain Hill stood and faced Jake. The older man had a couple inches reach on Jake, and twenty or thirty pounds. Jake would have to be fast to avoid getting hurt.

Captain Hill advanced and swung.

Jake ducked, danced forward, and punched Captain Hill in the stomach. But it was a lightweight punch; Captain Hill barely paused before he struck downward toward Jake, hitting just below the shoulder blade. Jake collapsed, face first into the water. Captain Hill grabbed the back of Jake's shirt and dragged him toward deeper water. Jake kicked and struggled, but he couldn't get his footing. Captain Hill shoved his face into the water, holding him there, trying to drown him.

Fortunately, the water was deep enough that Jake's underarms—and his gills—were submersed, too. Jake pulled his legs under him until he felt the creek bottom. Suddenly, he shot upward in a tremendous thrust. Captain Hill staggered and turned loose.

Jake slung water from his hair and clothing, shaking like a dog.

When he finally cleared his face, Captain Hill was already across the water and jogging along the opposite shore. Dad was beside Jake, saying, "You okay?"

It was Jake's turn for his eyes to glint in anger. "Let's get him."

Together, they forded the river: Dad slipped once, but Jake supported him and as the water became shallower, they ran faster and faster.

"Where's he going?" Dad asked.

"Marisa's house," Jake nodded to the distant A-frame. "Maybe Mom is there."

Saving his breath, Dad just nodded and sped up.

From somewhere inside, Jake found more energy to push harder and faster. A brisk wind was rapidly cooling his wet clothes, but his magma-sapiens blood kicked in to keep him warm, and he barely noticed.

Ahead, Captain Hill was already climbing up the embankment toward the Tullis's house, using his hands to help pull him upward. He disappeared over the top.

Dad panted, "Careful. Might ambush us. Careful when we climb that bank."

Jake glanced around and nodded. "Look. I'll climb up there." The spot was in a slight curve, and Jake thought it would be hidden from the house. "I'll crawl through the bushes, keeping low. It'll surprise him."

Dad had never looked more military than when he sized up the situation, looking from the river to the house and back to the bank where Jake had pointed. "Good idea."

Jake almost expected him to add, "Good idea, soldier."

Instead, Dad reached inside his shirt and pulled out—

"What's that?" Jake gasped.

"A Sig Sauer P 226."

"A gun?" Jake's breath caught. This was escalating too quickly.

Dad nodded. "Navy issue."

That's right. Dad was a military man, and he knew what he was doing. And they had to get Mom back from this lunatics. Dad bent and picked up a couple fist-sized rocks. "If I need a distraction, throw these and break a window or something."

Jake stuffed them into his t-shirt, against his belly, and tucked the t-shirt into his jeans to keep them in place. In one of those odd moments where you remember something that's totally not important, he realized he'd forgotten his jacket back in the car. Jake gritted his teeth and said, "Let's roll."

Dad kept low, below the edge of the bank, and dashed toward where Captain Hill had climbed up.

Meanwhile, Jake shinnied up the steep bank and crouched low. He'd remembered correctly: small shrubs and grasses were scattered about, so he could stay out of sight.

Ahead, Dad climbed up the bank.

Suddenly, a gunshot rang out, echoing from the mountains. Coach Blevins shouted, "Don't come any closer!"

Shock and disappointment ran through Jake. It wasn't just Captain Hill; his father was here, too. He must've left school immediately and come to warn his son. That's why Mom must be here and not at Hill's cabin.

Three more rapid gunshots rang out, punctuated by another yell, "Stop!"

The pit of Jake's stomach ached. This wasn't TV or a game. This was Mom's life.

Dad belly-crawled forward, apparently too low for Coach or Captain Hill to see him.

Jake was close enough now to see Coach Blevins in the dining room window. It was a double-hung window frame with double thick insulated glass. The top half of the window was down, and Coach was off to the side behind the wall, watching the riverbank. His baseball cap was on backwards, and he held a pistol.

Reaching into his shirt, Jake pulled out a rock and hefted it in his hand, waiting.

Dad reached a large tree and slowly eased into a crouch where he could take an aim at the window. He turned, scanned the brush and spotted Jake. He nodded, and mouthed, "Now."

Jake threw the rock at the window, as hard as the opening pitch of the World Series. With a crash and tinkle of falling glass, the window splintered.

Startled, Coach Blevins pulled back and exposed himself.

Dad shot.

Coach Blevins cried out. And then, it was silent.

Dad and Jake regrouped and considered what to do next.

In the end, they had no choice. Dad said, "We have to go in."

Jake nodded his agreement.

Keeping low, they ran to the house's foundation and crept around the side. Everything was dark as Dad and Jake stormed the porch and burst through the front door. Jake, who'd been here before, motioned Dad upstairs to search for Mom, while he cautiously felt his way in the dark hallway to check on the Coach.

Peering around a corner, moonlight streamed through a window into the dining room. Captain Hill knelt beside Coach Blevins who was slumped against the wall, his face pale and slack, his eyes unfocused. His arm dripped blood.

Jake closed his eyes in relief. Coach wasn't dead; Dad had just winged him.

He opened his eyes to see Captain Hill pointing a gun at him.

Jake said the first thing he thought of, "What's that?"

"A Glock 34."

"A gun?" Stupidly, Jake thought, Two guns in one night.

"ELLIS Force's issue." Captain Hill clicked something, probably taking the safety off.

Afraid to move, Jake's nostrils flared in fear. "I'm just a kid."

"And who shot my Dad?" Captain Hill stepped forward.

Now Jake did move, spinning away, and stumbling toward the kitchen. Desperately, he looked around for something to protect himself, but the wan light of the moon made it difficult to see anything. Over the bar hung racks of pots and pans. He ran a hand across them, making them clang and clank, until he recognized the feel of a heavy iron skillet. He turned just as Captain Hill entered the room. Darting to the side, Jake swung the skillet for Captain Hill's head, but missed, and the skillet went flying through a window, breaking it with another crash and tinkle of falling glass.

Captain Hill glanced over at the window, which let Jake pick up a kitchen chair and swing toward the man's head. Captain Hill raised his arm and deflected the chair, and it, too, fell aside. The momentum, though, pulled Jake off balance and he fell heavily. Captain Hill raised a booted foot and stomped, trying to smash Jake's head. Quick reflexes saved him, as Jake rolled like a sausage across the floor to stop against the kitchen cabinets. He shoved up and stood.

Captain Hill slipped his gun into his shoulder holster and advanced with arms held up like a boxer. Jake wanted to run, but he'd backed himself into a corner, literally.

From the other room, though, Coach called. "Cy. It won't stop bleeding."

Reluctant, Captain Hill stopped and almost snarled in frustration.

"Cy," came the low moan.

"Damn!" Captain Hill turned and ran back to the dining room.

Jake scrambled for the front hallway and dashed upstairs calling, "Mom! Dad!"

Coming toward him down the hall were dark figures. He recognized the silhouette of Dad—and Mom! Mom was okay! She was okay! She was okay.

Behind her was Colonel Lett, her bodyguard. He was okay, too.

Jake slumped against a wall and let himself slide down, holding his head and wanting to cry. Mom was okay. He could breathe again. Water dripped off Jake's clothes and puddled below him. Already, though, his magma-sapiens metabolism was drying out his clothes. It was his squishy, wet shoes that bothered him the most.

Dad leaned over and asked, "What happened downstairs?"

It wasn't over, yet. Jake had to pull himself together, and they had to get out of there.

"You winged the Coach. Captain Hill is doing first-aid stuff. We need to go."

Dad nodded and turned to Colonel Lett, "We've got to get back to our car, which is at a cabin upstream. Stay here. After we leave, neutralize anyone who's left and then call the Embassy for help." He tossed the Risonian soldier his cell phone. "We'll be back if possible. Otherwise, evacuate as you can."

The Colonel nodded, and Jake was sure the Risonian solider could take care of things here.

Dad led the way downstairs. Mom's hair—which was messy, almost straw-like, as if she hadn't washed it in a week—was tied back with a red scarf. When she'd been kidnapped, she'd been wearing that red scarf and a blue blazer with some jeans. Now, the blazer was gone, her white shirt was dirty, and she stank of sweat and onions. But her dark eyes flashed, and she reached over to squeeze Jake's hand, to give him a nod of encouragement.

They snuck downstairs and out the door without seeing anyone. Jake assumed that Captain Hill was still doctoring his father, but he didn't take the time to look around the wall into the dining room. Outside, the sky was brilliantly lit with a full moon that dimmed the Milky Way but left the major stars sparkling.

Dad and Mom held hands as they pounded toward the river. They had to get back to the Hill's cabin where Dad and Jake had left their SUV, so they could get away and take care of Dolk's TAG-GIMS. Commander Gordon was right to insist they bring it. They'd have a chance now to deploy it.

At the bank, Mom bent and tried to climb down, but she cursed in Risonian and said, "I'm so stiff. I was tied up."

Dad went down first, and she half fell into his arms.

Jake looked back at the Tullis's cabin and groaned. Apparently, Captain Hill had evaded Colonel Lett and now stood on the porch, shading his eyes and looking for them. When he saw Jake, he jumped off the porch and came for them.

Lett would take care of Coach Blevins, but that left the captain for them.

Jake leapt off the bank, landing heavily, but was up instantly, running full tilt toward the ford. But suddenly, he stopped.

A herd of elk was lazily crossing just at that point. Two or three dozen of the large animals ambled across the water, one stopping to drink, and another looking up at them. The white-rumpled bull whipped his head around, his antlers wide and deadly.

It didn't matter. They had to cross the river and get to their car.

Mom yelled and flapped her arms, but the bull elk held steady. Dad charged straight for the bull, but after ten steps, he stopped, too, because the bull hadn't budged. The bull was waiting for his herd to cross, and like a ship captain going down with his sinking boat, apparently this animal was going to be the last to move. The elk cows were moving quicker now, though.

Then, from behind, a gunshot.

At the sound, the bull bucked, then bugled loudly, a high-pitched, "Oh-wee-ooo." Then he darted away and the herd stampeded after him.

Looking back, Jake saw that Captain Hill pointed skyward with his gun; he pulled the trigger again and again and again. He only meant to scare the elk herd and not hurt any. Relief shot through Jake.

Captain Hill was getting closer now, though. They had to hurry.

Mom and Jake dove through the deep water, swimming more rapidly than they could run, and gained the opposite side easily. Dad had to run for the shallow ford and splash across, Captain Hill right behind.

Again, luck was on their side as Captain Hill slipped and fell onto his butt.

Stunned, he sat there a moment, giving Dad a chance to get away.

The Roses clawed and pulled their way up the bank and darted to their SUV. Dad juggled his keys to find the right one and started the car before Mom and Jake were even seated, pulling out as they slammed the doors shut.

Jake hoped that Captain Hill would stop right there and go back to his father. And Colonel Lett. Jake watched out the back window while Captain Hill darted into the cabin and immediately came back out to jump into his own SUV. Captain Hill's white vehicle leapt after them, just as the bull elk had leapt away.

"Jake," Dad said. "We need to find a high place where I can use the drone to drop Dolk's packet into a fumarole near the crater."

Jake shrugged. The only place he knew was Snow Lake Trail. It had several high spots just off the parking lot. Or Dad could even go to Bench Lake, where Hill had used the drone, because it gave a clear view of Mt. Rainier.

Dad drove expertly, pulling out smoothly onto Highway 12 and heading northeast toward the visitor's center. Ahead, against the velvet sky, towered Mt. Rainier. Still smoking.

Watching behind, Captain Hill's vehicle lights turned onto the highway behind them.

Jake warned Dad, "Here he comes."

Dad drove faster, pushing the speed limit, taking curves at wicked breakneck speed. Mom gripped the armrest, her hand turning white. Her lips were tight and thin, but she said nothing. Silently, Jake sat back, and reached for his seat belt and buckled in.

As a crow flies, it might have been 10-15 miles from Packwood city limits to the park. But they had to travel east on Highway 12 and pick up some winding forest roads before they came out on Steven's Canyon Road. It was a tense drive, longer than they wanted with Captain Hill on their tail and driving faster than they should.

As they drove, Mom explained what had happened: "They caught us on the way to the airport." She and the Colonel had been tied up and only untied a few minutes a day to eat and go to the bathroom. She'd expected to die when the mountain erupted.

Finally, Dad whipped the SUV into the parking lot for the Snow Lake Trail. Jumping out, he threw open the back and grabbed the heavy case that carried their drone. Mom stopped him with an outstretched hand.

He understood and pulled his gun to hand it to her. She checked the clip and said, "We'll give you time to get the Dolk's TAG-GIMS where it needs to go."

The brilliant maple vines of a couple weeks ago were bare, and the mountains were cloaked now in just evergreen trees and the brilliant white glaciers that gleamed softly in the moonlight. At this altitude, a brisk wind blew. Jake was cold—and he was never cold. But his mother held a gun, and with that anger in her eyes, she meant to use it. That chilled his heart. Legs spread for stability, she leaned over the SUV's hood, pointing the gun at the entrance to the parking lot.

When Captain Hill's white SUV slowed and pulled in, she didn't hesitate: she shot.

The right front tire went flat. The car jerked to a stop, reversed and peeled away. They heard it for a few minutes, and then, it went silent.

Mom groaned, "He's parked somewhere down the road and will try to go through the woods to stop Dad."

"You stay here," Jake said, "and make sure he doesn't come back to the parking lot. I'll go and warn Dad."

She pulled him into a quick hug—she was sweating with tension in spite of the cold—and he darted into the woods. A few hundred feet away, though, he slowed and turned off the path. He could go and warn Dad, but that would only mean that Captain Hill would find them, and Dad wouldn't have time to deploy Dolk's TAG-GIMS.

Instead, Jake could sneak back through the woods and ambush the Captain. Even if he lost, it would give Dad more time.

He pushed off the path, through shrubs and vines, trying to head to where he last heard Hill's SUV. He tripped on a fallen log that he hadn't seen in the dark. Lying there, doubts overwhelmed him; should he go back to Dad or try to cut Hill off?

Nearby, he heard the crunch of dead, dry leaves.

Jake rolled silently to his belly and tried to see through the shadows under the trees. His heart pounded with fear. There. A man was running.

Under the dark forest canopy though, Jake wasn't sure he could recognize anyone. It didn't matter: no one else was out here.

Jake rose to a crouch and waited. Just as the figure approached, he sprinted out and tackled him. They rolled over and over, and Captain Hill wound up on top. He drew back a hand to hit Jake, but pause to glance upward. A buzzing sound from overhead was coming closer.

Dad's drone skimmed away toward the crater.

"No!" Captain Hill screamed at the sky.

He looked down again, ready to hit Jake, but was surprised when Jake reared up and threw a punch straight at his chin.

Before, when he'd hit Captain Hill's belly, it was Jake's first time in real combat, and he'd held back. This time, he threw his weight into it, and it landed with a bone-jarring thud on Captain Hill's chin. The Captain fell back, momentarily stunned.

Jake rose, shaking out his aching hand knuckles. He didn't like hand-to-hand combat: it hurt.

Hill leapt up, though, and charged at Jake, shoving him aside and pounding through the bushes toward Dad and the drone's controller.

Jake had been here before—and lost. This time, he'd make sure that Captain Hill didn't make it to Dad.

Hill had lost the advantage of surprise, but he was still stronger and faster than Jake, who trailed along as quickly as he could. Hill couldn't be exactly sure where Dad was sitting: all Dad had to do was be quiet and motionless.

Except for the glow of the controller's monitor. In the dark, that would be a giveaway even from a distance. Even as Jake thought that, Hill gave a cry of triumph.

Dad had remembered Jake's story about Bench Lake and the vantage point of the rocks. He stood on top of a rock silhouetted against the moon and facing Mt. Rainier.

Hill scrambled up the rock, but Jake grabbed his boots and yanked. Hill fell hard on his belly and face, and when he rose, blood spurted from his nose. Still, he summoned Jake with his hand. "Come on, baby shark," he taunted. "I can take you."

Jake knew it was true. But he had an advantage that Hill didn't have. He stormed toward the ELLIS Forces officer, and his momentum carried them toward the water. Jake fearlessly thrust Hill under and didn't resist when the bigger man pulled him under, too. His breathing switched almost instantly to water breathing. Other mountain lakes had fish kill but so far, this one had escaped. The water was so pure, it was hard not to stop and revel in it—and he knew he had Hill right where he wanted him.

The water shone brilliantly under the full moon, and myriads of stars reflected on the face of the lake.

Jake was like a shark, now, just as Hill had feared. Hill thrashed in the water and finally surfaced, gasping at air. Jake circled him lazily. When Hill started to swim for shore, Jake thrust hard to reach out and grab Hill's feet and tug him under again. Deep.

Hill's eyes were wide and his cheeks puffed out in an effort not to breathe underwater. He kicked hard for the surface, and Jake let him go, returning to a slow circle of his prey. He toyed with the man, allowing him to rise to catch a breath—because he didn't want to kill Hill, just keep him out of Dad's way—but then pulling him back under. Hill kicked and struggled, but his movements were weaker and weaker each time.

Above them, silhouetted against the star-lit sky, Dad pumped his arm: "Victory!"

Dolk's Tungsten Anti-Gravity – Gradient-Index Meta-Surface was inside Mt. Rainier.

Suddenly, Jake realized that the cold was making Hill sluggish, so he reluctantly pushed and pulled the man to shore.

Hypothermia, he thought in disgust. He'd forgotten that humans were so cold-blooded.

THE FACES OF RISON

Jake stood in the middle of his room, closed his eyes, and rolled his glass marbles between his hands. Carefully, he chose just one, and screwing his eyes shut tight, he dropped the marble. It missed the jar and bounced wildly under the bed.

It was odd, Jake thought, that one of his most important lessons on Earth came from his enemy, Coach Blevins. The discussion about statesmen versus politicians had struck home, though, and Jake knew he had to face this issue squarely. With Rison on the brink of collapse, they had no room for politicians, only statesmen.

Both Blevins and Hill spent a couple days in the hospital recovering from the gunshot—just a flesh wound—and the hypothermia. After Mt. Rainier stopped smoking, and it was obvious the volcano had subsided, the father and son disappeared, clearing out both houses and probably leaving the country. But before they left, Captain Hill released to the press Jake's identity as the Risonian Ambassador's son. Inevitable. It was the only place left to strike at the Quad-des. But Jake was tired of hiding anyway.

His heritage as son of Dayexl Quad-de and stepson of Swann Quad-de meant that he had to stop being a child and step up himself. They had another Thanksgiving dinner on Thanksgiving Day, and this time, the whole family talked: Sir, Easter, Mom, Dad and Jake.

The thing that Jake noticed the most: they were all honest with him, holding nothing back. When he spoke, they listened. Like when he told Mom, "I won't hide any more."

Mom had agreed, "We'll be the Faces of Rison. Together."

The only thing they would still keep secret was the identity of his biological father, Commander Blake Rose. No one needed to know that Jake was half human because that would open up too many questions.

Jake murmured, "Mother and son. It'll be good for Earth to see that we have families just as strong as theirs."

Together. They had to turn the tide of opinion so other Risonians could join them.

□ ☆ ☆

"Action!"

Jake and Mom strolled along the shore while the cameraman walked backward holding the camera, giving the taped segment a casual feel.

Mt. Rainier loomed in the background. The press didn't know that Jake and his family had reversed the sabotage of the volcano; the press didn't even know there'd been sabotage. Captain Hill was still walking around free and would never be charged. But Jake had wanted Mt. Rainier in the background of this new video, "The Faces of Rison." For him, Mt. Rainier had become a symbol of planet Rison's future destruction and the Risonian people's future salvation.

Mom didn't just recite the script; instead, she took the dry words and put passion into them: "We want the same thing you want. To raise our children, to watch a sunset, to invite friends to a party. To live."

Jake took up the dialogue, "I want to graduate from high school and go to college. With our people here, the Earth's economies will be booming, and I'll join other graduates in exciting new professions."

They had an audience: the cameramen and security detail had established a perimeter and allowed no one within it. But just outside were a couple dozen photographers. They were a staple of Jake's life now; everywhere he went, photographers followed. He was getting used to seeing his face on the Internet, in print and on TV.

After that taping, Dad pulled Jake into a fierce hug. Then he held him at arm's length and whispered, "You risk your life with this video."

Echoing his mother, Jake said simply, "Life is a risk. I choose life."

□ ☆ ☆

It was a small party, just a dozen friends from school but it was a start.

Scared but determined, Jake took off his sweat pants and stood there with just khaki shorts on; everyone pretended not to stare. To defuse the tension, Jake sat and stretched out his legs and called, "You can come and look if you want."

David Gordon, of course, led the group. David wore a tight-fitting ankle-length swimsuit, like several others; just because Jake had "come out" didn't mean David had to. He leaned over Jake's lounge chair and used his index finger to point at Jake's calf. "OK, if I touch it."

Jake rolled his eyes, but nodded.

David ran a finger down the line of villi and whistled, "Weird."

Other's joined him, and Jake felt like a cat being petted by everyone in the room. And like a cat, he was suddenly tired of it all. He shoved back, startling a couple of people.

"Sorry," he said. "I just need to cool off."

With two steps, he was at the pool's edge and dove cleanly. His legs automatically Velcroed together, and his gills took over. To please the skeptics, he sat on the bottom for a while, watching the warped images of people walking above him. Of all the people on Earth, he missed Em. Still no word on where her family had gone. Or why.

Finally, bored, he shoved off the bottom and pulled out on the edge of the pool. Shaking like a dog, he brushed aside comments:

"Wow!"

"Seven minutes, 13 seconds. I timed it. No human could do that."

Instead, he checked with Sir in his pink apron. Of course his family was still keeping secrets: if he called Sir and Easter his grandparents, someone might eventually figure out that it was literally true. Instead, the Navy thanked them publically, loud and clear, for hosting an "exchange student" from Rison. Newspapers and talk shows interviewed the kind souls who had acted as foster parents for the Ambassador's son while he went to high school. Living with them gave Jake a lower profile and a chance at a normal high school life. Or so the story went. And since only science fiction nuts or conspiracy theorists would believe that alien species could interbreed, it was mostly believed. In the public view, Jake was the son of Swann and Dayexi Quad-de. Exactly as they wanted.

Sir's shiny baldhead nodded when he came up. "Good show. The burgers are ready."

"Hey!" Jake shouted to his friends. "Let's eat."

"Yeah," someone called. "I'm as hungry as a shark."

PHOKE

The moonless night sky dazzled Jake with the display of stars: the Milky Way truly looked like spilled milk tonight. The air was brisk, cold. Jake walked determinedly through the neighborhoods until he stopped at the Tullis's house.

Dark. No lights.

As he had with the Blevins's house a few months earlier, Jake tried the garage door. Locked. No one had seen the Tullis family—not father, mother or two girls, Marisa or Em—for two weeks. He was determined to find some clue, some scrap of information that would tell him where they went. He snuck around to the back and tried the door there. Locked.

But the dining room window was unlocked. It screeched when he opened it, the wood protesting. He paused, waiting to see if anyone heard. A dog barked in the distance, just a normal neighborhood sound.

Jake heaved himself over the windowsill and tumbled into the room. Awkwardly, he stood and climbed the stairs. He paused at the first bedroom, but it smelled wrong. The last bedroom, though, smelled like Em: coffee and swimming-pool-chlorine. He sat on the bed abruptly and thought about how she hummed all the time, not trying for any melody in particular, just enjoying the sound of her own voice. Where was she?

He switched on a small flashlight—he'd come prepared—and wasn't surprised that the room was littered with books, paper, clothes and shoes. Em never knew how to keep a neat locker or a neat gym bag, so it made sense that her room was messy, too.

Where to start? He sat down at the desk and flashed the light onto the bulletin board. Startled, he saw a photo of himself and Em together. She'd taken a selfie of them together on the sly!

She grinned at the camera in a swim team t-shirt, and a headband held back her dark hair. He was looking away—that's how she managed to take it—but she caught his profile.

He pulled the thumbtack from the photo to take it with him. But another card fluttered to the desktop. It had been thumbtacked behind their photo. Jake's heart pounded suddenly. Had she left him a clue to where she went?

Curious, he picked up the card. Small, rectangular, it was a regular sized business card, like all Earth businesses used. Laying it flat on the desk, he shone the light onto it and read, "Maximillian Bari, M.D. Family Practice." There was an address of the doctor's office and a phone number. Why was that behind their picture?

He turned the card over, and at the four words scrawled in Em's tiny handwriting, he stopped breathing:

Jake –

Help! Phoke!

Em

ABOUT THE AUTHOR

Translated into nine languages, children's book author **DARCY PATTISON** writes picture books, middle grade novels, and children's nonfiction. Her books, published with Harcourt, Philomel/Penguin, Harpercollins, Arbordale, and Mims House have received recognition for excellence with starred reviews in Kirkus, BCCB and PW. Three nonfiction nature books have been honored as National Science Teacher's Association Outstanding Science Trade books. *The Journey of Oliver K. Woodman* (Harcourt) received an Irma Simonton Black and James H. Black Award for Excellence in Children's Literature Honor Book award, and has been published in a Houghton Mifflin textbook. She is a member of the Society of Children's Bookwriters and Illustrators and the Author's Guild. For information on new releases, teacher's guides and more, join Darcy Pattison's mailing list:

Join our mailing list: MimsHouse.com/MoreBLUE

OTHER BOOKS BY DARCY PATTISON

Saucy and Bubba: A Hansel and Gretel Tale
The Girl, the Gypsy and the Gargyole
Vagabonds
Liberty
Abayomi, the Brazilian Puma:
Wisdom, the Midway Albatross:
Searching for Oliver K. Woodman
The Journey of Oliver K. Woodman
I Want a Dog: My Opinion Essay
I Want a Cat: My Opinion Essay
The Aliens, Inc. Series
- ***Book 1: Kell, the Alien***
- ***Book 2: Kell and the Horse Apple Parade***
- ***Book 3: Kell and the Giants***
- ***Book 4: Kell and the Detectives***